Praise for the n<!-- obscured -->

"A strong story with a lot of excitement and action added in."
—*Once Upon a Romance*

"A wondrous adventure, full of action and suspense, which will enchant readers." —*Romantic Times*

"The history, the characters and the plot blended flawlessly for a well-rounded story and hard-won happily ever after."
—*Night Owl Reviews*

"I couldn't put this book down once I started it. I highly recommend *Rising Wind* be added to your must-read list."
—*Fresh Fiction*

"A fast-paced, romantic adventure filled with laughter and danger . . . The pages turn very quickly and their story of adversity keeps the reader absorbed." —*Romance Reviews Today*

"A delightful western romance . . . The storyline is at its best when it concentrates on the lead couple, especially during humorous interludes." —*Midwest Book Review*

"Cindy Holby takes us on an incredible journey of love, betrayal and the will to survive. Ms. Holby is definitely a star on the rise!" —*The Best Reviews*

"Like no other book you'll read, and you owe it to yourself to experience it." —*EscapetoRomance.com*

"Ms. Holby has created a delightful and fast-paced medieval fantasy full of characters that felt real and poignant."
—*Romance Reader At Heart*

Colorado Heart

Cindy Holby

BERKLEY SENSATION, NEW YORK

THE BERKLEY PUBLISHING GROUP
Published by the Penguin Group
Penguin Group (USA) Inc.
375 Hudson Street, New York, New York 10014, USA

Penguin Group (Canada), 90 Eglinton Avenue East, Suite 700, Toronto, Ontario M4P 2Y3, Canada
(a division of Pearson Penguin Canada Inc.) • Penguin Books Ltd., 80 Strand, London WC2R 0RL,
England • Penguin Group Ireland, 25 St. Stephen's Green, Dublin 2, Ireland (a division of Penguin
Books Ltd.) • Penguin Group (Australia), 250 Camberwell Road, Camberwell, Victoria 3124, Australia
(a division of Pearson Australia Group Pty. Ltd.) • Penguin Books India Pvt. Ltd., 11 Community
Centre, Panchsheel Park, New Delhi—110 017, India • Penguin Group (NZ), 67 Apollo Drive,
Rosedale, Auckland 0632, New Zealand (a division of Pearson New Zealand Ltd.) • Penguin Books
(South Africa) (Pty.) Ltd., 24 Sturdee Avenue, Rosebank, Johannesburg 2196, South Africa

Penguin Books Ltd., Registered Offices: 80 Strand, London WC2R 0RL, England

This is a work of fiction. Names, characters, places, and incidents either are the product of the author's
imagination or are used fictitiously, and any resemblance to actual persons, living or dead, business
establishments, events, or locales is entirely coincidental. The publisher does not have any control over
and does not assume any responsibility for author or third-party websites or their content.

COLORADO HEART

A Berkley Sensation Book / published by arrangement with the author

PUBLISHING HISTORY
Berkley Sensation mass-market edition / November 2012

Copyright © 2012 by Cindy Holby
Cover art by Jim Griffin
Cover design by George Long.

ISBN: 978-0-425-25110-2

BERKLEY SENSATION®
Berkley Sensation Books are published by The Berkley Publishing Group,
a division of Penguin Group (USA) Inc.,
375 Hudson Street, New York, New York 10014.
BERKLEY SENSATION® is a registered trademark of
Penguin Group (USA) Inc.
The "B" design is a trademark of Penguin Group (USA) Inc.

PRINTED IN THE UNITED STATES OF AMERICA

10 9 8 7 6 5 4 3 2 1

For the men in my life, each one a hero.
Rob, Josh and Drew.

ACKNOWLEDGMENTS

A special thank you to my agent, Roberta Brown, my editor, Kate Seaver, and the members of HCRW for all the sound advice through the years. And of course my wonderful were-armadillos who share all the ups and downs this crazy business throws at us every day.

ONE

Winter, always a deceptive mistress, had been down-right brutal this year, especially in the mountains of Western Colorado. Certainly there were days when she was a calm and gracious lady, painting the valleys and ridges with gentle snowflakes and crisp air in a sky so blue that it hurt the eyes to look at it. But then there were days when she was vindictive and mean. She sent howling winds that would slice right through a man like the sharpest sword and swirling snow that could disorient you so quickly, that if you weren't careful, you'd fall right off a mountain. During her bad spells the days were so dark that you couldn't tell if or when the sun was up or down, and if you were lucky enough to have some sort of shelter, you could easily lose track of the days.

Jacob Reece stared out of his office window at the drifts of snow that made him feel like a prisoner in his own home.

Winter had hung on too long, there was work to be done and a life to be lived and Jake was itching to do both. He felt as if he'd been frozen in the snow all winter, but now that spring was on the horizon, he was like a bear waking up from hibernation. He was hungry for something; he just couldn't figure out at the moment what it was.

Jake had spent many a winter morning trudging the path that led to his barns and bunkhouse in a seemingly endless circle to check on his stock and his men, who were more than willing to lie in their beds and sleep after they had finished the minimal chores that could be done, considering the weather. The early afternoons he spent walking the polished wooden floors of his sprawling ranch house, while outside the snow blew and swirled until it drifted up to the eaves. Most late afternoons he cleaned the guns that filled his case and cussed at his cook, Fu, who cussed back in Mandarin while banging the pots and pans in the large kitchen of Jake's house that was the Chinaman's domain. In the evenings he read the many books that filled the shelves on either side of the large stone fireplace in his wood-paneled office. But mostly Jake just stared out the windows of his lonely home and waited for the snow and the howling wind to cease their brutal attack.

The nights were the worst. He lay alone in his big feather bed with its abundance of pillows and quilts and thought about what he would do when the weather broke. He made plans for his ranch but those plans didn't do anything to alleviate the strange longing that seemed to fill his soul. Something was missing in his life; he just couldn't put his finger on what it was.

He thought he'd be married by now. It was part of his plan, but fate changed that for him in a hurry. The woman he thought to make his wife fell in love with another man. *Love.* As far as Jake was concerned, love was for fools. It didn't pay the bills and it most certainly didn't get the work done. It might keep a body warm on a cold and snowy night, but that was about all it did.

Now March was over and at last he had something to look forward to. As Jake marked the days off his calendar, he took some comfort in the knowledge that soon he would not have to fight his way through the blowing snow that had drifted up to the rooftops, just to do the simplest chores. Soon he would be able to simply walk to the barn to check on his horses, and his men, who were growing fat and lazy with the forced confinement in the bunkhouse, would go back to work and earn their keep. Now that it was the end of March, winter, which had held Angel's End in its grip since the end of October, would soon be over.

With April came the thaw, and they could all go back to work. Then he would know how many of his thousand-plus cattle had survived the winter. Where Jake was concerned, not knowing was the worst of it. If he didn't know, then he couldn't plan. Planning ahead was what got him to this place in his life. He'd scraped his way up from nothing, to owning his own ranch and a thousand head of cattle, all by the time he was thirty years old. It took hard work, planning, and never taking your eyes off your goal.

"Ready to eat, Mr. Jake?"

Jake turned from the window in his office, and a final March evening of musings, to where the Chinaman stood in the doorway in his silks and braid.

"It depends," Jake said. "Is it beans again?"

"It is beans," Fu said.

Jake sighed. All of his careful planning wasn't enough

to get him through the worst winter in years. Jake was tired of beans, tired of bacon and especially tired of the long and lonely winter evenings.

Fu stood in the doorway of Jake's office with a large spatula in his hand. Jake eyed it warily. Fu had been known to throw things when he was angry. As long as it wasn't a knife, he figured he was safe. The man could pin a fly to the wall with a paring knife if the notion took him.

"If you want something else then you need go to town to bring me something else to cook. I can't make magic in kitchen when nothing in larder but beans and bacon."

Fu had been singing that same song for a week. "If I could get to town then I wouldn't have to worry about you making magic in the kitchen." Jake felt his temper rising. "I could just eat there! The company would definitely be better."

"It not Fu's fault that snow is waist deep," Fu argued back. The two men had definitely spent too much time together of late. Just the sound of Fu's voice grated on Jake's nerves.

"Tomorrow, Fu," Jake returned. "I'm going to try to make it to town tomorrow."

"There is a crazy donkey outside."

"Donkey?" Jake looked at Fu like he was crazy, which he might very well be. Being cooped up did strange things to a person. Made them see things or talk to people who weren't there. "What donkey?"

"Same donkey come to see Mr. Jake last year when miners die," Fu said. "Same donkey standing by barn right now."

Jake followed Fu to the kitchen and looked out the broad window that faced the barn. Sure enough a gray donkey with an oversized backside stood by the barn door, twitching her tail while she brayed to be let inside.

"What in the hell?" Jake grumbled. "What is that fool

donkey doing out here, and how did it manage to get here all the way from town?"

"Last time donkey come, it bring bad news. Maybe it bring bad news again," Fu said.

Jake was afraid that Fu was right. The donkey should have been safe and sound in Jim Martin's livery in Angel's End. Had something happened in town? There was only one way to find out. He kicked off his slippers and yanked on the knee-high, buffalo-hide boots he kept by the back door for when the snow was deep. He pulled on his long wool coat and bundled his scarf several times around his neck. A toboggan over his ears and his thick gloves over his hands completed his outfit.

"You got any recipes for donkey?" he asked Fu before he opened the door.

"Fu have no magic to make donkey taste good."

"That figures," Jake grumbled as he opened the door and stepped into the dimming light. Not that he planned on actually eating the donkey.

The wind had lost its sharp edge since he was out this morning. It no longer cut through a body like a knife; instead it swirled around his coattails like a mischievous child, teasing him and then running away, only to come back and tease again. The snow held its crusty surface, even though bits of it slid loose into the path he'd beaten down in his daily treks to the barn and bunkhouse. Jake kicked some from his path and it flew out in every direction before it spattered onto the frosty blanket that covered everything within sight.

The one thing you could count on in his small valley was that winter would inevitably loosen her grip, even if her fingers had to be pried off, one at a time. At least what he saw was a start. The sky was clear and the moon, behind the spiky ridge of the mountains, promised to be bright in the sky when it finally made its ascent.

"Libby!" Jake called out to the recalcitrant donkey who stood with her nose pressed to the crack between the double doors of the barn. "What are you doing here?"

Libby turned to Jake, laid her ears back and let out a hoarse, honking, teeth-baring bray. Jake plowed onward to the barn until he was able to grab onto her halter. "Don't tell me you came all the way from town," he said as he pushed open the door wide enough for them to slip in.

Or so he thought. The donkey's huge backside was too big for the opening and she brayed her annoyance. "What has Jim been feeding you?" Jake asked as he wrangled his way around Libby and pushed the door open wider. She trotted in with an indignant shake and went immediately to the feed bin while the chickens squawked their annoyance as they fled from her path.

Oscar, his huge yellow barn cat, crept out of a stall, stretched, meowed and twined his way around Jake's ankles. His horse, a golden palomino called Bright, put his head over the stall door and neighed in recognition to Libby. The rest of the horses looked curiously at the interloper as they lazily stretched and shook themselves awake from their afternoon doze.

"What brings you here?" Jake asked the donkey. He ran expert hands over her flanks to check for injuries and sniffed her coarse bristle mane for the scent of smoke. Fires were always a hazard, especially in winter. A fire at the stable certainly would have sent the donkey running for the hills. Fortunately, or unfortunately for his nose, all he smelled was donkey and something else that was unfamiliar and disturbing. It belonged to an animal, he was certain, and did not hold a threat. He dismissed it as not worth the bother at the moment, and something Libby had probably picked up in her flight. Still something was amiss. Why else would the donkey be here?

Libby nuzzled through the feed bin, which was for the most part empty, and once more brayed her displeasure. Jake scooped a handful of feed into the bin and looked the donkey over once more.

"Why do you always come here when something is bothering you?" he asked. He didn't expect an answer but that didn't stop the nagging worry. Libby had shown up on his property last fall and led him to the mining camp in the mountains above Angel's End. Jake, upon following her, had found the entire population of the camp dead from a measles epidemic. It was a gruesome scene and not one that Jake cared to repeat.

Lib responded by planting her hoof on top of his foot and bearing down.

"Dang it!" Jake shoved her aside and hobbled around the barn as pain shot through his foot. The buffalo hide was good for staying dry, but it didn't offer much protection from stupid critters that were put on earth to torture him.

"That's it," Jake said when his foot finally stopped throbbing. "I'm taking you back where you belong."

Lib opened her mouth wide and hee-hawed in his face. Jake pushed her aside and went down the line of stalls and opened the one that housed Skip. Skip was a scrappy little mustang the color of mud. There was nothing appealing in any way about his looks, but he was solid and strong and had a *don't quit* attitude that Jake loved. He'd much rather ride Skip through the deep snow than Bright, who was too valuable to risk on the fool's mission he had planned.

After saddling Skip he went back to the house to change.

"Mr. Jake going to town?" Fu asked as he followed Jake

upstairs. "Night coming. Mr. Jake will freeze or fall into snowbank, even fall off mountain," Fu chattered on as Jake stepped onto the thick rug that covered his bedroom floor.

"Dang it, Fu, I'm not going to ride over any mountains. I'm just going to town. If that stupid donkey can make it all the way up here, then I sure as hell ought to be able to make it back down." Jake unbuttoned his shirt with sharp jerking motions.

"Fu make list." The Chinaman pulled a piece of paper from the sleeve of his shirt and handed it to Jake.

"You knew I was going all along, didn't you?" Jake asked as he dropped his shirt on his high bed. He would more than likely miss its comfort in an hour or so. With luck he'd be in town by then. And not freezing to death in some drift.

"Mr. Jake need to drink whiskey and talk to his friends," Fu said.

The rest was lost to Mandarin as Fu left the room muttering to himself.

Jake changed into a warm pair of long johns, a heavy flannel shirt, a thick knitted sweater and a sturdy pair of pants. He pulled on two pairs of socks and stuffed his feet into his boots. He went into his office and retrieved his Colt .45 and holster from the rack. Hungry wolves didn't care if their prey had two legs or four, and he wasn't about to make things easy for them. He finished up by putting on a short heavy jacket, followed by his duster, leather gloves and toboggan. He shoved his hat on top of the toboggan and got a Spencer from the gun rack next to the front door.

"Here's hoping I don't freeze to death," he said to the reflection he saw in the mirror of the coat stand. "Dang it, Fu is right. I do need some company since I'm standing here talking to myself." Jake shook his head at his foolishness and walked out the front door, shutting it securely behind him.

"You heading to town, Mr. Jake?" Two of his hands, Randy and Dan, came out of the bunkhouse as he approached the barn, both dressed for the weather. Jake knew they were as antsy as he was.

"Yes," Jake said. "I'm worried something might have happened down there, since that fool donkey showed up here."

"We'll ride with you," Randy said.

"If you don't mind," Dan added.

"Suit yourself," Jake said. He didn't mind the company, especially if the snow was bad. More than one man had died a cruel death in this weather, and there was safety in numbers.

It took no time for his men to saddle up and join him. Jake gave Libby's lead to Dan and they started out, but Skip had only taken a few steps when a horrible ruckus started. Jake turned to see Libby sitting on her haunches in the snow with her front legs planted while she brayed her distress at the top of her lungs.

"Now what?" Jake groused. He dismounted and as soon as his foot hit the ground Libby got up and trotted to him. She butted her head against his side and hee-hawed again. Dan and Randy both cracked a smile.

"Looks like she's sweet on you, Mr. Jake," Randy said.

Dan handed him the lead. "Only one way to find out for sure." His face twisted in an effort not to laugh.

Jake sighed. If Libby followed him without a fight he was never going to hear the end of it from his men. Who knows, maybe he'd get lucky and Libby would just lie down in the snow and refuse to move.

Jake swung up on Skip and gave a tug on the lead. Libby trotted right up next to his leg and shook her body indignantly, as if Dan's hold had been an insult.

"Smart-ass," Jake said to the donkey.

Dan and Randy burst into laughter.

"Not another word," Jake threatened good-naturedly as they set off. Skip settled into the trough that the donkey had plowed on her way to the ranch, with Libby following behind and Randy and Dan bringing up the rear.

"Too bad she didn't show up sooner," Randy said.

"Would have kept Mr. Jake from spending all those evenings alone," Dan rejoined.

"Yup, she probably would have curled up on the rug in front of the fire like a big dog," Randy added.

"I'm going to shoot both of you and leave you for the coyotes if you don't shut up," Jake said.

"That's the biggest ass I've ever seen in more ways than one," Dan said.

"Hey," Jake barked. "Now you're getting personal."

"Yeah, Dan, don't you know you're never supposed to talk about a lady's personal . . . er, accoutrements?"

"That donkey ain't no lady," Dan observed.

"Where in the heck did you learn a word like *accoutrements*?" Jake asked Randy.

"I wasn't always a cowboy, Mr. Jake," Randy said. "Sometimes circumstances dictate a fellow's future, no matter what else he's planned for."

Jake raised an eyebrow. "Circumstances?"

"Don't ask," Dan said.

"It was all because of a girl," Randy said.

"Isn't it always," Jake said.

They moved on, down the trail that led out of the wide valley that was home to Jake's spread, the Rocking J. The going got easier the farther they rode out of the mountains. The moon rose up behind them and the reflection off the snow was bright.

"Looks like she wandered a bit before she showed up," Dan said. He pointed north and Jake saw the packed-down snow that showed signs of something Libby's size passing through.

"She's lucky she didn't wind up as a meal for a wildcat or the wolves," Randy observed.

"What were you up to out here?" Jake asked the donkey. Libby twitched her ears and showed Jake her teeth.

"Yup, she sure is sweet on you," Dan said.

They were almost out of Jake's valley and to the main road. To the south and east the road led out of the mountains and eventually to Denver, after a week of hard riding. To the north and west was the small town of Angel's End. Other valleys branched off the road on both sides, most all of them home to various ranches. Higher up in the mountains, beyond the ranches, were scores of mines, some with gold, others with silver. Mining was hard work and too much of it depended on luck. It wasn't the life for Jake; he knew good and well that he didn't have the patience for it.

It had been awhile since Jake talked to the other men in the local Cattlemen's Association and he wondered how they had all fared during the long hard winter. Raymond Watkins, who had the valley opposite Jake's, had the biggest spread. He considered himself the head of their association, even though Jake had been elected this year to run it. Some men liked to be in charge and Jake figured he'd get along better with the man by letting him be rather than standing up against him. It just wasn't worth the trouble to challenge him. Watkins's crew was bad news. Jake wouldn't have hired any of them, but since they weren't on his payroll it was none of his business. They didn't bother him, so he minded his own business and was happy that Watkins chose to do the same.

The Castles lived south of Jake. They'd only been around for a few years. Jared, his wife Laurie and their daughter Eden. They had a younger son who Jake had only seen once and who went to school in the east, and a three-year-old granddaughter by an older son who was rumored to be in prison. Both the son in prison and the granddaughter had Indian blood in them. There was a story there, but Jake didn't know the Castles well enough to ask. They were good people from what little he did know and Jake often envied the obvious affection between Jared and his beautiful Laurie. Their daughter, Eden, was the image of her mother but walked with a limp from a twisted leg that came with her birth.

They came to the main road. There was evidence of traffic as the snow was beaten down and packed tight. A wagon couldn't make it through the deep snow, but riders had passed this way and not too long ago. The sky above was cloudless and endless, with innumerable stars scattered across. It made one feel small and insignificant to look at it. It made one feel lonely.

Jake took a deep breath. It was time to leave the winter doldrums behind. The air was crisp without that bone-chilling slice that cut right through a person. Spring was definitely on its way. Jake could only hope that it wouldn't take its own sweet time arriving.

He turned Skip to the north and the town of Angel's End. The road split here, dividing off toward Watkins's Bar W ranch to the left and Angel's End to the right. Signs were nailed to the trees at each cutoff, identifying the name of the family and their brand. The three men rode on, lost in their own thoughts and the quiet magic of the beautiful night.

The valley on the north side of Jake's and closer to

Angel's End was currently uninhabited. It had belonged to Sam Parker, a crotchety old geezer who would just as soon shoot you as look at you. He had run a few head of cattle and always contributed his part to the annual drive to market. He had up and died sometime the winter before last and no one had even realized it until the spring thaw when his cattle showed up mixed in with Jake's. Jake had gone looking and found him sitting in a rocking chair by his fireplace. He'd been dead for a while. They'd buried him under a pine and sent a letter to a daughter-in-law, whose name and address Jake had found scribbled in an old Bible. The place had been empty for well over a year. Someone would show up eventually to claim it, or else it would be sold off. It was the way things were out here.

"Stop right there!" a gruff voice called out.

Jake cursed himself for a fool for getting so lost in his musings that he didn't see anyone coming their way. He looked up the trail and didn't recognize the appaloosa or the rider who was currently pointing the business end of a Spencer rifle at his head. The rider was small and new horses turned up all the time. Could it possibly be one of Jim's older twin boys? But surely the twins would recognize him. And why would they be robbing him?

Jake raised his hands. He kept a hold on Libby's lead. He heard Dan and Randy pull up behind him.

"Boss?" Randy asked.

"Let me see what's going on," Jake said. He knew the three of them could take whoever it was but he wanted to avoid bloodshed if possible. It was too pretty of a night to have to shoot someone, even if they were stupid enough to try and steal from him.

"Turn loose of that donkey," the rider said. The voice wasn't as gruff this time. It was a boy trying to disguise himself by speaking lower than natural. Then the words sunk in to Jake's mind.

"Wait." Jake tried to keep a straight face. "Are you trying to steal my donkey?" He stretched out Libby's lead. "This donkey?"

The rider cocked the rifle to show he meant business. "No. You are stealing my donkey."

"What the hell?"

"Watch your language. And let her go."

"I think there's been some sort of misunderstanding," Jake started.

The rifle raised a notch. "I'm guessing you understand *this*, don't you?"

"You want us to do something?" Dan said quietly from behind him.

"I got it," Jake responded. "The last thing I want to do is kill some fool kid." He raised his hands higher so the idiot with the rifle could see that he wasn't holding a weapon, and with a squeeze of his knees, Skip moved forward, slowly, with Libby walking along by his side.

The rider, whoever it was, wore a coat that was way too big for him. It reached from neck to ankles and was made of heavy wool. His wide-brimmed, flat-top Stetson was pulled low over his face, and a heavy knit scarf wrapped around his neck, covering any hint of skin. The rider was so laden down with trying to stay warm that Jake knew he could take him out before he had a chance to twitch his finger on the trigger.

"Take it easy," Jake said as they approached. "I'm bringing the donkey, although I don't know why anyone in the world would want to steal the fool thing. She's more trouble than she's worth."

"Like I said before. It's my donkey."

The rider sat on a small rise in the road. The moon was directly overhead and his features were lost in the shadow of his hat, but the gloved hands on the rifle were small, albeit steady, and the tips of the boots that stuck out from beneath the folds of the coat barely showed.

"What are you? Twelve?" Jake asked as Skip stopped about a head's length from the appaloosa.

"What are you?" the thief said after he cleared his throat. "Stupid?"

Jake tapped his heels and Skip charged full bore into the appaloosa. The appaloosa reared and Jake wrenched the rifle from the rider's hands as he tumbled backward from the saddle.

Libby hee-hawed and kicked out and the appaloosa spooked, taking off up the trail toward Dan and Randy, who quickly cut the horse off and grabbed its reins. Libby trotted a few steps away and turned to watch.

Jake jumped from Skip's back and jabbed the business end of the rifle in the chest of the kid who lay sprawled in the snow.

"Ow," a much more feminine voice said. Jake used the tip of the rifle to push the hat away from his . . . no, her face. The moonlight spilled down on delicate features and skin that looked like it should be on a porcelain doll. Her mouth was pursed into a pout that made his lips twitch with the urge to press a kiss against their fullness. Lush lashes formed crescent moons on her cheeks before she opened them to stare up at him with accusing blue eyes. Her pale hair was short and wispy, and stuck out in every direction like tufts of grass.

"Who the hell are you?" he asked.

"Language," she said as she pushed the rifle away.

"What are you, a Sunday school teacher?"

In the next instant Jake was lying on his back in the snow and she was standing over him with a .45 pointed at his chest. He heard Randy and Dan chortling in the background. He had to admire her. Tiny as she was, she'd managed to sweep his legs right out from under him with one of the slickest moves he'd ever seen.

"I'm the owner of that donkey that you stole," she said vehemently.

"I didn't steal her. She came to me."

She raised a skeptical eyebrow and the pistol she held in her left hand did not waver a bit. She was so petite he wondered how she could get her hand around it, but she did, and it was obvious she knew which end meant business.

"Yeah, Libby is madly in love with him," Dan said.

"You're fired," Jake said. He didn't take his eyes off the woman. He wasn't worried for his life and he knew Dan wasn't worried about his job. Jake was aware his two men could take her out if they wanted to and were just cutting up, as he was, to put her at ease, so she didn't do anything stupid.

She raised the gun and took her finger from the trigger. "You do know her name . . ."

"And now you do too," Jake said. "That doesn't mean you knew it before."

Her pale eyes changed. "What is that supposed to mean?"

"Do you mind if I stand up? My ass is freezing."

"Do you always talk like this?" she asked with a sigh.

"Only when someone tries to rob me and then dumps me in the snow."

Randy and Dan snorted with laughter. The woman backed up a few feet but kept a tight hold on the pistol as Jake clambered to his feet and made a production of brushing the snow from the back side of his duster. She picked up her rifle while Jake cleaned himself off, and stuck the pistol in the pocket of her oversized coat.

"You can put the rifle away too," Jake said as she stepped far enough back so that she could keep the rifle leveled on all three of them. "If I wanted to hurt you I would have done it already."

"Well excuse me if I've heard that before."

Jake found his hat and brushed the snow from it. "Lady, I don't know who you are or where you are from but I can tell already that you have an attitude problem. So I suggest we both go to town and clear this up."

"I'm not going anywhere with you," she said indignantly.

"Then tell me who sold you the animal." If she said Jim's name he'd gladly turn Libby over to her. But he wasn't about to give the donkey up just because some woman waved a gun in his face.

Her tone turned defensive and her hold on the rifle slackened. If Jake wanted to, he could jerk it from her hands. "I got her last fall from the livery in town. I don't know his name, as it was a friend of mine who bought her."

"Well that sure does prove a lot," Jake said. "How about we both go to town and we'll see what the sheriff has to say about this."

"What?" she spouted. "Like I said, I'm not going anywhere with you."

"Suits me," Jake said. "If this donkey is indeed yours then you can pick her up tomorrow at the livery. If she's not . . ."

"Oh she's mine," she said. "And maybe I'll have a word with the sheriff about how you wound up with her."

"Fine," Jake said. "You can both find me at the Heaven's Gate." As he didn't trust her with the rifle, he kept his eyes on her as he spoke to his ranch hand. "Randy, you can give this fine lady back her horse now."

The tiny woman gave an exasperated sigh and clicked her teeth together. The appaloosa responded by shaking his head. Randy let go of the reins and the little horse trotted over to her owner. "Stand back," she said.

"Gladly." Jake raised his arms wide. She guided the appaloosa to a rock buried in the snow and used it to gracefully swing into her saddle. "Believe me, I plan on staying as far away from you as possible," Jake added.

She slammed the rifle into her scabbard. Without a backward glance she took off up the trail to Sam Parker's spread.

"Well now, don't that beat all," Randy said as they watched her ride away.

Jake let out a heavy sigh before he slammed his hat onto his head and mounted Skip. "Boys, I am in desperate need of a drink."

TWO

"All I know is the man who bought Libby was Mexican," Jim Martin, who owned the livery, said. "He didn't say where he was from or where he was going. He just came into the stable around the first of December and asked if I knew of anyone who had a donkey for sale. I showed him Libby and he offered me two dollars for her. It sounded like a deal to me so I took it."

"Has anyone said anything about someone moving into the Parker place?" Jake asked. "Because that's where she was headed last we saw of her. If it's family, it seems like I should have heard from them since I sent out the letter."

Cade Gentry, the sheriff, and Ward Phillips, owner of the Heaven's Gate Saloon where the men were happily enjoying a drink, both shook their heads.

"I sure would have loved to have seen her put you in the

snow," Ward said with a laugh as he poured the four men another round of shots.

"It was a pretty slick move," Jake admitted. "Whoever she is, if she's not careful she's going to try that on the wrong person and wind up dead."

"I reckon I should ride out to the Parker spread tomorrow and see what's going on," Cade said.

"Who knows," Jake said. "Maybe she'll show up tomorrow to claim the donkey."

"And swear out a complaint against you?" Cade asked.

"She's welcome to try," Jake said.

"How long ago was it you sent that letter?" Jim asked.

"Almost two years," Jake said. "You think if he had any family they would have shown up a long time ago." He looked at the swallow left in his glass. "And you'd think I'd know since I have the key to the house." He drained his glass. "They must be squatters as well as thieves."

"We'll figure it out tomorrow," Cade said. "You're welcome to come along if you want." He tossed back his shot. "Now if you gentlemen will excuse me, I've got a wife to get home to."

"Yeah, I'd better go too, before Gretchen sends out a search party," Jim said, and he followed Cade out the door.

"So she was a looker?" Ward asked when the door was shut firmly behind the two men.

"Yes, she was pretty," Jake admitted. "Even though she looked liked she got scalped with a dull knife." He slammed his glass down on the bar. "Pretty don't mean much when you've got a gun pointed at your head."

Ward grinned as he poured another shot into Jake's glass. "It's much better than having a gun pointed at your head by an ugly outlaw," Ward pointed out. "Why didn't you just let her keep the donkey? It's not like the animal actually belongs to you."

"I guess I just wanted to make her mad to see what she would do next."

Ward grinned, so Jake turned his back on him, as he had a pretty good idea of what his friend was thinking. He didn't want to hear it, so he concentrated on what was happening in the Heaven's Gate Saloon. There wasn't much there to distract him.

Dan and Randy sat at a table by the potbellied stove with Priscilla, one of the waitresses, who giggled mightily at something Dan said. Talking about him and how he was attacked on the trail by a slip of a woman, no doubt. Six puppies, three black and white, two solid gray and one a mix of all three tumbled about beneath the tables. One chewed on Randy's boot and he picked the pup up and put it on his lap. Lady, Ward's dog, watched her offspring carefully as she lay next to a box close to the stove.

"How old are those pups?" Jake asked.

"Old enough to leave if you're interested."

"Nah," Jake said, although he was tempted as it had been awhile since he'd lost Sonny, who'd been with him for years. A good dog was hard to come by.

"Speaking of pups and such," Ward said. "Had you heard that Leah and Cade are expecting?"

Jake tossed his drink back. "That didn't take long." He didn't want to admit that losing Leah to Cade Gentry still hurt his pride a bit. "I reckon they're happy and such."

"They look it."

"I'm glad for her then," Jake said.

"Still hurting?" Ward asked.

"I wouldn't call it hurting," Jake said. "Leah didn't love

me and I reckon when you get down to it, I didn't love her since it didn't really make me all that mad after I thought about it for a while. Sometimes I'm just a bit lonely is all."

Ward raised his glass in salute. "I certainly know what that feels like, my friend." Jake drained his glass again and turned it upside down on the bar. He was done with whiskey for the night. Ward re-corked the bottle and put it away on the shelf that held his private stock.

Jake caught sight of his reflection in the mirror that hung behind the bar and stared at the man who gazed back at him with steely blue eyes that looked hollow and lost. The winter had taken its toll on him. He'd worked hard all his life and now he had something to show for it. But it didn't mean much when there was no one to share it with.

"Maybe I should take a trip down to Denver," Jake said. "See the sights."

"And find a bride?" Ward asked.

"Maybe," Jake admitted.

"You sound like a man who wants to fall in love," Ward said. He poured Jake a beer from the large keg that sat on the end of the bar.

"Love?" Jake scoffed. "I'm pretty sure that's something the poets and Shakespeare made up."

Ward grinned. "We'll see," he said.

Jake shook his head and rolled his eyes at his friend. It seemed strange, but he felt a bit better about things. Almost optimistic. Fu was right, not that he'd ever admit it to the Chinaman. He just needed to get out of the house for a bit. And there was no reason why he couldn't make a trip to Denver after the spring roundup. There were plenty of women there. Plenty of women just dying for a man to provide for them. He just needed to look at it like a business deal. Take a trip down to Denver or maybe wait until the fall drive and go on to Kansas City, or St. Louis. There were women everywhere. Surely he could find someone who knew how to take care of a house and home. She wouldn't even have to cook since he had Fu around. And it wasn't as if he was such a bad catch. He was young and he was strong and he'd been told he was handsome more than once by women who weren't related to him.

Jake smiled at his own ego. Enough planning for tonight. He picked up his beer and decided to join his men for the rest of his drink.

Instead he almost fell flat on his face.

"Dang!" One of the pups had gotten tangled up between his feet. It rolled sideways as he stumbled and landed on its back. It blinked up at him with one brown eye and one blue eye, and promptly leapt on his boot with a cute little growl.

Cute. Now where in the hell had that come from? *Cute* wasn't a word that came up a lot in his vocabulary, yet he had to admit the tricolor pup was the epitome of the word. Jake knelt down and picked up the pup that was in the process of killing the evil creature that was his boot and scooped it up to check its sex.

"That one's a girl," Pris informed him. She came to his side and leaned close enough that Jake could see the pale white skin of her breasts as they brushed against his arm. She rubbed the pup's head. "I just love her eyes," she added.

The pup tilted her head sideways as she considered Jake with her different-colored eyes. The fur on her back was a mix of black and gray, and her belly and legs white with a few brown spots scattered around. A white blaze split her face and carried over to surround the blue eye, which made it all the more startling in her sweet face. Both eyes bespoke the intelligence of her sire and the faithfulness of her dam.

"Change your mind?" Ward asked.

"I believe I have," Jake said. He tucked the pup into the crook of his arm. "I reckon we'll turn in now," he said. Ward lifted his glass in a good-night salute as he sat down at his piano.

"Are you sure?" Pris asked. The invitation shone in her eyes, on her mouth and in the way she stood with her hand on her hip. Behind him he plainly saw the disappointment on both Dan and Randy's faces.

It would be so very easy to say yes. To drag her upstairs and lose himself inside of her. But just as much as he knew it would be easy to do, he also knew that the morning would be filled with regret. He'd spent a long and lonely winter keeping regret at bay. He wasn't about to do anything to make it turn up here. "I'm sure," Jake said, and moved toward the steps.

"Suit yourself," Pris said, and went back to his men. The sound of Ward's playing accompanied him up the stairs as Jake went into the room he always slept in when he stayed in town. It didn't take him long to strip down to his long johns and climb beneath the thick pile of quilts. The pup seemed content, and with a squeaky yawn she curled up in the crook of his arm. Luckily she slept through the bed banging against the wall in the room next door, along with the normal sounds that accompanied such things.

Jake wasn't as lucky, nor was he content, and it was a long time before he drifted off to a sleep that was haunted by a woman with ragged hair and kissable lips.

THREE

Angel's End, Colorado. One look at the angel statue in the middle of the street told Cassie Parker everything she needed to know about the origin of the town's name. Where the statue had come from was another story altogether. Maybe if she stuck around long enough she'd find out. Odds were against it though. Sure she'd love to have a place to call home, a place where people would just leave her alone and let her be, but her recent history had proven that it wasn't likely to happen anytime soon.

Cassie had pushed her family hard last autumn to get to the small valley and the ranch her grandfather had left her before winter set in. Since then they'd kept to themselves, content to hide beneath the several feet of snow that fell day after day. But now with spring on its way, and the better weather, she had to show herself in town. Supplies were low and they needed to eat.

She did a slow survey of the street as she dismounted in front of Swanson's Mercantile. She quickly noted the sheriff's office and the saloon, where she was certain the idiot she met on the trail was hiding. Libby the donkey was probably in her stall at the livery. The way her luck was going, Cassie would probably have to buy her again, even with the bill of sale Manuel had luckily kept.

Three men and a dog came out of the saloon as she waited for Manuel to tie the mules to the hitching post. She recognized the shortest of the three as the man from the trail. Her eyes were sharp enough to spot a star on the chest of the tallest man, which meant he was the sheriff. The third was more than likely just nosy.

"Are you sure you'll be all right?" Cassie asked Manuel.

He patted his pocket where he kept the bill of sale. "I will be fine," he assured her. "Will you be all right?" he asked in return.

Cassie patted the pocket of her coat where she kept her pistol. "I will be fine also," she assured him and she went inside.

The heat from the potbelly stove in the center of the store was welcoming. Cassie felt as if she'd been cold forever. Neither a fire nor the many quilts she slept beneath gave her comfort. She was always cold. With luck, when summer came the long hot days would chase away the terminal chill that filled her body.

Cassie unbuttoned her heavy wool coat that covered her from ears to ankles. She took off her wide-brimmed hat and gloves and placed them on a chair by the stove. She ran her fingers through her chin-length hair. She shouldn't have cut it off the way she did. Grabbing the knife and sawing off her braid had been impulsive, but when she'd done it she wasn't thinking properly. Now it was mostly in the way as it was still too short to pull back. She did the best she could with it, fluffing the silky strands with her fingers until she was certain it wasn't plastered to her head before she turned to face the enormous woman who stood behind the counter with a phony smile stretching across her round face.

"Just passing through, deary, or are you new to Angel's End?" the woman asked.

Cassie took a deep breath. *She can't hurt me . . .* Cassie reminded herself as she stuck out her hand to get the formalities over with. "I'm new to Angel's End," she said. "I'm Sam Parker's granddaughter and I've come to claim his land."

The woman's mouth and eyes both rounded in surprise before she came around from behind the counter. The floorboards creaked mightily with her weight as she grabbed Cassie's hand and pumped it up and down. "Sam's granddaughter. Well I never even knew he had children, much less a granddaughter." She studied Cassie's face looking for some resemblance. Cassie could only wonder if she found any as her memories of her grandfather were dim. "Imagine that," the woman continued. "Of course the man never said much of anything to anyone that I can recall."

Cassie couldn't say she expected anything different. The relationship between her mother and her grandfather was a tenuous one after her father died. She never knew what happened between them. She didn't even know where her grandfather had gone off to until the letter, addressed to her father, found them. By that time her grandfather had passed away well over a year before, but the timing was providential where Cassie was concerned. She needed a place to go, a place to hide, a place where she could safely care for her mother, and a place that, God willing, she could eventually call home.

Cassie had a vague memory of her grandfather from when she was a small girl. Sitting on his lap and looking in his pocket for hard candy. It felt like the memory belonged to another person as it was so long ago and from a time when her grandmother and father were both alive. Still, it was a fine memory, when she could stand it, which wasn't often, as it reminded her too much of what she'd lost and what she'd never find again.

She could still see the corn towering over her head on the farm in Illinois where her parents and grandparents had all lived together. She remembered spinning beneath the sky and chasing butterflies before her father scooped her up to sit on his shoulders so she'd be closer to the clouds that drifted across the sky. Twenty years felt like several life-times to Cassie, and yet the memories were still fresh, when she allowed them to come out.

"Well bless your heart you are a tiny thing," the woman said as she looked her over. "Sam's granddaughter. And what might your name be?"

"Cassandra Parker."

"Well now, isn't that just the sweetest thing? Your father was Sam's son?"

"Yes, ma'am, he was. He died in the war and my grand-mother soon after. My grandfather came west after that." Cassie did not volunteer any other information.

She should have known better. The woman stuck her nose right in the middle of where it didn't belong. "And where is your mother?"

"At the ranch," Cassie said, determined not to share any more.

The storekeeper's gaze was questioning as she looked Cassie over from the top of her shorn head to the tip of her boy's boot. "And you never married. Now isn't that a shame?" she said with a smile.

It didn't matter the town or the territory. People were the same no matter where you went, always interested in everybody else's business. Still, her marital state or lack thereof was none of this storekeeper's business, so Cassie ignored the comment. She knew trouble would find her soon enough; she didn't need to invite it in.

"Gus! Gus come out here," the woman called in a shrill voice through an open door at the end of the counter and then turned back to Cassie. "I'm Bettina Swanson and my husband is Gus, the mayor. He can tell you where to go to claim your granddaddy's land."

Cassie double-checked to confirm that she was alone in the store and no one blocked the exit. She had no reason to be worried about the storekeeper; still, she put her hand in her left pocket to make sure the pistol she always kept on her person was handy, just in case.

"Thank you, ma'am." Cassie relaxed when she saw the shop owner was small and unassuming with a friendly smile and a worn-down countenance. His wife ran roughshod over him. Cassie was good at reading people. She'd had to be to survive.

"Gus, this is Sam Parker's granddaughter. And she's here to stay. Already moved in." While the grocer's wife explained to her husband how Cassie had inherited her grandfather's land, Cassie studied the contents of the store.

You could tell it was nearing the end of winter just by looking around. Everything was picked over and the candy jars on the counter were low, with just a few pieces left in each of them. Cassie surely had a weakness for candy and her sweet tooth ached at the thought of reaching into one of those jars and pulling out a piece of peppermint, or even better, indulging in a bar of chocolate. It had been awhile since she'd had either.

The dry goods looked as picked over as the candy. Bolts of fabric in drab colors were spread out on a table. A container of more gaily colored ribbon stood in the middle of the table, as an encouragement to add a finishing touch to whatever material you chose.

Cassie didn't own a dress or a skirt. Boys' clothing suited her just fine. There was a time in her life when she would have run her hand over the fabric and held up the ribbons to a mirror to see which would flatter the pale blond color of her hair, but that time was behind her. She had no desire to call attention to her hair or any other part of her body.

Another table held a supply of jeans and heavy shirts of flannel and denim. Cassie had heard there were mines in the area and the clothes befitted the population. A shelf along the wall held an assortment of pots, pans, plates and mugs made from tin and covered over with blue-spotted enamel. Another shelf held boots of different styles, all lined up according to size. Then there were blankets and coats and all the other accoutrements of everyday life. The counter where the Swansons stood held glass bins that were low on dried beans, while the shelves behind them held crocks marked with other necessities such as sugar and coffee. A few sacks of flour sat on the floor around a large barrel.

The pickings were slim but it would be enough to get them through until the store had a delivery.

"Jake said he found instructions in a Bible about who to notify when he found Sam," Gus said. "It looks like the letter found you."

"You never told me that," Bettina interrupted.

"It wasn't anything you needed to know," Gus replied.

Cassié arched an eyebrow. Maybe Gus wasn't so hen-pecked after all.

"Jake lives in the next valley over. He was the one who found your grandfather and wrote the letter," Gus explained.

Cassie nodded. She had the letter in her pocket, just in case she needed it to claim the property. It was thorough and to the point and signed by a man named Jacob Reece. Sam had sat down in his chair and died and he'd been buried beneath a tree behind his cabin.

"There's over a year's worth of taxes due," Gus added.

"If you'll send me in the right direction I'll take care of it," Cassie said. She hoped it wasn't too expensive. She had a bit of money, but not much, and she had to make it last for a while.

"The tax records are kept in the sheriff's office," Gus said. "We'll have to look it up."

"Here's Cade now," Bettina trilled as the bell rang over the door. Cassie quickly moved behind the large barrel where the flour was kept. "And Ward Phillips, and low and behold, Jacob Reece. Imagine that," she said to the last man to walk through the door. "Were your ears burning, Jake?"

"Should they be?" the man from the trail said with a charming grin. He went to the counter and handed Bettina a list. "I can wait," he said. "Until you're done with her," he added with a tilt of his head in her direction.

His manners hadn't improved any since last night. Cassie put her hand in her pocket as she studied the three men. She needed to feel the security of the gun, as they seemed to fill up all the space in the general store.

She hadn't gotten a real good look at Jake Reece the night before. She'd been too angry to pay attention to how he looked. But she knew he was solid from the way he landed when she'd swept his legs out from under him. His clothes were well tended, and she had to admit he was handsome with his short-cropped hair and cleanly shaven jaw. But one look at his eyes as he turned to face her unsettled her. They were as gray as a stormy sky and the look he gave her made her insides twist up. Cassie fought the urge to run her fingers through her hair again to make sure she didn't look like a hoyden. She was surprised when a puppy with one blue eye and one brown stuck its head out of the neck of his jacket.

"So I'm guessing Libby actually does belong to you," he said as he stroked the ears of the puppy.

"She does," Cassie replied coldly. "My friend went to the stable to collect her. With the bill of sale as proof," she added. The puppy was so cute that she wanted to touch its soft fur but she wouldn't dare. She'd never allow herself to get that close to a man, intentionally.

The other two men grinned at each other as if they shared a private joke. The one Bettina called Ward Phillips was tall and strongly built beneath his expensive suit. His brown hair was neatly trimmed and his warm dark eyes studied her. A large gray dog with a friendly face stood by his side. Cassie relaxed a bit. She trusted animals more than she trusted men. Still, there was something about this man, something that said he saw more than you wanted him to see. She'd have to be careful around this one. Since she didn't plan on spending a lot of time in town it shouldn't be too difficult.

It was the sheriff who made her palms sweat inside the confines of her pocket. He was taller than the other man, rangy, with whipcord muscles that disguised his strength. His hair was the deepest of browns and his eyes so brown they were almost black. The gun he wore on his hip looked like a natural extension of his body. It was his eyes that frightened her. They held so many secrets, secrets just like hers. It was almost like looking in a mirror. Almost. His eyes held something else that she knew was missing in hers. A sense of peace, or dare she call it *hope*? Both were things she knew no longer existed for her.

"Welcome to Angel's End," he said, and gave her a friendly smile. She relaxed a hair, nothing more. "I'm the sheriff, Cade Gentry."

"Cassandra Parker."

"Miss Parker is Sam Parker's granddaughter," Bettina cooed.

"Well I'll be damned," Jake said.

"I see your language hasn't improved any since last night," Cassie said.

"Oh it's been known to get a lot worse," Ward said. "We're glad to have you in Angel's End. How long have you been here?"

"Since middle of November," Cassie replied. "We arrived right before the snow started."

"I camped near your place around that time," the sheriff said. "I never saw a soul, but I did see something strange." Cassie's shoulders tensed at the sheriff's words. Someone had been that close to her place and she didn't know it.

"What was that?" Ward asked.

"I could have sworn I saw a sheep." The sheriff continued with a shrug. "I just put it down to God's providence as I was struggling with a decision at the time."

"The Lord does work in mysterious ways," Gus intoned.

Cassie kept her mouth shut. Things would be out in the open soon enough and there was no need stirring the pot as long as it was simmering so nicely.

"And look at how well that turned out for you," Ward said with a sly grin. "The town got a sheriff and you got a wife, a son, and a baby on the way."

"Well, I'm not so sure about all that," Bettina said with an indignant sniff.

Cassie stole a look at the group. There was some sort of history there and something that meant all was not entirely peaceful in the town of Angel's End. But every town had its stories, just like the one in West Texas from which she'd fled.

The sheriff and his friend casually dismissed Bettina's comment with grins.

"I own the saloon, if you feel the need," Ward said.

"I won't," Cassie assured him. A saloon full of drunken cowboys was the last place on earth you'd catch her, with hell being a preferred location.

"Suit yourself," he said casually as he wandered over to look at the boots lined up on the shelf. Cassie moved around the barrel so she could keep everyone within her line of sight.

"I was told you have the tax bill on the property?" she asked the sheriff.

"I'll bring it around when the snow melts," he said with an easy smile.

"I can pay it today . . ." Cassie began.

Cade help up his hand. "I'll have to hunt it down and I know you want to get back before nightfall. There's no rush. I know where you live."

That was exactly what she was afraid of. While she'd been talking to the sheriff, Jake Reece had closed the distance between them. Being surrounded by three strong men, all of whom were considerably bigger than her, made Cassie very uncomfortable, yet she was determined not to show it.

"If you had taken the time to introduce yourself last night, instead of waving that gun around, it would have saved us both a lot of heartache," Jake said.

"I didn't expect the man who wrote to me about my grandfather to also be a thief," Cassie retorted.

Jake shook his head and looked toward the ceiling. "I didn't steal your donkey. She came to me. It's a bad habit she has. Every time she has a problem she comes running to me. So obviously she doesn't like you. It must be your charming personality."

Cassie opened her mouth to reply and then stopped when she heard the soft voice of Manuel at the door. He stood hesitantly at the entrance of the store, not sure if he was welcome. Cassie wasn't sure of his welcome either. There were places in West Texas where a Mexican would be shot just because he dared to speak.

"Come on in where it's warm," Cade said, and opened the door for her man. Bettina let out an impatient huff and Cassie couldn't help but notice that her husband gave her a stern look.

Manuel took one step inside and then one to the right of the door so he was out of the way. He kept his eyes on the floor as he spoke. "I have the donkey," he said. "Do you need help with the supplies?"

"I haven't purchased them yet," Cassie explained. She walked past Jake, who grinned as if he was vastly amused.

"I will wait outside," Manuel said, and went out as quietly as he'd come in.

Cassie gave her list to Mrs. Swanson, who studied it for a moment and then handed it to her husband. "We're low on supplies right now," he said. "But we can take care of the necessities." The two of them went to work, gathering stores.

"Where did you live before you came here?" Cade asked.

"Texas." Cassie knew her answer was vague and Texas was a big place. Easy to get lost in and hopefully easy to lose. It was better to be honest than not. Not answering would have made the man just more curious.

Ward worked his way around her and leaned casually on the end of the counter close to the door. His dog stood beside him and looked between her and his master as if she were considering a threat. Between the three men and the big dog Cassie was having a hard time staying calm. She could tell by Ward's lazy smile that he knew she had a history, and it had only taken him a few minutes to figure that out. So much for lying low. When you had to eat and people were relying on you, there was only so much hiding you could do.

"Well, we'll let you get your shopping done," Cade said. "And I'll drop by after the melt with that tax bill."

"Thank you, Sheriff," Cassie said.

"It was nice meeting you," Ward said. He took off his hat and gave her a courtly bow.

"Try to keep your donkey in line, Miss Parker," Jake said as he followed the other two men out the door.

Cassie narrowed her eyes at the man as he grinned at her. She should have followed her instincts and shot him last night.

FOUR

"Now that was curious," Ward remarked to Cade as he stepped onto the porch where Ward sat with Lady. Now that it was warmer, Ward and Lady liked to engage in their favorite pastime, which consisted of watching the goings-on in Angel's End, or as Pris called it, being nosy. Neither one of the men spoke as they watched Cassandra Parker and Manuel ride out of town with the spare mule loaded down with supplies and the donkey trotting somewhat stubbornly by her side.

"Which part?" Cade asked as he leaned against the porch post. "The part where she's trying to hide the fact that she's a woman?"

"You caught on to that?"

"Well her hair looked as if she'd sawed if off with a dull knife. That was a sign. But any woman that pretty who wears that many downright ugly clothes doesn't want to call attention to herself."

"Is she gone?" Jake interrupted them as he came out of the saloon with the puppy safely tucked in his arms.

"She just left," Ward said.

"I'll go and collect my supplies then," Jake said. "If there's anything left. I settled up the bill inside," he added.

"I'll be out that way in a few days," Cade said.

"You're welcome to stop by," Jake replied and stepped off the porch.

"Wait," Ward said as a thought hit him. "Didn't you say you'd opened an account for Sam's heirs down in Denver?"

"Yes, I sold his stock and put the money in the bank. Actually in that bank," Jake said as he pointed to the Curry and Hayes sign across the street. "I see that they've taken over the stage route."

"And the post office too," Cade said.

"Don't change the subject," Ward declared. "Why didn't you tell Miss Parker about the money?"

Jake shrugged. "I didn't feel like it," he said, and went on his way.

"Well don't that beat all," Ward said as he watched Jake walk away.

"It appears to me like Miss Parker got on the wrong side of Jake in a hurry," Cade said.

"If it comes down to a battle of stubborn, we're going to be in for a treat," Ward said.

"You think so?" Cade asked.

"She had that tilt in her jaw." Ward leaned his chair against the wall and put his legs up on the porch post. "I used to know a girl with hair that color," he mused. "The color of corn silk. Hair that color makes me think of summertime and picnics on the riverbank and stealing sweet kisses in the moonlight."

Cade grinned as he turned from his perusal of the street. "Sounds like you had a nice time growing up. Which river was that?"

"None of your damn business," Ward growled. His past was his own and not something he'd seen fit to share with anybody since coming to Angel's End. It kept things simpler. He'd come here to escape it, not share it with the world. Something Cassie Parker had in common with him, he was certain.

Cade laughed out loud. "I'm betting Cassie Parker would rather not be kissed. By any man, yourself included."

Ward thought about it for a second and that was it. While her lips were kissable, there was something about her, a sense of tragedy and an air of hostility that put him off. "While it may be tempting, once she fixed her hair and put on a dress, I'm guessing that pistol she kept fondling in her pocket would be enough to warn anyone off, including me." While he did occasionally long for the companionship of a good woman, he already knew that Cassie Parker was not for him.

"You saw it too?" Cade turned back to watch the woman disappear from sight.

"I saw that she had a tight hold on something in her left pocket and wondered more than once if she was planning on shooting her way out of the mercantile."

Cade easily dismissed that notion with a shrug. The sheriff was fast, Ward had seen proof of it. Cade could have taken her down without killing her. "What's the story with her grandfather?"

"He was a grouchy old son of a bitch." Ward considered

what he recalled about Sam Parker. "He could put Dusty to shame on one of his worst days. Didn't want anything to do with anyone. He was here before I got here and the only thing he seemed happy about was the fact that I opened the saloon. I never saw him talk to anyone beyond acknowledging their presence."

Ward pulled the remnants of his cigar from his pocket and lit it again. He took a long drag before he continued. "He ran a few head of cattle, got along all right with the rest of the ranchers, if you can call not talking being cooperative. Jake found his cattle mixed in with his, spring before last, and went to check on him. He was sitting up dead in his rocking chair and had been there awhile." He stopped for a moment, out of respect for the dead, grouchy and otherwise.

"Jake had him buried, checked around and found a son's name and address in a Bible and wrote him a letter. That was the last any of us thought of it. Jake made sure the house was closed up, sold off the cattle and livestock and put the money in an account in case anyone showed up. I believe that flock of chickens pecking around in your yard came from Sam Parker's place."

"And Jake didn't bother to tell her about the money?" Cade asked as he once more checked the streets, looking up one end and down the other, as was his habit.

"Nope," Ward replied. "Not that he won't. Jake is as honest as the day is long. He's just mad that she got the best of him on the trail last night. I reckon this is the first she's talked to anyone around here."

"Why do you suppose that is?" Cade asked

"I think she might be the reason you thought you saw a sheep."

Cade's mouth dropped open at the thought and he looked at Ward incredulously. "Surely not."

Bringing even a single sheep into cattle country was one of the deadliest sins one could commit. Ward knew it and Cade knew it. Dang near everyone knew it. "There's got to be some reason she's acting so squirrelly," Ward said.

Cade looked in the direction the small party had gone. "I reckon there's only one way to find out."

Ward blew a perfect smoke circle into the cold air and watched it drift downwind. "Let me know when you ride out. I think I need the exercise."

Cade crossed his arms, leaned against the post and shook his head. "Jake isn't going to like it. Isn't he the head of the Cattlemen's Association this year?"

"Yes. And he can just put it on his list of things he don't like," Ward said. "But Jake isn't the one you should be worried about."

"Watkins?" Cade asked. Watkins ran the biggest spread around, with Jake's coming in a close second. Watkins felt the size of his ranch coincided with the size of his worth and was always trying to throw his weight around, especially when it made him a dollar. He hadn't been too pleased with the fact that Cade was appointed sheriff. Ward knew it was because he'd wanted to bring in one of his own men, someone who would secretly be on his payroll. The few times trouble had been able to make it through the deep snow to town it was in the form of Watkins's men, and Watkins didn't take too kindly to Cade putting them in jail to cool off. Luckily for everyone around, Cade had the grit to stand up to Watkins's veiled threats, and gave back as good as he got.

"Watkins," Ward said in affirmation.

"I reckon I'll have to attend a few meetings of the Cattlemen's Association too," Cade said. "Just to get to know everyone."

"And head off trouble before it shows up?" Ward asked.

"Something like that," Cade said. Cade stepped off the porch and walked toward the cozy little house he shared with Leah.

The bell in the church steeple clanged crisply in the chilled air. Children poured out of the building like water in a chute. Leah's son Banks saw Cade and ran for him with a wide grin on his face. Cade ran his hand through the boy's blond hair when the boy joined him and the two of them continued on companionably into the house. The rest of the kids came on down the street in Ward's direction. He recognized the Martins' tribe of three sets of twins and a few others' children whose names Ward didn't even know. The schoolmarm, Margy Ashburn, followed along after them. She held her skirts up around her ankles to keep them dry from the melting snow and marched onward, looking neither right nor left. She was much too pious to even look in the saloon's direction, which gave Ward considerable amusement. With her nose up in the air she kept going until she passed the mercantile and went into the Swansons' house where she rented a cold and lonely room.

The town of Angel's End was peaceful and Cade Gentry, as sheriff, was determined to keep it that way. But Ward had a feeling that peace might be a hard thing to keep since Cassandra Parker showed up. And part of him hoped he was right, just so things would be interesting.

FIVE

When would she learn? Was the stupid donkey worth the trouble it caused? Cassie slammed the bolt on the stall door in hopes that it would keep the recalcitrant Libby where she belonged. Libby looked up at Cassie with her big brown eyes and brayed loud and long, a sad and mournful song for her lost freedom.

Trying to fool yourself made you the biggest fool of all. Libby hadn't caused the ruckus; she was just doing what came natural. Cassie had to admit to herself that it was her own stubborn stupidity that made her act as she did on the trail. She leaned her head against a wooden post and thunked it one time, in the desperate hope that it would knock some sense into her. All it did was add fuel to the fire of the ever increasing headache that pounded in her temples.

"You have got to think." She gave voice to the things that tumbled in her mind. "And quit letting fear rule you." The image of a pair of moonlit eyes flashing silver as they stared down at her in surprise ran through her mind. He didn't know she was a woman until he saw her lying in the snow. There was no threat in his eyes, but there was something there, something that unsettled her to her core. Cassie couldn't help but wonder what might have happened if she hadn't gotten her gun back. She'd made herself vulnerable. She'd shown her hand too soon and now Jake Reece was suspicious of her. Another problem to add to the ever increasing pile that plagued her.

It hadn't always been this way. There had been a time in her life when she would have laughed at the actions of the foolish Libby, and would have greeted the man on the trail with friendly caution instead of hostility. There had been a time in her life when she trusted and laughed and was filled with optimism. Now the only people she trusted were her mother and Manual and his wife Rosa, and the only thing that filled her with optimism was her never-ending practice with the guns. As for laughter, the kind that sprang forth from deep within, the kind that meant your life was full of joy and happiness, that was something she barely remembered.

"It will take time, Cassie," Manuel said as he came into the barn with his faithful dog Max by his side. "The donkey must think she belongs or she will continue to run."

I know just how she feels . . .

"Do you think she will run to the same place again?"

"If she has good memories of this man, then yes."

"So we need to mix her in with the herd as soon as possible?" Cassie asked.

Manuel grinned. "The flock."

Cassie couldn't help but smile back. "Sorry. Still getting used to it." The soft baa's of the sheep drifted around the barn. How far would it carry in the still night air? How long until the local ranchers found out there was a bunch of sheep right in the middle of cattle country?

She shouldn't even worry about what just happened. It was nothing compared to what might happen in the near future. When the word got out, and it would eventually, trouble would come calling in a hurry.

"Put her in a pen with some of the ewes so she'll get used to them," Cassie said. "And spoil her so she doesn't think she'll have it better someplace else."

"Like Rosa does with me?" Manuel's dark eyes sparkled as he unsaddled Puck, Cassie's appaloosa.

"Like Rosa does with you," Cassie agreed.

"Perhaps Rosa should take care of Libby also," Manuel teased.

"Go tell her," Cassie teased back. "I'm sure Libby will enjoy your company when Rosa runs you out of the house."

Manuel's laughter rang out joyously. Puck tossed his head along with the laughter and Max joined in with a woof. Cassie smiled, grateful for the laughter that came so easily to Manuel, even after all his tragedy. She hoped someday she would feel joy like that again.

They walked in companionable silence back to the house with Max following along beside them. The air was crisp without the frigid bite that left Cassie shivering most of the time. There were nights when she was so cold she was certain that her bones would shake loose from her skin. She hoped those nights were behind them for a while.

She could honestly say the heat was the only thing she missed about Texas. Texas had been the biggest mistake of her life, but there were some small blessings because of it. She'd met Manuel and Rosa there. Without them, she would have thought there was nothing left in the world but evil.

They stomped the snow from their boots and opened the door to mouthwatering smells. Cassie's stomach rumbled in anticipation of the meal that Rosa was preparing. It had been a long, hard winter and they were all looking forward to something other than beans and rabbit stew.

The cabin, like the outbuildings, was nice. She hadn't expected much but was pleased with what she found when they arrived shortly before the first snow hit last fall. It sat close to a stand of tall pines that did much to shelter it from the howling wind that roared down from the mountains. It was well built and snug, without any cracks that let in cold air. It had needed a thorough cleaning, which Rosa had attacked with ferocity, until she discovered a family of raccoons living beneath the floorboards. Manuel had deemed them harmless, saying as long as the coons were there the snakes would probably find another place to hibernate. That was all Rosa needed to hear and the raccoons stayed. The sound of their chatter led to much frustration on Max's part but he'd finally gotten used to it and mostly ignored it by flopping on the floor over the source with a huff before adding his snores to the symphony.

Three rooms covered the main floor. One was large and stretched from front to back. It contained the kitchen and living area. A huge stone fireplace split the cabin with doors on either side that led to bedrooms. Opposite the fireplace was a narrow staircase that led to a large loft. Cassie could only assume the cabin was here when her grandfather came west. She couldn't imagine any other reason why he needed that much room as he'd been all alone, as far as she knew.

The furniture was functional, shabby, yet sturdy, as if it had traveled far and been around for a long while. A large built-in hutch ran along the wall in the kitchen area. Between the odds and ends her grandfather had and the few pieces that survived the trip from Illinois to Texas and then to Colorado, there was plenty here for their housekeeping needs.

Cassie quickly shed her outer garments and traded her boots for a pair of fleece-lined moccasins.

Her mother sat in the rocking chair by the fire. She was wrapped in a thick shawl with her hands lying loosely in her lap and she stared at the fire, seeing nothing, as she had since that day that changed everything for both of them. Still, Cassie, always hopeful, went to her, knelt by her side and touched her right arm.

"How are you today, Momma?" she said as she picked up her right hand. Max looked up from his place on the rug and his dark eyes reflected the sadness that Cassie felt whenever she looked at her mother.

Her hair, once a pale blond like Cassie's own, was now faded and gray, turning that way overnight in Cassie's mind, although in reality it had been two years since the stroke that left her mother an invalid. Her blue eyes, once brighter in color than Cassie's, were vacant and the left side of her face pulled down from paralysis. Her body slumped to the left as that part of her was dead, along with her ability to speak. Cassie wondered again, more times than she could count, if her mother was still there, inside, or if she had simply gone away after the horrors of that day and left nothing behind but an empty shell.

"She is the same as always," Rosa said simply. "I've already fed her, so sit and eat."

Once more Cassie felt the crush of disappointment. The lost hope of a miracle that would never be. How many mornings had she awakened and thought, *Please God, let my mother be better today*? How many evenings had she come in hoping that today there would be some sign of her mother?

A slight tightening of her hand when she grasped it. A look of recognition in her eyes that said "I'm still here."

Cassie took her place at the table and let Rosa fill her plate. As always, Rosa took her hand, and then Manuel's, and Cassie obliged and completed the circle because she would never hurt these two people, not intentionally. Cassie closed her eyes and listened to the familiar words as Rosa prayed for the soul of their only child, a son who'd been killed shortly before his twentieth birthday. Then Rosa kissed the silver cross that hung about her neck and it was time to eat.

The rest of the evening passed as usual. Cassie helped Rosa clean up after the meal. Manuel repaired a harness and Rosa picked up her knitting when the kitchen was done. Cassie read from a well-worn volume of Shakespeare and they all listened to the sounds of the raccoon family as they stirred beneath the floorboards. Finally Manuel turned Max out for the last time before bed and Rosa and Cassie led her mother to the room they shared.

Her mother was compliant as always. No change in her face as they went through the motions of putting her to bed. She no longer had control of her bodily functions so she wore a diaper, like an infant. She was changed and cleaned and a warm gown put on her before she was tucked beneath the covers. Rosa, always patient, did more for her mother than anyone should have to and Cassie was grateful. Before she left, Rosa sat on the edge of the bed and said a prayer for her mother.

Even though a chamber pot was handy, Cassie bundled up again to make the nightly trip to the outhouse. Using the chamber pot meant more work for Rosa and she did enough, in Cassie's mind. Rosa had cared for her and her mother ceaselessly since Manuel found them, urging them to stay when they had nowhere else to go. Rosa's heart was made of gold as far as Cassie was concerned and her place in heaven well earned.

Max bounded up to her as she stepped out onto the back stoop. The moon hung bold and bright in the crisp sky. Cassie still wasn't used to having to look for it as it played hide-and-seek with the mountain peaks early in the evenings. Cassie had decided soon after arriving that she liked it better here. The sky seemed closer and it wasn't as vast. One could lose oneself in a West Texas sky. She nearly had.

One of the sheep bleated and another answered it. A dark shape dashed behind the outhouse. A coyote? Max looked in the direction of the shadow and his ears rose as he listened. Cassie heard the chatter of a coon and saw the tracks in the snow. Max let out a slight whine, a sign of his never-ending frustration at not being able to rid his home of the unwanted guests. Cassie touched the top of his head to console him before she stepped onto the worn path. If it was a coyote lurking about, Max would give chase.

Cassie shivered uncontrollably as she went about her business and hurriedly arranged her clothes back into place. Since they came here, it seemed as if she couldn't wear enough clothes or get close enough to the fire.

Max followed her into the house and went to his place on the rug by the banked fired so he had a clear view of all the doors in the cabin. If anyone came in or went out, he would know about it. Max took good care of his family.

The soft sounds of night always gave Cassie a hollow feeling inside. The murmur of Manuel's and Rosa's voices, so cozy within their room, only served to accent her own loneliness.

Her mother's eyes were closed. Whether she was asleep or simply lying there Cassie could never tell, as she was always the same. Never better, never worse, just there. Cassie often wondered if her mother was even conscious of the fact that she lay beside her each night and listened to the sound of the air going in and out of her lungs, while her prayers alternated between hoping they would stop and then begging God not to take her. The problem was he already had.

Cassie had been told by a well-meaning pastor, not too long ago, that God would not give you any more troubles than you could bear. She then searched the Bible from front to back, in hopes of finding something to offer her comfort. The closest that she could find to what the pastor said was 1 Corinthians 10:13. *There hath no temptation taken you but such as is common to man: but God is faithful, who will not suffer you to be tempted above that ye are able; but will with the temptation also make a way to escape, that ye may be able to bear it.*

What tempted her? Nothing. Cassie would not allow herself to be tempted. The only thing she truly asked God for was peace for her mother and the wisdom to understand what that might be. Surely this nonexistence she led could not be construed as peace.

SIX

Jake looked out over his valley. The snow was gone, either by melting or by the trampling of his herd. It still clung stubbornly to the mountains, covering the peaks with a bright white blanket that gave a chill to the air. But the sun was warm and the ground, soft with moisture, promised a coming bounty of bright green grass. His men and their horses went about their work with joy as they shook off the lazy bindings of winter.

By his count, close to a thousand cattle were spread across his valley. It hadn't been an easy job, scaring them out of the canyons where they took shelter during the winter. Not all had made it. They'd found many dead, either from wolves or the weather. And not all of the cattle were his as they were yet to be sorted. Jake and the other ranchers knew cows did not recognize brands. Until all of the ranchers got together and figured out which cow belonged to whom, there was no way of knowing how he or anyone else had fared.

Thinking about the other ranchers brought his mind around to Cassie Parker. Had she really been here all winter long without a soul knowing it? After he'd found Sam Parker dead, Jake had poked around his place a bit and found an old family Bible. Like most Bibles, it held the history of the Parker family. It turned out Sam had a wife, once upon a time, and a son. From the dates written within, it appeared as if both died during the war. The son had a wife named Loretta and there was a daughter, Cassandra. Stuck within the pages he found a letter from the son to Sam. Jake hated to be nosy but he read it anyway. The son was a doctor for the northern forces. And he missed his wife and daughter.

Jake sent a letter to the address on the letter he found, notifying them of Sam's death. And he couldn't help but wonder why Sam left Illinois. Why his son went to the war. Why those who remained behind hadn't stuck together.

If he had ever had any family that's what he would have done.

Josie, who'd spent the two weeks since Jake brought her home chewing on every boot he owned, stuck her head out from his jacket and gave a curious woof at the spectacle before them.

"Not yet, little girl," Jake said. "Those cows would stomp you into a puddle before you knew what hit you." He rubbed the top of her head with his fingers and she proceeded to chew on his glove.

"Dang it, I'm not going to have anything decent left if you don't soon outgrow this chewing stage," he said as he pulled his finger from her mouth. Josie's mouth followed his fingers until her eye caught the button of his coat and she went to work on that.

A shout from one of his men caught Jake's attention. Two riders were coming from the direction of his house. Jake quickly recognized Ward's big bay and the pale horse that Cade rode. With a flick of his heels he urged Skip forward to meet the two men.

"What brings you two out?" Jake asked when they were within speaking distance.

"I'm paying a visit to your new neighbor," Cade said. "Thought you might want to tag along." The three of them met up and their horses stood nose to nose so the riders could talk. Josie whined and tried to claw her way out of Jake's jacket when she caught sight of Ward. Ward reached over and rubbed her head. She caught a fit of the wiggles so Jake handed her over to Ward. Ward settled Josie into his lap where she promptly started chewing on the horn of his saddle.

"I thought it might be a good idea," Ward volunteered as he tried to pry Josie's teeth off his saddle. "Kind of a good-news-bad-news thing. And while you're there you can invite her to the Cattlemen's Association meeting. Have you set a date for it yet?"

"Yes, this Thursday," Jake said. "And what the heck does good-news-bad-news have to do with me?"

"Gus, being the mayor, is all worried about Miss Parker paying her back taxes," Cade explained. "And since you got the information on the account you set up in Sam's name after you sold off his stock . . ."

"It wouldn't seem so downright rude," Ward finished for him. "I can't imagine anyone would be too sociable when the first thing you tell them is that you're there to collect money."

"She sure as heck wasn't worried about rude when she ambushed me on the trail two weeks ago," Jake said.

"Seemed to me she was more worried about my cussing than whether or not I was being polite."

"Jake, seeing as how I've heard you cuss, I can't say that I blame her," Ward said with a grin.

"I think we can all agree that Miss Parker isn't the friendly sort," Cade said. "But like it or not, she still owes taxes on her property and Gus sent me out here to make sure the town gets paid. And if the town gets paid that means I get paid, so I'm kind of personally invested in the entire process. You can come with us, or we'd be happy to deliver the news about her money, if you want to give us the details."

"I'll ride along," Jake said. "Your company is better than what I've had lately. Just let me swing by the house and pick up the bank book."

"It looks like the pup is working out all right," Ward said as he handed Josie back.

"Josie?" Jake rubbed her head as she attacked the button of his coat once more. "I'm pretty sure I'm going to have a shortage of good leather boots, and all my table and chair legs look like they've been chopped with an axe."

"So you're saying she's a chewer?" Ward said dryly.

"Just a bit."

"Give her some bones to gnaw on," Cade suggested. "Something with gristle."

"Next time we butcher, I will," Jake said. "If my house lasts that long. Did you find homes for the rest of the puppies?"

"Jared Castle took two of them. A miner showed up and his pretty daughter took a liking to one and took it with her. Believe it or not, Zeke took one and the stage driver took the last one home to his wife."

"Sounds like they all got homes," Jake said. "'Cept maybe the one that Zeke took."

"I don't know," Cade said. "The first time I ever saw him smile was the day he picked up that pup."

"Wait, Zeke actually smiled?" From experience Jake knew the assayer, Zeke Preston, wasn't the friendliest person around. He also had a bad habit of saying exactly what he was thinking, which most of the time wasn't good.

"Like he was lovesick," Cade replied.

"A good dog is worth its weight in gold," Ward said. "And considering the parentage, you gotta know these pups are all winners."

"Why Ward, if I didn't know you any better, I'd think you were in love with Lady."

"I've never had a woman look at me the way that dog does," Ward admitted.

Cade and Jake both laughed. Jake glanced casually at the sheriff as they rode along. He'd been determined to hate Cade Gentry since he had lied about who he was, and, mostly, because he'd stolen Leah from him, but he seemed to be decent enough, no matter what his faults. Lord knew Jake had enough of his own. This was the first time he'd ever had a relaxed conversation with Cade. He couldn't be all bad if Leah loved him, which she did, and her son seemed to have taken to him really well.

So maybe he wouldn't hate him. Maybe he'd tolerate him for a bit until he figured out if he was as good as Leah and Ward seemed to think he was. But if he ever hurt her . . .

"Quite a spread you got here Jake," Cade interrupted his musings.

"Thanks." Jake nodded his head.

Ward laughed.

"What's so funny?" Jake asked.

Ward shook his head. "I'm just happy to be alive, that's

all. Speaking of . . . I'm surprised that crazy Chinaman hasn't killed you yet."

"He gave it a good try this winter," Jake admitted. "Or at least made things interesting."

"Where did you find a Chinaman all the way out here?" Cade asked. "I thought I was dreaming when he walked out on the porch and told us where to find you."

"More like a nightmare," Ward said. "He was carrying one of those big knives of his."

"Yeah, you don't want to mess with Fu when he's got a knife. He's downright deadly with them. And to answer your question, he found me," Jake said. "In Denver. The first year I drove down to market. He was hanging around the stock pens looking for the skinniest round eye he could find, or so he says. He figured whoever was real skinny was in desperate need of a cook, and he was right. There are a lot of things I can do but cooking isn't one of them."

"It takes a great man to admit his faults," Ward observed.

"Why should I bother when I got you and Fu pointing them out to me all the time?"

"You're welcome," Ward said.

They'd reached the house and the two men waited on their horses while Jake took Josie inside and got the bank book from his desk drawer. They were soon on their way again, out of Jake's valley and up the road to the turn to the Parker spread.

"How did everyone fare the winter?" Ward asked. "Jared said he found a lot of carcasses up in the small valleys."

"It was rough," Jake admitted. "Lots of them got trapped when the first snow came and couldn't get out. I'm almost afraid to count. There's no way of knowing until we get them all together and start separating them out, which should be done by the end of this week."

"Will this be at Watkins's place?" Cade asked.

"Always is," Jake said.

"I'll be around then. It will be a good chance for me to meet all of the ranchers."

"Not me," Ward said. "Being around all that work makes me downright uncomfortable."

"Just admit it, Ward," Jake said. "It's all that castrating that you can't stand."

Ward shifted in his saddle. "You got that right."

"It'll be good for Miss Parker to attend the Cattlemen's Association so she can get a handle on how we do things around here."

"Yep," Ward said. "I bet everyone will be anxious to meet her."

Jake gave Ward a look. He'd been acting funny since he showed up. Like he had a secret that he just couldn't wait to tell everyone. Knowing Ward, there was no sense in asking. He'd let him in on it when he was good and ready, so there was nothing to do but just sit back and wait. The three turned up the trail that led to the Double P. With the P's standing back to back, Jake always thought that the brand looked like a tree.

"That is if she's planning on raising cattle," Ward continued.

"What else would she be doing on a ranch?" Jake asked.

"Lots of things," Ward said. "Just because it's a ranch doesn't automatically mean you've got to raise cattle."

"What else would she raise?" Jake asked.

"Silkworms?" Ward suggested

"Silkworms?" Jake said. "What in tarnation?"

"Ask Fu," Ward said. "They have them in China. Where do you think silk comes from?"

"I don't know, Ward," Jake said. "Silk's not something I think about a lot."

"That's something I'd like to see," Cade said. "A herd of worms. Do you think they put tiny little brands on them?"

Jake raised an eyebrow at the sheriff, who grinned widely at the notion. He felt like the butt of a joke. "Is there something you're not telling me, Ward?"

"Nothing that I know for certain," Ward admitted. "But I have a feeling."

They rode around a bend over a rise and Parker valley opened before them. Strange that it was still covered with snow, but upon a closer look, Jake realized the snow was moving. And it stunk to high heaven.

"Well I'll be damned," Cade said. "I didn't imagine it."

"I thought so," Ward said.

Jake looked between the two men. "What?" he asked.

Cade pointed at the house that sat up against the trees, at the barn and other outbuildings and at the snow that shifted beneath the warm sun.

"Sheep," Cade said with a grin.

Jake blinked. "Holy hell," he said.

"Exactly," Ward summed up for the three of them.

SEVEN

A bark from Max alerted Cassie to the prospect of visitors. She shaded her eyes against the bright sunshine and watched as three riders stopped on the rise. She knew exactly why they stopped. The last thing they expected to see in the middle of cattle country was three hundred sheep. There was no hiding it now. Her secret was out and there was nothing left to do but own up to it.

Manuel was on the opposite side of the sheep pen, which they had hastily erected last fall by weaving tree branches together. Libby, short for Liberty in Cassie's mind, stood in the middle, seemingly oblivious to the milling of the sheep around her legs. Cassie waved to Manuel to get his attention and pointed at the riders. Manuel nodded and whistled for Max.

Cassie walked toward the visitors, who were moving once again, coming down the drive to meet her. Her short jacket hung on a corral post and she put it on. She checked to make sure the revolver was still in the pocket. She picked up her rifle, which was leaning against the post, and continued on, around the corral where Puck and the two mules pricked their ears with interest toward the approaching riders. Cassie glanced up at the house and saw Rosa had come out. Cassie's mother sat in a chair on the porch, wrapped in a shawl with her face turned to the sun. Rosa went to her side. Cassie stopped beneath the big oak tree that sat at the foot of the rise to the cabin and waited.

Even though she'd only seen them once, Cassie recognized the lean silhouette of the sheriff and the broader frame of the saloon owner. Which meant the third rider was Jake Reece.

Libby must have recognized who it was at the same instant as Cassie. She brayed long and loud and charged to the side of the pen. Cassie cringed at the sound of snapping wood. Their quick job last fall was enough to hold the sheep, but it wasn't much against a determined donkey. Libby kicked her way through the loosely woven branches and passed Cassie in her haste to get to the riders. The men pulled up as Libby charged up the road, braying with all her might. She stopped when she got beside the horses and lipped at the boot of the man Cassie had accused of stealing her. At least now she understood why the man had her in his possession. Obviously Libby was in love with him. That knowledge, while humorous, didn't make the situation any less humiliating.

The sheep discovered the opening in the pen and milled about, adding their questioning baas to Libby's brays. Max ran to the front of the flock and proceeded to nip at the sheep in his gallant efforts to herd them back into place. The sheep were torn between their devotion to the donkey and the strictness of the dog, and they jumped over each other and turned back and forth until the entire flock was nothing more than a big fluffy mass of confusion that tumbled back and forth until the three riders, the donkey and Cassie were nothing more than sentinels in a sea of wool.

"Well this has turned into a fine day," Cassie muttered. There was nothing left to do but keep going, although she felt a bit foolish with the rifle in her hand. If the three men wanted to shoot her on sight she'd have to say they were justified.

"Good afternoon, Miss Parker," Ward called out over the constant baas. "Fine day, isn't it?" The man seemed to be having a good time. The sheriff looked cautious while Jake looked downright furious. All of the horses stood with their ears laid back at the noise and general confusion. Cassie felt like she was in the middle of a kettle that was fixing to boil.

"I guess that depends on why you came calling," Cassie yelled back. The situation might be next to impossible but it was still her place and she didn't recall inviting anyone to drop in. "Why are you here?"

The sheriff took a piece of paper from his pocket and waved it. "Is there someplace we can talk?" he yelled.

Cassie looked up toward the house. Rosa had gotten her mother inside while all the madness was going on. She knew the piece of paper was about her taxes. She could only hope that she had enough money left to pay them. If not, the lot of them would be kicked out of here in a hurry because of the sheep.

"Up at the house," she said and pointed. The men turned their horses and started for the house. Libby followed. The sheep followed Libby. Max barked and circled in an effort to herd the sheep, the donkey and the riders into the pen. Cassie watched the disaster and wished that the earth would just open up and swallow her. Finally Jake motioned his friends onward. He turned his horse and loosened the rope that hung from his saddle. He quickly and effortlessly looped it around Libby's neck and led her to where Cassie stood. The sheep followed and Max nipped at their flanks to keep them moving.

Jake handed her the coils of rope and looked down at her with his flinty eyes, while the sheep milled around them. "You have got to be the most gol-durn woman I have ever met," he said.

Cassie grabbed the rope close to Libby's neck and pulled her close. She was having a bit of trouble hanging on to the donkey with one hand and the rifle with the other while the sheep jostled her. The presence of the overbearing man on the horse right before her didn't help much either. Still, she refused to be intimidated.

"Well at least I now know where this donkey learned her manners from," she said.

What was it about him that set her on edge more than any other man she'd come across? For the most part she ignored men, only dealing with them when it was necessary. She made sure she was free of any unwanted attention by the way she dressed and the threat of her guns, but this one . . . it was the third time she'd met him and it seemed as if his plain purpose for being on this earth was to harass her.

"Are you comparing me to an ass?" he asked incredulously.

"If the ears fit . . ." Cassie smiled sweetly. It was a nice revenge for the way he'd been haunting her dreams lately also.

"At least I've got more sense than to bring a bunch of sheep into cattle country."

"Oh, is it cattle country?" Cassie responded. "I don't recall seeing any signs. Not once did I see anything that said *sheep unwelcome* or *shepherds keep out*."

"You know good and well that this is cattle country or you wouldn't have snuck this herd in here last fall without saying a word to anyone."

"What business is it of yours if I have sheep?" Cassie's voice raised a pitch at his audacity.

"I'm the man who wrote you the letter telling you your grandfather was dead," Jake snapped back. "So everyone in the country is going to blame me for you and your gol-durn sheep."

"You are the one who found him?" Cassie said in surprise. The kind and thoughtful letter didn't match her imaginings of the man sitting before her.

Jake took off his hat and wiped his gloved hand over his hair. It was light brown in color, thick, and cut short and neat. For some reason, when she'd thought about the man who found her grandfather and written the letter, she'd imagined someone older and kinder. Not someone like Jake Reece, who seemed to be put on this earth just to agitate her.

"I am," he said. "And if you'd quit waving a gun in my face every time I come close I might tell you about it sometime."

She really couldn't argue with that since he was right. She'd met him three times and two of those times he'd see a gun in her hands. Still, it was hard to let go of both the gun and her pride. They were the only things that kept her safe.

The sheep were finally under control again. Manuel and Max had them rounded up and back in the pen. Half a day's work was wasted as they'd been trying to separate out the pregnant ewes when the men rode up. Cassie led Libby to the corral. She leaned her rifle against the boards, opened the gate and sent Libby trotting inside with a slap on her rump. Cassie lifted the lasso off as the donkey went by and coiled it up. She walked back to where Jacob Reece waited and handed the lasso up to him.

She took a deep breath and looked up at the man who seemed to tower over her from his horse. "I'd like to hear about it, and see where you buried him, if you don't mind," Cassie said.

"I'll show you when the sheriff is done with his business," he said. Then to her surprise he held a hand out to her. "Want a ride?"

Cassie was taken aback by the offer. His eyes on her were steady yet cautious. The thought of climbing up behind him, of being that close to him . . . not just him but any man. She couldn't show her fear.

"No thanks, I'll walk," she said.

"Suit yourself." If she hadn't been standing so close she wouldn't have seen the slight twitch of his knees that told his horse to move. The horse jumped forward at a trot and flicked its tail right in her face. Jacob Reece rode up to her house without a backward glance.

EIGHT

"Now that wasn't a bit neighborly," Ward said as Jake dismounted from Skip and joined him and Cade on the porch of Cassie Parker's house.

"Which part? The part where she showed up carrying her guns or the part where we were surrounded by sheep?" Jake asked.

"The part where you just rode off and left her," Ward said.

"I offered her a ride and she didn't want it," Jake groused. "Of course it might be because she's loco. She'd have to be to bring sheep into cattle country."

"Maybe we should hear her side of the story before we pass judgment," Cade said.

"I don't know," Ward said. "No matter what her reasons, it's still not a good decision. I imagine the reaction when the Cattlemen's Association finds out there's a couple of hundred sheep around won't be good."

"Yeah, and I'll be the one that will have to deal with it," Jake growled. "What difference does it make to you anyway?" he asked Ward. "It's not like you've got a dog in this fight."

"My income depends upon the happiness and well-being of everyone in this valley," Ward said. "And since things seem to come to a head in the Heaven's Gate, I'd like to know what's going on so I can keep the peace and my furniture."

"Well I got a feeling things are going to get a whole lot worse before they get better," Jake said as Cassie stepped onto her porch. Once more he was struck by how small she was. She barely came up to his shoulder and he was six feet tall. Next to Ward and the sheriff she looked downright miniscule. Yet she was feisty. She'd put him on his back quick enough on the trail and she knew how to hold a gun.

"I'm sorry about the sheep," she said right off as she leaned her rifle against the wall. "Not that they're here," she quickly amended. "Just that they got out and in your way. It's not the usual way I welcome visitors."

"You don't have to explain yourself to anyone," Cade said. "As long as you can pay what you owe you've got the right to do whatever you want with the property." He handed her the tax bill.

"Wait just a doggone minute," Jake began. He could not believe that the sheriff wasn't protesting the presence of sheep. But then again, why would he? After all, the man had posed as a preacher. Allowing sheep in cattle country wasn't that much of a reach after that.

"Don't you have something for Miss Parker too?" Ward interrupted.

"Tell me again why you're here?" Jake asked Ward, who was having entirely too much of a good time. Jake took a moment to work his jaw when he realized it hurt from being clenched so tight. Something about Cassie Parker had him all twisted up inside. In the past few weeks he'd just put it down to her getting the best of him on the trail but after the recent events, he was certain she had come to Colorado for the express purpose of aggravating him.

Right now she looked a bit paler than normal as she perused the tax bill. It had to be high, with the property being two years in arrears. Maybe she didn't have enough, even with what was in the bank.

"Can't a body be neighborly?" Ward said in reply to Jake's question. He gave Jake a look that would have shamed a lesser man. But a lesser man didn't have to worry about having sheep on his range. Still, Jake was an honest man, even if he was feeling a bit stubborn at the moment. He dipped in his coat and pulled out the bank book.

"After your grandfather died I took his stock to market with mine. I sold them and deposited the proceeds in an account in Denver at the Curry and Hayes bank. It turns out they just opened up a branch in Angel's End when they took over the stage line. All we have to do is go to the bank and I'll add your signature to the account and take mine off and the money is yours."

There. He felt better about telling her, especially when he saw the relief on her face when she realized how much money was in the account. Still, he couldn't help but think maybe it wasn't a good thing that she had the money. Without it she'd have to go. There were a whole lot of people who weren't going to be happy about her sheep and Jake knew good and well that Raymond Watkins would be one of them. Eventually the word would get out. It was impossible to keep this many sheep hidden, especially now that spring was here and the hands would be out, searching all the ridges and valleys for strays.

"It's so much," she said. Her blue eyes were full of gratitude when she finally tore them from the bank book and looked up at him. "Thank you." Her words were genuine but guarded and her eyes quickly changed when she realized that perhaps she'd given too much away. Jake took it as a challenge. She could let her guard down, when she wanted to. What could he do to bring back that look? But more important, what was it that she was hiding? Cassie Parker was a mystery, a tiny woman with secrets and a herd, no, they didn't call them herds, it was a flock. A dang flock of sheep.

"If you two don't mind working out a time to go to the bank I'll let the mayor know when he can expect the money," Cade said. He tipped his hat as if in apology. "Just doing my job, ma'am."

"Whenever it's convenient for you," Cassie said to Jake.

"How about tomorrow morning," Jake said. "Say nine?"

"I'll be ready," she said.

"I'll let Gus know," Cade said and in one graceful motion stepped off the porch and onto his mount. Ward, always one to take his time, walked to the edge and looked out across the valley. Jake had to admit it was a pretty sight, even with the sheep. The land rolled a lot more than his. The house sat snug against a line of pines that served as a windbreak. The barn and corral and a few outbuildings lay down a small rise to the left, while the road out curved up and to the right. A stream ran behind the house and barn and split the valley. A flat bridge, wide enough for a wagon, went over it, and the overgrown trail led to the ridge that separated their property. The stream meandered on down and ran parallel to the road they came in on. Eventually it crossed Watkins's land. Even though it wasn't his only source of water, Watkins would have plenty to say about the sheep fouling up his water when he found out. And eventually he would.

"You live out here by yourself?" Ward asked.

"No," Cassie said. "I have Manuel." She waved at the Mexican who walked toward the house with the dog at his side. "And his wife, Rosa."

"I thought I saw two women on the porch when we rode in," Ward continued.

"My mother." Cassie, with her will-o'-the-wisp hair sticking out in all directions, looked directly at Ward and spoke in a tone that would put a momma grizzly to shame. "She's not well, and she doesn't take to strangers. They upset her."

"I'd be the last one to do that." Ward put his hands up in surrender. "Just wanted to make sure you were well taken care of." He stepped off the porch and mounted up beside Cade. "Ranching is a hard life for a woman on her own."

Cassie shaded her eyes against the sun that poured onto the porch as she looked at the two men. "As you can see, Mr. Phillips, I'm quite capable of taking care of myself and all of those in my care."

"Some might think it's too big of a burden for such narrow shoulders." Ward's tone teased.

"Those who think so can keep their opinions to themselves." She might be tiny but there was no fear in her. She reminded Jake of a honey badger he'd seen in a traveling zoo. The critter came all the way from India and was as feisty as they came. He'd felt sorry for the creature when he saw it, at the way its keeper kept poking into its cage with a stick. But it never gave up; in spite of all the odds being against it, it kept on fighting. Still, Cassie Parker needed to know what she was up against if she was determined to stay.

"That's because no one realizes you've got these sheep up here," Jake said.

"Why, Mr. Reece, if I didn't know any better I'd think that was a threat."

Yup, she was definitely a honey badger. "Confound it," Jake sputtered, "you've really got no idea what kind of trouble will be coming your way once everyone finds out there are sheep up here."

She turned to face him. "As the sheriff said, what I do on my property is my business."

"You see that stream?" Jake pointed. "It comes down from those mountains. Before it gets here it runs underground and then out again, right before it hits your boundary. The water in it is as pure and sweet as water can be. It goes clear across your property, and then it crosses the road, running onto a property owned by a man named Raymond Watkins. And I know for certain that Raymond Watkins will have something to say about your sheep fouling up his water."

It took Jake a moment to realize that he was practically shouting at her. There was something about Cassie Parker that agitated him to no end. Especially when she stood before him, no bigger than a minute, with her arms crossed as if she were daring him to cross some invisible line. It also didn't escape his attention that Ward and Cade were both sitting on their horses watching the two of them as if they were putting on a show. He felt like the keeper in the zoo, poking the stick at the honey badger. Poke. Poke. Poke.

If she was aware of the two men watching them, she didn't show it; instead, she drew herself up as if she could sprout a couple of inches and came right back at him. "That's the most ridiculous thing I've ever heard," Cassie said. "Are you telling me that there is no other water on Watkins's property? There's water all over the place here. That's one of the reasons we came here, plenty of water, plenty of land and plenty of room for everyone and everything."

"Oh he's got water, and plenty of it," Jake came right back at her. "He's also got the most land and the most hands and the most cattle and the most money, which means if he don't like something he's got the power to make sure it's gone, and I guaran-damn-tee you that he's not going to be happy about your sheep."

"Language, Mr. Reece," she said in a voice that was suddenly silky smooth. "You seem like an educated man. Can't you come up with a better way to express what you're feeling?"

Jake opened his mouth and shut it again. She had to be the most frustrating woman ever put on this earth. Why was she here of all places?

"I don't know, I thought that was pretty creative." Ward grinned. "How about you, Sheriff?"

"Definitely creative," Cade agreed. "But after my brief time as a minister, I also have to agree with Miss Parker. Cursing is just a lazy way of saying what you're thinking."

Jake had to resist the urge to shoot both of them on the spot. "Neither one of you is helping," he said.

"And you consider this to be constructive?" Ward asked. "It's like watching the rams butt heads up in the high country."

Ward was right. There was no talking to this woman. There'd been no talking to her the night he met her on the trail and there was no talking to her now. She'd figure it out soon enough and with luck she'd pack up her sheep and her people and hightail it back to wherever it was she came from. Maybe he'd even offer to buy her out, to make it easier on her. *Why would I even care?*

Jake took a deep breath, took off his hat and ran his gloved fingers through his hair. In a much softer and polite tone he offered, "If you can spare the time right now, I'll show you where your grandfather is buried."

He caught her off guard. Cassie blinked and nodded. There it was. The unguarded look that showed there was another side to her. "I would greatly appreciate it," she said in a tone that matched his.

"You can go now," Jake said to Ward and the sheriff. "I'm not likely to kill her today."

"Make sure that you don't," Cade said, and the two men rode off, Ward wearing a big grin. Jake was certain he'd be the subject of much conversation, but it wasn't the first time Ward had a good laugh at his expense, and it probably wouldn't be the last.

They stood on the porch for a moment with an uncomfortable silence growing between them until finally Cassie spoke. "Just give me a moment to check on my mother."

"No problem," Jake said while she slipped through the door as if she were afraid he'd follow her. "Well don't that beat all," he mumbled to himself when the door shut firmly behind her. Jake walked to the end of the porch that offered the view of the mountains.

Cassie and the sheriff were right. It shouldn't be anyone's business what she did on her own property. He knew good and well that he'd resent it if someone tried to tell him what he could and couldn't do, but still . . . sheep . . . it was like she was asking for trouble, yet it was also like she was hiding. Was she so skittish because of the sheep? Or was there more to it? Dang it all, he was the one who was going to have to deal with all of the backlash since he was the head of the Cattlemen's Association. Jake huffed out a breath of air.

Manuel and the dog arrived at the house. The Mexican seemed as cautious and standoffish as his employer. "Hello," Jake said as the man stepped onto the porch. "I'm your neighbor, Jake Reece." He crouched down and motioned for the dog. The dog looked at its master for a moment. Manuel made a slight motion with his hand and the dog went to Jake slowly and cautiously. Jake removed his gloves and let the dog sniff his hand. The dog's tail wagged a few times as the animal allowed Jake to pet him. "I love a good dog," he said. "And you are a fine one indeed." He looked up at Manuel. "What's his name?"

"Max," Manuel responded. He lifted a finger and Max returned to his side.

"Well trained too," Jake said. If he could get Manuel to talk, maybe he'd reveal some things about Cassie. Obviously it wasn't going to be easy. "I just got a pup a few weeks ago. Right now she's more interested in eating my house than learning anything."

That got a smile from the man. "Like everything else, it takes time." He spoke English well, in a soft-spoken way, with just a slight accent. The man was educated. So what was he doing so far away from home with a herd, no, dang it, flock of sheep?

"Something to remember with animals and people," Manuel added. Jake nodded in agreement, wondering if the older man was offering advice about Cassie.

The door opened and Cassie came out and Manuel and the dog went in. The revolver was no longer in her coat pocket and she left her rifle on the porch as they silently stepped off the porch and walked around the house.

"Looks like you've got some varmints sharing your quarters," Jake said as he saw a bushy tail disappear between the stones that served as the foundation of the house.

"Yes, it's a family of coons," she said. "We left them there to scare off the snakes."

"Practical," Jake said. "They probably moved in when the house sat empty for so long. You're lucky you didn't find them inside, although I locked it up real well, or so I thought." A sudden realization came to him. "Just exactly how did you get in? I still have the key at my place."

"I broke out a window. It was easy to repair, as there was some glass in the shed."

"Why didn't you just come get the key? I'm pretty sure I mentioned in the letter that I would hold it." He wished he could see her eyes, but as they were walking side by side and she was so much shorter, he couldn't. "Was it because you didn't want anyone to know you were here?"

She stumbled over a rock and Jake quickly grabbed her arm to keep her upright. It took Cassie a moment to regain her balance and when she had, she shook off Jake's hand like he was a leper and kept on walking.

"Does that mean I was right about you not wanting any-one to know you were here?" Dang it, he should have ignored it but there was something about her that made him want to pick and prod like he was poking at a hornets' nest with a stick. Poke. Poke.

He knew he'd probably get stung, or thrown on his back in the snow, but still he did it.

"What difference does it make?" she snapped.

"It doesn't, if you've got nothing to hide. But it seems to me like you knew people would be unhappy about the sheep so you were trying to keep them secret for as long as possible."

"It's not news to me that people would be unhappy about the sheep. It's one of the reasons why we came here in the first place."

"Because the people in—where is it you came from?—were unhappy about the sheep?"

"Texas. We came from Texas." Talk about a vague answer. Jake shook his head.

"Texas is a big place. You want to narrow it down some?"

"West Texas."

"That narrows it down some." Jake couldn't help but laugh. Getting answers out of Cassie Parker was next to impossible.

"What difference does it make?" she asked again. "We're here now. Where were you before you came to Colorado?"

"Many different places," Jake admitted. "But originally Boston."

"Boston?" She almost stumbled again and she turned to look at him when she'd regained her footing. "Really?"

"I have nothing to hide," Jake said. There he went again. Poke. Poke. "Why not Boston?" They'd come to the row of pines that sat along the back of the house. Snow still lay beneath them, as the ground beneath was sheltered from the sun. Jake walked to one that had lost its lowest branches. The bark was scraped from elk and deer rubbing their horns against it, and the ground beneath littered with pinecones and sticks. There was a rock beneath the snow that marked the head of the grave.

"It just doesn't seem to suit you," she admitted.

"As West Texas doesn't seem to suit you," Jake replied. He nudged a pile of snow beneath the tree with his boot. "This is the place."

"Oh," she said. Cassie stared at the ground as if she could see what lay beneath it, and then she knelt in the cold snow. She picked off the leaves and pinecones, and with her bare hand smoothed over some rabbit tracks that crossed over it.

She looked vulnerable kneeling there, with the pale skin

of her neck exposed as she bent her head and said a silent prayer. She sighed as if she held the weight of the world on her narrow shoulders. Maybe she did. Jake didn't know enough about her to know what burdens she bore, but it seemed like a lot.

A lot of things that she hid from the world.

"Tell me about it," she said. "Tell me how he died."

Jake closed his eyes against the gruesome scene that he'd found. There was no need for her to know her grandfather had sat there for a few days. "Near as I can tell, his heart just gave out. He just sat down in his rocking chair, closed his eyes and died. It seemed like it was peaceful."

"The chair by the fireplace?"

"Yes." Jake toed a pinecone off to the side. "It was springtime and the ground was soft so I brought him out here."

"You buried him?" She turned and looked up at him. Her eyes seemed bluer in the dim light beneath the trees. "By yourself?"

"I did." He dragged his boot around the snow, curving it as if to make the edge of the grave. "I didn't see any need to get anyone else."

"Did you know him well?"

Jake shrugged. "As well as anyone around here I guess. He wasn't . . ." Jake scratched his chin as he searched for the right words. He didn't want to say anything bad about Sam Parker. The man had been in this valley before he arrived and as far as Jake knew he always kept to himself. "He didn't seem to want to get close to anyone."

Cassie nodded her head in agreement. "It makes sense. My mother said it was like the light went out in him when my father was killed and then my grandmother died soon after. It couldn't have been easy for him. He seemed to shut out the world after that."

"Were you close before?" he asked.

Cassie looked off into the distance, out of her valley and past the mountains, to the east, as if she could see all the way to Illinois. "We were," she said. "Before the war came."

"Illinois seems a bit far from the battlefields. What made your father go?"

"He was a doctor. He had friends he went to school with who enlisted. He felt like that was where he was most needed."

"Your grandfather kept a letter he wrote in his Bible. That's how I knew where to send it."

"Bible? There's no Bible in the house."

"It's at my house. I didn't want to leave it. I wanted to make sure it was safe in case someone showed up. I didn't even think about it until now."

Cassie turned her pale blue eyes upon him. "It's a good thing you did," she said. "Keeping the money for me and writing the letter. Most people wouldn't have bothered."

Jake was surprised to feel a blush creep up his cheeks. "You must have run across some bad people," he said. "I find most are honest, or at least I like to think so." Jake always wanted to see the best in people. He needed to see the best in people, but he knew better than to expect them to behave that way. There were plenty of selfish ones, and more than a fair share of bad ones out there. "In my experience what goes around comes around so I like to keep the odds in my favor by trying to do the right thing."

"If only more people were that way." She grew silent and looked away. Jake realized something had happened to her, something bad enough that she wanted to keep the entire world at bay. Something that had her carrying a gun and an attitude that said shoot first and ask questions later. She started to rise and Jake held out his hand to help her. She wouldn't take it. Instead she wrapped her arms around her body as if she were cold.

Whatever had happened to her, it was bad, and the thought of it only made Jake more curious. The desire to poke was still there, but maybe he'd be a bit gentler when he did it.

"Thank you for everything," Cassie said, and just like that, Jake knew he was dismissed. He didn't mind. He had work to do.

"I'll see you in the morning," he said and left her there, standing by the grave. As he mounted Skip, he felt as if there was something else he could or should do, but for the life of him, Jake couldn't figure out what it was.

What he did know was that things were going to get ugly. If only he could find a way to stop it, but he might as well tell the wind to quit blowing. And it was a cold wind that pushed at his back as he rode home.

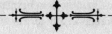

NINE

Cassie sat straight up in the bed. It took her a moment to realize where she was. The dream had taken her so strongly that she was disoriented. As her heart slowed from its panicked gallop, she heard the slow and steady breathing of her mother and reality surrounded her once more.

Dawn would be here soon. Cassie sensed it more than saw it. She was afraid to close her eyes again, afraid that she'd be caught once more in the dream, so she eased out of bed.

The advent of spring had helped with the coldness that always surrounded her. She didn't feel the need to wear as many clothes or wrap up in her heavy coat now, but she did put on her robe as she walked to the window and pulled aside the heavy curtain.

As she expected, it was still full dark, but dawn was there, close at hand. She'd thought the dreams were behind her. Like Texas, she'd put them in her past, locked up tight in a box and buried deep in a hole. For some reason they'd surfaced again and it was too much of a coincidence that they'd begun again right after meeting Jake Reece on the trail.

But why? Cassie had learned to trust her instincts. The one time she didn't was the one time things went horribly wrong. Her instincts were telling her now that Jake Reece would not hurt her. So why was she so terrified of him?

There were no answers to be had in the empty darkness around the cabin. Cassie put on her clothes, picked up a lantern and went to the barn. She heard the skitter of tiny feet as she opened the door and stepped inside. "We need a cat," she said as she held the lantern before her to make sure all the creatures that came out at night knew she was there.

Puck and the mules stirred in their stalls. Libby, who'd been put in a stall to make sure she didn't take off again, gave out a squeaky bray at the interruption to her dreams.

"I'm beginning to think you are more trouble that you are worth," Cassie said as she walked by her stall. Libby responded by turning away from Cassie so that she was talking to her backside. "I'm not impressed," Cassie responded.

There were a pair of goats across from Libby and a milk cow between, all of whom made the trip with them north from Texas. Cassie was pleased that they'd all survived, down to every chicken, both rooster and hen. She'd formed a partnership with Manuel when she realized she had a place for them to go. Manuel and Rosa needed a refuge and Cassie needed a reason to go on living.

She stopped when she arrived at Puck's stall. The horse came to her, as he always did, since the first time she'd met him. They'd both needed healing. Cassie found the quiet presence of the horse a soothing balm for her fractured soul and she knew in her heart that Puck felt the same. Cassie went into his stall and wrapped her arms around the horse's neck. Puck shifted his weight so that they leaned into each other. He was small enough—only fifteen hands or so—that she could easily mount him, and there'd been many a times when she'd done just that, slowly building his trust and conquering his fear, after the abuse he'd suffered.

She named him Puck after the character in Shakespeare's play, *A Midsummer Night's Dream*. She thought the name fit the appaloosa's odd markings and his whimsical nature. Manuel deemed the horse hers, as he said she was the one responsible for healing him. She hoped, here in Angel's End, they would all be able to heal. Manuel and Rosa had managed well enough before Cassie and her mother moved in with them, but after, when she was the sworn enemy of the richest and most powerful man around, life had become impossible for all of them. Jake Reece's letter, when it finally found her, seemed like an answer to her prayers. Still, Cassie couldn't help but wonder, as she picked up the currycomb and went to work on Puck, if there would be more trouble here. One good thing about Angel's End: she wouldn't have to worry about running into the man who raped her here.

Cassie met Jake at the bottom of her valley, where it joined the main road. She was dressed in the clothes she usually wore, but for some reason, when his storm cloud eyes glanced at her, she felt inadequate. Especially when she noticed that he was dressed nicely, in a brown leather jacket, a plaid shirt and a clean and pressed pair of jeans. His boots shone from a brushing and his jaw was clean shaven.

She caught herself twisting the flyaway ends of her hair

as if she could make it grow faster. At one time it had been down to her waist and someday it would be again, if she left it alone. Right now it was just at an awkward length, too short to pull back but long enough to be in her way. In the wintertime she wore a knitted hat to keep it tame. But now, with the warm weather, she just wore the wide-brimmed Stetson that kept the sun off her pale skin, as she had a tendency to burn.

"Pretty day," Jake said. He was riding a different horse this morning, a beautiful palomino stud that was full of himself, if his arched neck and flowing tail were any indication. Cassie eyed him dubiously as she fell in beside Jake on Puck.

"Don't mind Bright," Jake said as he rubbed the golden neck with evident affection. "This is his first trip out this spring so he's feeling his oats."

"Bright," Cassie said as she admired his lines. "That's a good name for him."

"I thought it suited him," Jake said. "That's an interesting mount you've got. I haven't seen many appaloosas up this way."

"This is Puck," Cassie began.

"As in Robin Goodfellow?"

His quick answer surprised her. "You read Shakespeare?" Cassie asked.

"The winters are long and lonely," Jake answered. "And I have plenty of books."

"Yes they are," she replied without thinking. "Unfortunately I only have the one book of Shakespeare's plays."

"When you come by to pick up the Bible, you can help yourself to any book on my shelves," he offered.

She was completely taken aback. "Thank you," she said finally. She hadn't considered going to his place and picking up the Bible. She just assumed he would bring it to her. He'd given her a reason to go, but was she brave enough to risk it?

He looked at her as they rode, once more studying her. Cassie was glad she had her hat pulled down low on her forehead to shelter her face from the sun, which blazed warmly against her side. "You're not used to that," he said.

Cassie looked up at him from beneath the brim of her hat. "Used to what?"

"People being nice to you."

Was he teasing her again? His face was inscrutable. "What makes you say that?" Cassie asked.

"Because every time somebody is nice to you, you look surprised."

Cassie's first reaction was to protest. Then she noticed he was grinning at her. It was almost as if he enjoyed antagonizing her. Or could it just be teasing? It had been so long since Cassie had interacted with a man besides Manuel that she wasn't sure how to react. When she saw his grin, she had a sudden desire to reach over and smack his arm, just because he was enjoying himself so much.

Her fear, so easily found, wouldn't let her. It controlled everything she did. As long as she stayed in her safe little circle, she was fine, but when she was out, and around other people, it ruled her life. Would it be that hard to let her walls down, just a little?

Not every man was a rapist. But how could she tell? She never would have considered Paul Stacy capable of the deed. The best way to stay safe was not to let her guard down, as tempting as it might be to do so with Jacob Reece.

As she couldn't go around waving her gun in his face, she relied on her other weapon to keep the walls up. Words could build walls just as easily as weapons and she knew from experience that they could sting just as much.

"Are you always this nosy?" she asked. "Or is it just me?"

"I wouldn't call making an observation being nosy," he quickly replied. "And believe me, you're going to have a lot of people in your business once they find out what you've got in your little valley."

Cassie refused to look at him. She didn't want him to know that she was worried about the reaction to her sheep. "As long as I keep my sheep in my valley it shouldn't be anyone's business what I do."

"Suspicious and defensive," Jake said. "That's an interesting combination in a neighbor."

Why did he agitate her so much? Was it deliberate? Was he trying to get a rise out of her? She shouldn't respond and yet she couldn't help herself. "I don't recall asking for your opinion or your approval," Cassie retorted. "I've managed just fine the past couple of years without either."

"And how is that working out for you?"

"And once again, you've come back to being nosy," Cassie said. "Like your constant use of bad language, it's a bad habit."

He put his hand over his heart as if she'd shot him. "Why, Miss Parker," he drawled. "I've been a perfect gentleman this morning. Nary a curse has left my lips."

He was teasing her, yet she couldn't help but think that there was also genuine concern there. That may have scared her more than anything. Cassie shook her head and rolled her eyes. "I think it best if we not talk anymore."

"Ever?"

"Don't tempt me," Cassie said. "Until we get to town. And only when it's necessary."

"I am wounded to my very core."

The look on his face let Cassie know that his imaginary wound wasn't serious. He grinned at her and arched an eyebrow in question. The grin was nice, and it cleared the storm clouds from his eyes like a fresh wind. It would be so easy to soften her edges, to enjoy the back-and-forth of conversation, to sink into knowing Jake Reece like she used to sink into a good book, but she couldn't. She was weak and she wouldn't survive it again. She could not let him in.

Instead she concentrated on the scenery around her. She'd not had a chance to pay attention to such things since she'd only been out of her small valley the one time, and she'd been too angry then over the incident with Libby to notice her surroundings.

Colorado was beautiful. The majesty of the snowcapped mountains, the varying shades of green that blanketed the ground, the clear purity of the water that tumbled through the stream along the side of the road. Everywhere she looked made her think of God as an artist with a great canvas and a pallet full of glorious colors. The wonder of it hurt her eyes.

What would her life be like if she'd received the letter about her grandfather's death before the decision was made to go to Texas? What would she have done? If she had known what lay before her, then no, she wouldn't have gone, but if she had known there was another option at the time, would she have chosen Colorado?

Cassie had to admit she still would have gone to Texas. How many attorneys offered a woman a chance to study law? It was all she'd wanted for as long as she could remember. Both her parents were educated. Her father had been a doctor, and her mother a teacher at a very exclusive school in Chicago, a position she found after Cassie's father's death. Cassie was able to attend the same school and could have taught there if she wanted, but she wanted to be an attorney. When she'd received the letter from Arthur Gleason saying he would take her on, she'd been thrilled.

"Did you forget the way to town already?"

Cassie pulled up on the reins to stop Puck. She'd been so lost in thought that she'd forgotten where she was and who she was with.

"I know I'm not supposed to talk, but if you want to get to town you've got to take this fork," Jake said.

He was right. They'd come to the fork in the road and the sign was plainly marked "Angel's End."

"You can go that way if you want," he continued. "Maybe that's part of your plan. You can go up there and jump some claims and get the miners mad at you too."

"With an attitude like yours it's a wonder the entire community isn't at war," Cassie replied as she turned Puck in the right direction. "Maybe if you talked about peace as much as you do fighting, there wouldn't be any problems."

"Oh no," Jake said. "You've got no one to blame but yourself for what's coming."

"Thank you for being the voice of doom," Cassie said. "Did it ever occur to you that if I just sat down and talked with the rest of the ranchers and explained to them that I plan on keeping my sheep within the confines of my valley that there won't be a problem? Or is everyone around here as unreasonable as you?"

He laughed and shrugged his shoulders good-naturedly. "Don't say I didn't try to warn you." Cassie shook her head in disgust, and with a gentle nudge of her heels sent Puck into a slow trot, intent on leaving Jake Reece behind. But he easily caught up and fell in beside her.

"The voice of doom," he said. "That was a good one. And you are?"

"The voice of reason," she said. "Which has been sorely missing if you are any indication."

He chuckled some more. It was a nice sound. Pleasant

and comforting. He was a hard man to stay irritated with—
and that frightened her more than anything.

The road curved and rose in a gentle slope and the town
stood before them. Smoke poured from a chimney and the
sound of a hammer hitting iron echoed off the buildings.
Cassie recognized the lean form of the sheriff as he walked
across the street with a black-and-white dog on his heels.
There was a wagon in front of the store, and a pair of horses
stood at a hitching post in front of a building past the saloon.

" 'Devil's Table Café'?" Cassie read the sign as they rode
past the mercantile.

"Yes," Jake said. "It belongs to Dusty. He considers himself a rebel, but the food is good, so no one complains."

"It's an easy guess how the town got its name," Cassie
said as she looked at the statue of an angel with outstretched
arms and wings that stood on a pile of stones in the middle
of the street. "But where did the angel come from?" she
asked.

"It was here when the town was first settled," Jake said.
"The only thing we can figure is someone tried to take it
across the passes and realized they weren't going to make
it so they left it here."

"It must have killed them to leave it," Cassie said. She
stopped Puck before the statue and looked up at the face of
the angel. It was worn smooth by the wind, but the features
were still there, offering welcome and forgiveness for any
who needed it.

"It would have killed them to take it," Jake replied. Bright
stood next to Puck, but when Cassie looked over at Jake, he
wasn't looking at the statue, but beyond, at a house on the
end of the street, right before the church. He must have realized she was watching him because he suddenly turned to
her. She had grown accustomed to his eyes being a stormy

gray, so she was surprised to see them verge on blue when he stared into hers.

"Sometimes you've just got to leave your burdens behind," he added.

If only she could. Jake Reece was getting too close for comfort. Cassie felt as if he knew things about her, things no one should know. There was no way he could, and yet his words often seemed to carry a hidden message. It made her uneasy. She couldn't afford to let anyone get close to her. "Where's the bank?" she asked.

Jake pointed to a building on the right, just past the statue. "Curry and Hayes Stage Line and Bank" was scrolled importantly on the sign.

They dismounted in front of the bank and tossed the reins over the rail. Cassie hung her hat on the saddle horn and tugged at the ragged ends of her hair. She really should have worn better clothes. If she wanted to be taken seriously as a landowner then she should dress the part. That didn't mean she had to wear a dress, but maybe she should invest in some better quality clothes for business gatherings.

Jake stopped and studied Puck.

"He's not good around strangers," she warned him.

Jake indicated the scars on Puck's flanks. "I can see that he had a bad time before he came into your care."

"He did," Cassie said. "There were some who said he should be put down."

Jake held his hand out, palm down, beneath the white blazed nose of her horse. "It would have been a waste," he said. "You can tell by looking into his eyes that he's intelligent and has a lot of heart."

"That he does," Cassie agreed. She watched carefully as Puck's nostrils flared and the horse snuffed at his hand.

Finally Puck dipped his head and allowed Jake to rub his neck.

"I'd say he's lucky you took him in," Jake said as he turned.

"The feeling is mutual," Cassie said in wonder. It was the first time she'd ever seen Puck let anyone touch him. He was even skittish around Manuel, except when she was close by.

"Well." Jake looked around as if he were searching for an excuse not to go inside. He must not have found one, so he opened the door for Cassie as if she were dressed in silk and satin. "Let's get this over with," he said.

Cassie stepped inside. Apprehension gripped her. Signing the account over to her might be an ending for Jake, but it was a beginning for her. How it would turn out was another matter entirely.

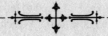

TEN

There were two clerks inside. One served as a postmaster and worked the stage office, and the other one worked the bank. The postmaster was middle-aged and wore a wedding band. The other was around Cassie's age, gangly and tall with thin black hair that he wore slicked back from his forehead. He gawked at Cassie when she ran her fingers through her hair to fluff it up. Jake went to the window with the bank book in hand.

"I need to transfer this account from my name to Miss Parker's," he said.

The clerk looked at the book and his brows rose up close to his hairline.

"Will you be making a withdrawal, ma'am?" he asked. "I have to send to Denver for the money if it's over one hundred dollars."

Cassie joined Jake at the window and opened the tax bill

for the young man to see. "I need to have this amount paid to the town for taxes," she said. "Whichever way the town prefers is fine with me."

"I'll ask the mayor," he said. He went to a desk and moved some papers. Jake turned and leaned against the ledge so he could see the door. Cassie kept her eyes on the bank clerk. She wasn't anxious for any more conversation with Jake. He left her too unsettled.

The bell rang over the door and Jake shifted suddenly, straightening up from his casual stance. Cassie turned to see what had his attention.

A very pretty and very pregnant woman came through the door. Her light-brown hair was neatly swept up in a twist and she wore a beautiful shawl against the cool springtime air. She looked so much a lady that Cassie decided then and there that she was going to the mercantile to find something decent to wear.

"Leah," Jake said casually. "It's good to see you." There was something in his voice that caught Cassie's attention, and she studied him while he looked at the woman. His eyes were once more that stormy gray that intrigued her so.

"It's good to see you too, Jake," Leah replied. "I see you fared well over the winter."

"As did you," Jake replied.

Leah's hands went to her burgeoning belly. "Yes, we did," she said. "Cade and I are very happy."

"I'm glad for you, Leah." His words sounded genuine and he smiled at her.

"Thank you, Jake. That means the world to me to hear you say so."

Well that was interesting. There must have been something between them at one time. And now Leah was married to the sheriff. Leah's green eyes settled on Cassie with expectation and without judgment. Cassie wondered if she should speak or maybe give Jake a quick kick to remind him of his manners.

"I'm sorry," Jake said. "This is Cassie Parker. She's Sam's granddaughter."

"I heard you've taken over his spread." Leah held out her hand to shake Cassie's. "My husband is Cade Gentry, the sheriff."

Cassie hesitated a moment and then took her hand. It had been a long while since she'd been around such friendly people.

Leah squeezed it gently. "I'm so sorry about your grandfather. He used to come into the café where I work. He was always a gentleman."

"Thank you," Cassie said. "It's nice to hear people talk about him so kindly."

"Since you're in town, why don't you come by the café for lunch? It's a great place to get to know the townsfolk."

"We'll see," Cassie said. "I've got a lot of work to do at home."

Jake suddenly choked. Or was he laughing? Cassie eyed him suspiciously. Leah looked between the two of them with a slight smile on her face.

"Is there something wrong?" Cassie asked.

"Oh no, I'm fine," he finally croaked. He cleared his throat. "Here's the paperwork," he said.

"It was nice meeting you," Leah said. "Take care, Jake."

"You too, Leah," Jake replied. "Tell Banks I said hello. And my promise of a horse for him is still there."

"I'll talk it over with Cade," Leah said, and went to the opposite window to talk to the postmaster.

"Banks is her son," Jake said by way of explanation when

he joined Cassie at the bank teller's window. "He's six . . . no, he would have turned seven over the winter."

"She seems very nice," Cassie said.

"She is," Jake agreed. He picked up the pen and signed his name and handed the paper to Cassie. His handwriting was very neat and concise, a lot like the man. Cassie signed her name where the clerk indicated. They repeated the process two more times.

"Is that it?" Jake asked.

"That's it," the clerk said. "I'll send two copies to the office in Denver and keep the other one here. Is there anything else I can do for you, Miss Parker?"

"Yes, I'd like to withdraw twenty dollars."

"Planning on shopping?" Jake asked.

"I'm pretty sure he said you were done," Cassie replied. The clerk gave her the money and carefully recorded the transaction in her book, even going so far as to subtract and write the still healthy balance on the line. Cassie put the money and the book into the inside pocket of her jacket. "So you can go on about your business and leave me to mine."

"Think you can find your way back home?" he asked with a grin. "Because you got lost on the way here."

"Your life must have been boring before I got here," Cassie replied. "Seeing as how all you've got to do now is antagonize me."

That set him back on his heels. His mouth opened and closed again and without another word he left. Cassie watched him go with a look of amusement on her face. It was fun leaving him speechless, but she regretted it as soon as the door shut behind him. She felt very alone.

She did have business to do. Leah had just finished with the postmaster and looked at Cassie with an amused expression on her face. Maybe she could help with the first thing on her list.

"Would you happen to know of anyone who has a cat they'd like to get rid of?" she asked. "I've got a barn full of mice."

"The Martins do," Leah said. "I'll take you there."

"No, just point me in the right direction," Cassie said.

"Nonsense," Leah said. "I can introduce you to the brood." She looped her arm through Cassie's, and Cassie realized Leah would not take no for an answer. Besides, it felt rather nice to know that the people of the town were so friendly. It certainly hadn't been true in the last place they lived.

"The Martins own the livery stable," Leah said as they walked outside. "Where you got Libby?"

"Actually my friend Manuel purchased Libby when we arrived last fall."

"It's a shame the weather wasn't any better. It was one of the worst winters we've had in a long time," Leah continued. "And the Martins have three sets of twins."

"Three sets of twins?" Cassie said. "I couldn't even imagine."

Cassie listened to Leah's conversation with half a mind while she searched the street for Jake. She saw his palomino standing in front of the Heaven's Gate Saloon.

"Isn't a little early in the day to be drinking?" she said without even realizing she spoke out loud.

"Jake?" Leah said. "You don't have to worry about him. He's one of the most levelheaded men I know. He and Ward are best friends, although sometimes when they talk to each other you wouldn't know it."

"I wasn't really worried," Cassie started to protest.

Leah smiled at her and continued on. "It's a shame Jake hasn't met the right woman yet. He's got so much to offer and I know he'd make a great father. He's always been good to my son, Banks."

Cassie managed to gracefully separate her arm from Leah's by stopping and pretending to search for something in one of her pockets. She really didn't care about Jake's marital status, although she'd just assumed he wasn't by the way he talked to her. And he had not mentioned a wife. But she was curious about some of the things Leah said and what she'd observed between Jake and Leah in the bank.

"Doesn't that bother the sheriff to have Jake offering his son gifts?"

"Cade is my second husband," Leah explained. "Banks's father died five years ago. Cade and I got married last Thanksgiving. And as you can see, we didn't waste any time." She touched her belly.

"It's really not any of my business," Cassie apologized.

"Nonsense," Leah said. "The entire town knows everything that happened. That's the way of it in Angel's End. We look out for each other and we care about each other."

They arrived at the house by the livery. Leah knocked on the door and then pushed it open. The sweet smell of roses assaulted her senses as Cassie tentatively followed Leah inside.

"Oh you're in luck," Leah said. "Nonnie's making some of her rose salve and soap. It's wonderful for dry skin." She showed Cassie her hands. "Mine sure do take a beating."

"It does smell good," Cassie admitted as she wondered who exactly Nonnie was and if they should have just walked into the house. Leah led her into a kitchen. The scents of roses and almonds filled the air. A long trestle table was covered with small crocks and baskets. An older woman sat at the table crushing almonds in a heavy stone mortar with a pedestal. Both pieces seemed ancient to Cassie but the smell coming from the large pot on the stove was enticing. A younger woman with red hair turned to greet them with a large ladle in her hand.

"Gretchen, Nonnie, this is Cassie Parker."

"Sam's granddaughter," Gretchen said in greeting. "And the owner of Libby," she continued. "Welcome to Angel's End."

"Thank you," Cassie said. "As far as owning Libby, it seems like she has a different version of ownership than I do."

Gretchen's eyes went immediately to Leah and she grinned widely. "Oh I do think I'm going to like having you as part of our little town," she said. The words were genuine and they made Cassie feel hopeful and welcome, but her cautious nature would not let her do anything more than smile graciously at Gretchen.

Nonnie pulled out the chair next to her. "Come." She patted the chair. "Sit."

"Oh, I can't," Cassie protested. "I must get home."

"We heard your mother is here also?" Gretchen asked.

"My mother is an invalid," Cassie said. "Which is why I need to get back."

"Oh, I'm sorry to hear that," Gretchen said. "Perhaps Nonnie and I could ride out and visit someday. And Leah also."

"Before this baby gets in the way of me traveling." Leah placed a hand on her burgeoning stomach.

Cassie hated to be rude but she didn't want anyone visiting her mother. They wouldn't know the vibrant and beautiful person she'd once been. They'd only see the empty shell she was now. She didn't want her mother exposed to their pity, yet how could she say no? Ever since she'd walked into the bank with Jake, she'd felt overwhelmed. Unsure whether to trust the friendly welcome she seemed to be receiving. Luckily Leah saved her from having to make excuses for why they shouldn't visit by changing the subject.

"Cassie needs a cat," Leah added.

Gretchen dropped her ladle and dried her hands on her apron. "Thank goodness," she exclaimed. "You have definitely come to the right place. It just so happens I have a spare. Actually I have four spares if you want more than one."

"Gretchen, the twins will kill you!" Leah said.

"What they don't know won't hurt me," Gretchen said with a laugh. The banter between the two women was so easy it made Cassie feel strange, as if she were looking through a window. It would be lovely to have a friend like that. Someone to talk to and to share her fears with. She was so used to keeping everything inside, everything private, that she could not even begin to imagine what it would be like to share confidences with someone. She'd thought friendships such as this only existed for schoolgirls.

"Actually I was just thinking, if you don't mind, you could take the momma cat," Gretchen continued. "There's less chance of her getting pregnant again if she's living out in the country. The last thing we need in this house with six children is more kittens underfoot."

"As long as you don't mind," Cassie started.

"Heavens no," Gretchen exclaimed. "You'd be doing me a favor. Come with me to the barn and I'll show you the momma cat. You can have your pick of the kittens too."

"I'll let you two get to it," Leah said. "I have to get back to work." She turned to Cassie and stuck out her hand. "It was so nice to meet you."

Cassie had no choice but to take it and Leah gave her a

reassuring squeeze. "It was nice meeting you also," Cassie said.

"Please stop by the diner before you leave town," Leah said as she left. All Cassie could do was nod in response.

"Before you go," Nonnie said to Cassie in her heavy German accent, "I have some things for you." She picked up a bottle. "This one for skin," she said, and placed it in a basket. "And this one for hair. Will make it grow faster."

"Nonnie!" Gretchen protested, clearly embarrassed.

Cassie resisted the urge to tug on the flyaway ends of her hair. She could do nothing about the embarrassed flaming of her cheeks however. "Thank you," she said, and gave the older woman a genuine smile. "That would be helpful."

Nonnie got up from her chair and went to Cassie. Like most everyone else, she was taller than Cassie and her body was surprisingly solid for her age. "May I?" she asked. Cassie had no idea of her intent but her presence was calming. She knew the older woman would not hurt her.

"Yes."

Nonnie placed her worn hands on Cassie's cheeks and looked into her eyes. Nonnie's eyes were the same pale blue shade as Cassie's, and they searched her face as she stroked her cheeks with her thumbs. "You must leave the sadness behind you," she said.

How does she know? Nonnie's words were shocking and Cassie had to fight every instinct that said run and hide. She willed herself to stay calm, willed her heart to regain its steady rhythm as Nonnie's eyes looked into hers.

"You must open your heart, child," Nonnie continued. "Only then will you find peace." She followed her words with a kiss to Cassie's forehead. She handed Cassie the basket and without another word went back to her work.

Cassie felt strangely better, almost as if she felt the peace that Nonnie mentioned, which made her feel even stranger, if that was possible. For the past two years she'd tried to stay as far away as possible from people in general, yet since she'd arrived in Angel's End this morning, she'd had several interactions that were extremely personal.

Gretchen shook her head at Nonnie's actions and waved Cassie toward her.

"I'm so sorry," Gretchen said as they walked down a hallway toward the back of the house. "I don't know what came over her."

"Don't worry about it," Cassie said.

"Nonnie's been such a help to me," Gretchen continued.

"She seems extremely kind," Cassie said as they walked outside. Behind the house was a forge where a man worked in his shirtsleeves. A horse was tied next to him, being fitted for new shoes, something else Cassie needed to take care of with Puck. She might as well do it while she was in town. Another man stood by the horse's head and talked to and stroked the animal while the blacksmith worked on a hoof.

"Come meet my husband Jim," Gretchen said.

It was turning into a day, Cassie realized. It wasn't something she'd considered when she left this morning. It had been her plan to dash back home as soon as she was done with the banking. But here she was, meeting people who seemed to be genuinely nice and friendly and without judgment. Of course, they didn't really know anything about her or her history and there was no reason for them to know. It was a strange feeling inside of her, it almost felt like hope. Hope for some normalcy in life. Hope for peace.

The blacksmith lowered the horse's leg, rubbed its flank and wiped off his hands on a towel as the two women approached the forge.

"This is Cassie Parker," Gretchen said. "Sam Parker's granddaughter. Cassie, this is my husband, Jim."

"I hear you're the one who took that crazy donkey off my hands," Jim said as he shook Cassie's hand.

"Maybe you should have paid me," Cassie said.

Jim held up his hands in surrender. "I'll call it a deal as it stands," he said. "This is one of your neighbors, Jared Castle."

Jared Castle was at least ten years older than Jim, and fit and extremely handsome with his rugged jaw and salt-and-pepper hair. "We live on the other side of Jake Reece," he said as he shook Cassie's hand. "I've heard you two have met."

"We have." Cassie didn't want to go into any detail, but from the look on Jared's and Jim's faces, she had a feeling they already knew about the incident with Jake on the trail. Whether or not Jared knew about the sheep on her land was another detail she didn't want to discuss.

"You should come to the Cattlemen's Association meeting," Jared said. "It's always the first Thursday of the month, which is day after tomorrow. It will be at our place at six. Jake can show you the way."

"I'd hate to bother him," Cassie began.

"Jake's the head, he'll be there," Jared assured her.

"I'll keep it in mind," Cassie said as she tried not to cringe. Jake was the head of the Cattlemen's Association? And he knew she had sheep. That didn't bode well. Not at all.

"My wife and daughter are at the mercantile. I hope you can meet them today also."

"I'll be heading over that way as soon as I'm done here," Cassie said.

"Cassie has come to get a cat," Gretchen said.

Jim grabbed her hand again and pumped it up and down. "Bless you," he said. "Take two while you're at it."

"If you're trying to get rid of them I can take one to Hannah," Jared said. "My granddaughter," he explained to Cassie. She felt like she was caught up in a whirlwind of well-intentioned people. She left the Martins' with Jared Castle carrying a basket with her new mother cat and a half-grown calico kitten inside. He insisted on escorting her to the mercantile, and Jim Martin promised he'd have Puck fitted for a new set of shoes by the time she was done with lunch at the Devil's Table, which was something else she hadn't planned on.

"You can have lunch with us," Jared said. Cassie was apprehensive about meeting more people. Surely everyone in Angel's End couldn't be as welcoming as those she had met so far. When she walked into the store and saw the two beautiful women looking at fabric, she nearly turned around to run back to the safety of her ranch.

"We have a new resident in Angel's End," Jared said. "This is Cassie Parker. Cassie, this is my wife, Laurie, and my daughter, Eden." A tiny girl with black hair ran to Jared. He swung her up in his arms. "And this is my granddaughter, Hannah."

Cassie was surprised that Jared claimed the black-haired girl as a granddaughter, especially since both Laurie and Eden had golden blond hair. But the striking blue eyes, more so in the face of the child, gave evidence of their shared blood.

"Welcome," Laurie said. She came to Cassie with genuine kindness on her beautiful face. Once again there was no judgment over her chopped-off hair or her hand-me-down clothes.

"What's in the basket?" Hannah asked, even though the piteous meows gave it away.

"A kitten for you, sweet girl," Jared said. "And one for

Miss Parker. I thought we'd drop it off for her since we have a wagon and she's on horseback. We wouldn't want her kitty to start off being mad at her for the rough ride to her new home."

"We'd be delighted to help out," Laurie said. Eden had stayed at the table with the fabric after giving Cassie a shy hello, but at the mention of a kitten she joined them, walking their way with an obvious limp. Hannah's excitement at the new kitten could not be contained, and soon the kitten was in her arms while the family surrounded her.

Cassie took advantage of their distraction to look at the ready-made clothing displayed on a table. The friendly chatter of the Castles made her suddenly melancholy for her childhood, and memories of the time when her family was all together came flooding back. There was no sense in mourning for something that was long gone.

You must open your heart, child . . .

What was it exactly that Nonnie expected her to do?

ELEVEN

"At this rate she's going to know everyone in town," Ward said as he rubbed his hand across Lady's head.

"We'll see how friendly people are when they find out about her sheep," Jake said. He sat next to Ward on the porch of the Heaven's Gate, watching the goings-on in the town, especially those that involved Cassie Parker. He was glad to see Leah had taken to her, but couldn't help but wonder why she'd gone in to the Martins'. It made some sense when Cassie returned and got her horse from in front of the bank and led him around to the forge. But what was in the basket she carried, and what was she doing with Jared, who carried another basket?

"I can't imagine Jared causing any problems," Ward said.

"Jared will be the one voice of reason," Jake said. He shook his head. Thinking about Cassie Parker and the problems that were sure to come was taking up a tremendous amount of his time. Time that should be spent taking care of his own ranch. Spring was the busiest time of year and here he sat with Ward like he didn't have a care in the world.

"How about you?" Ward asked. "Where will you stand?"

"I'm hoping things won't come to that," Jake said.

"But if they do?"

Cassie came out of the mercantile with Laurie, Eden and Hannah around her. Jared put the basket he carried in the wagon and stopped to talk to Gus, who placed a parcel in the wagon also. The women walked up the boardwalk on the opposite side of the street. Cassie carried a bundle along with her basket. It looked like the Castle women had convinced her to go to lunch with them at the Devil's Table. He smiled when he saw Cassie walking slowly with Eden, their two heads bent together in conversation.

Ward was waiting for an answer. "She's right," Jake said. "It's nobody's business what she does on her own property, and I'll fight for her right to do as she sees fit. But if she can't keep those sheep at home, then there will be hell to pay. And I have to do as the association sees fit. Not as I see fit."

"You think Watkins will start a range war?"

"I think he'll gladly start one, just for the hell of it," Jake said. He stood and stretched. "I'm hungry. How about we get some lunch?"

Ward looked down at the café, where Cassie and the Castle women were just walking through the door. "Are you sure you're hungry?" he asked Jake with a suggestive raise of one eyebrow.

Jake knew what Ward was thinking. He didn't like it that his friend could read him so well, but also couldn't help but be glad for it. It meant he wouldn't have to explain anything to him, especially since he didn't understand it himself.

"Dang it, Ward," Jake said. "Sometimes a man just can't help himself."

Ward stood up and stretched his long frame in the same manner Jake had. Lady jumped to her feet and did the same as her master. "Well then by all means, let's eat," Ward said.

.

It wasn't as if Jake had planned on riding back home with Cassie Parker. It just turned out that way. She was done with her business, he was done with his, and they were both headed in the same direction.

"Are you following me?" she asked when he fell in beside her on the outskirts of Angel's End. She had a parcel and a small basket tied to her saddle horn. Her hat hung on her back by its lanyard and her nose and cheeks were pinked by the sun that shone brightly overhead. Her flyaway hair curled up on the ends and her pale blue eyes danced with mischief as she sucked on a peppermint stick. Jake's eyes drifted down to her jacket, which was unbuttoned to the warm spring air. Her curves peeked out from between the open sides. There wasn't enough flannel in the world to hide them. Her boys' clothing made him wonder what she wore underneath. Was it something lacy or something practical?

She was a puzzle. Or maybe she was a challenge. Whatever she was, she kept his curiosity piqued. "Maybe you're following me," Jake replied. He liked playing this game with her and hoped she would join in.

She pulled the peppermint from her mouth and waved it behind her. "I left town first," she replied saucily before putting the peppermint back in her mouth.

"Just because we're headed in the same direction doesn't mean I'm following you." Dang, it was fun poking at her. "I see you did some shopping." Poke. Poke.

"I see that you hung out in the saloon all morning." She poked back.

She was playing along. Jake grinned, suddenly very happy with the day. The sun was warm on his face and the sky was as blue as he'd ever seen it. The grass that grew alongside the road waved gently in the breeze, and birds flitted to and fro, busy at the task of building their nests. Bright must have felt his mood because he stretched out his neck and flicked his tail as he trotted alongside Puck.

"Are you worried about me?" Jake held his hand up in front of his mouth and blew against his palm. "Do you want to check my breath for the scent of demon drink?" He leaned toward her.

Cassie punched him in the arm. "You are incorrigible," she said around her candy. She took it out again. "How do you get any work done if you spend your days sitting around?"

"Ow!" Jake rubbed his arm in mock pain. "How do you get any work done if you spend all day shopping and gossiping with women?"

"I wasn't gossiping. How can I gossip when I don't know anyone?" She turned her nose up in the air, as if she was insulted, and bit a chunk off her stick. It was intriguing. She might be dressed like the poorest of boys and nearly acting like one as she chewed on her candy, but she had a very proper air about her. "Besides, I don't gossip," Cassie continued after she'd swallowed. "It's like cursing. I try to abstain."

"You try to abstain?" Jake grinned at the challenge. "So it is possible for you to curse?"

The look she gave him would have frozen the nearest stream. "There are situations when I am sorely tempted."

"Indeed?" Jake laughed. "Is now one of those situations?"

"Your ability to state the obvious is a thing to behold, Mr. Reece."

"Please, after all we've been through, don't you think you should call me Jake?"

She rolled her eyes. "You neglected to tell me you were the head of the Cattlemen's Association," she informed him. She finished her candy and delicately licked the ends of her fingers. He had a hard time tearing his eyes from them, but he had to as she'd given him an opening.

"So you were gossiping!" he said with glee.

"Gossiping is embellishing something you've heard with your own jaded version of fiction. You being the head of the Cattlemen's Association is a fact."

"I can't argue with that," Jake agreed. "So if you weren't gossiping, what were you doing?" he asked, anxious to hear what she'd say next.

"I was meeting people. You should know as you were the one responsible. You introduced me to Leah Gentry."

"And she introduced you to everyone else in town?"

"No. She introduced me to Gretchen, who then introduced me to Jim, who introduced me to Jared Castle, who then introduced me to his family . . ."

"Who then took you to lunch," Jake finished for her.

She glanced at him, sideways, and Jake was struck by how long her lashes were, and how big her blue eyes were in her pixie face. It suited that she was familiar with Shakespeare's play *A Midsummer's Night Dream*. If he believed in such things, he would think her from the fairy realm instead of Illinois by way of West Texas.

"So you weren't wasting time," she observed. "You were spying on me."

"It's not like I had to make an effort, since you were in the middle of the street most of the time," Jake protested.

"Are you mistaking me for the angel?" She grinned and then turned her nose up again in that superior way she had.

"It *was* very nice of the *Castles* to take me to lunch." Cassie glanced at him again. "And they *were* the only *ones* who asked me."

Jake sputtered. Was she angry because he didn't ask her to lunch? "Leah asked you. I heard her."

"Yes she did."

"What exactly is your point?"

She turned to face him. "That it was nice to be invited to lunch."

"Are you suggesting that I should have invited you to lunch? Because I clearly recall you telling me that I was done."

"I find it hard to believe that a man who by all appearances is a successful rancher gives up so easily."

"Would you have gone to lunch with me if I had asked you?"

She sighed dramatically. "I guess we'll never know as the moment has passed us by."

Jake's jaw dropped open. How could she, sitting on her horse as easy as you please, condemn him for not asking her to lunch when she plainly told him to get lost? Unless . . . he enjoyed poking at her, had actually looked forward to it when he followed, yes, he admitted it, followed her out of town. Maybe she was just returning the favor. Maybe she liked poking at him too. And he knew just the way to call her on it.

"Let me make it up to you," he said.

"What?"

Clearly she wasn't expecting that. Jake grinned. "Come have dinner at my ranch tonight. I've got a great cook, Fu; he's Chinese."

"And that makes him a great cook?"

"No, but it does make me careful when he goes to throwing knives."

"And that's supposed to entice me to come?" Cassie asked.

"Well it is entertaining, as long as he's not aiming at you. And besides, you can pick up your grandfather's Bible and any books you'd like to read."

She studied him for a long moment as they rode along. Jake just grinned at her. Something about her, about being around her, made him happy. She was interesting; he never knew what to expect, what she was going to say next. If not for those gol-durn sheep . . .

Suddenly Cassie stiffened in her saddle and her hand went to her pocket where he knew she carried her gun. She pulled Puck to a stop. Jake stopped Bright and looked ahead. Three riders were coming their way. He quickly recognized the one in the lead as Raymond Watkins, with a couple of his crew riding behind him. One of them was dragging something behind his horse with a rope.

"Son of a bitch," Jake said when he realized what was being dragged. For once Cassie didn't correct him.

"Oh no," was all she said.

Watkins and his men stopped in front of Jake and Cassie. "Reece," Watkins said before his eyes turned to Cassie.

Jake didn't bother with introductions. "What are you dragging?" he asked, already knowing the answer. It was bloody and covered with dirt, but it was a sheep. Cassie dropped off Puck and ran to the sheep before Jake had time to react.

"You bastard," she yelled. "You killed her!"

"You're damn right I killed it," Watkins said. "We found it down by the stream. Baxter put a rope on it so we could drag it into town."

Just as Jake expected, things were going to get ugly quick. He dismounted and ran to Cassie, who was fumbling with the rope, trying to get it off the sheep's neck.

"Hang on there, girlie," Watkins yelled. "That's evidence."

"Evidence of what?" Cassie yelled. She stood in the middle of the trail, all five foot nothing of her with her hands clenched into fists as she faced Watkins. "That you and your men are monsters?"

"Evidence that someone has brought sheep into cattle country."

"No kidding," Cassie said, her voice suddenly calm. The tone scared Jake into thinking she might do something stupid, something rash. He moved behind her, ready to grab her in case she dug her hand into her pocket to pull out her gun. "Ride up into my valley and you'll see a couple of hundred more."

"Your valley?" Watkins asked. "Who in the hell are you?"

"My name is Cassie Parker and I'd appreciate it if you watch your language when you are in my presence."

If he wasn't so worried about her, Jake would have laughed. She'd just cussed Watkins herself. Instead, he placed a calming hand on her left shoulder, so she couldn't reach for her gun. Not that he thought Watkins would shoot her, but his men were another thing altogether. Jake considered himself to be handy with a gun, but these odds were definitely not in his favor. If there was any way he could stop this from escalating, he was bound to stop it.

"Cassie Parker," Watkins said. "As in Sam Parker?"

"I'm his granddaughter and I've claimed his land," Cassie said. "And it is my intention to raise sheep on it, whether you like it or not."

Watkins laughed. He braced his arm across his saddle and laughed long and hard. His men joined him. They had a good time between the three of them, laughing and guffawing until tears gathered in their eyes.

"Easy now," Jake said into Cassie's ear. Cassie jerked away from him and went back to her sheep.

"Did you know about this?" Watkins asked Jake when he finally stopped laughing.

"Just found out yesterday," Jake answered truthfully.

"And you didn't do anything about it?" Watkins asked.

"What was I supposed to do?" Jake said. "It's her land, free and clear. She's even paid the back taxes on it," he added because he knew how Watkins's mind worked. "She can do whatever she wants on it or with it."

"Not when her sheep will foul up my water," Watkins said.

"You've got plenty of water," Jake replied. "And you'd have to prove it."

"You wouldn't be talking that way if you lived downstream from her."

Cassie got the rope off the sheep. She coiled it up in jerking motions and flung it at the cowboy it belonged to. Jake saw the man's eyes flare, and his hand instinctively went to the gun on his hip. "Don't," he said as he held up his left hand while he kept his right one poised over the handle of his gun.

"Why, Jacob Reece," Watkins said. "Have you turned into a sheep lover?" His eyes flicked to Cassie. "Kind of a strange position for the head of the Cattlemen's Association, don't you think?"

"Maybe he's got a thing for little boys," Baxter said. "Or maybe he can't tell the difference."

"You need to watch your mouth," Jake said. "There's a lady present. Obviously you can't tell the difference."

Baxter jerked at the insult, and Watkins held out his hand to stop him from pulling his gun. "Leave it for now, Baxter,"

Watkins told his man. "We'll just ride on into town and have a word with the sheriff," he continued.

"Go ahead," Jake said. "But he already knows."

"Knowing something and doing something about it are two different things," Watkins said. "We'll see what kind of sheriff he is real quick." Without another word, Watkins kicked his horse into a gallop and, with his men following, took off to town.

"I got a feeling you're not going to like the kind of sheriff Cade Gentry is," Jake said quietly to their retreating backs. He turned to Cassie. She was on her knees next to the dead sheep. The animal looked ghastly after its horrible death. Its neck was nearly twisted off its body and its eyes bulged and its tongue hung from its open mouth.

"They choked her to death when they dragged her." She was fighting to hold back the tears as she touched the woolly fleece that was filthy with dirt and tangled with twigs and leaves. "How could anyone do something so cruel?"

Jake had no answer for that, as he didn't understand it himself. He already knew what Watkins was like. If the man had indeed found the sheep on his property, then he had every right to kill it. The manner in which he chose to do it was something Jake could never comprehend.

"Some people are just that way," he finally said. "That doesn't justify it. It's just the way it is." Her anger and grief were justified, yet he couldn't blame Watkins for being angry. The way he chose to show his anger was another matter altogether. There was no excuse for cruelty. None at all.

Cassie stood up. She wiped her hands down her pants and then used the back of her hand to swipe at the tears gathered on her cheek. "Well I'm sick of it," she said. "No matter where I go, it's the same thing. I was hoping things would be different here. I guess I should have known better."

She whistled for Puck, who came to her side. Then she dug her hands into the woolly fleece of the sheep.

"What are you doing?"

"I'm going to take her home." She straightened and pulled, but the dead weight of the sheep was too much for her small frame.

"Let me," Jake said. He bent to pick up the sheep, but she jerked the body away.

"I don't want your help." Her chin had a tilt to it that he quickly recognized.

"For a little thing you sure are stubborn."

"What's my size got to do with it?"

They were on opposite sides of the body, both crouching down with their hands in the wool. He wasn't going to argue with her. Cassie would just have to accept his help because he surely wasn't going to stand by and watch her try to wrestle the sheep's body onto the back of her horse.

"It has everything to do with it at the moment," Jake said. "You are too small to pick up this sheep. Being stubborn won't make you grow taller or stronger, but it will keep you frustrated. So you can accept my help or get angry about it. I'm going to pick up the sheep while you're deciding." Jake stared into her tear-filled eyes. Her eyes flared and he thought she was going to argue with him, but she didn't. She nodded and released her hold. "We can do it together if you'd like," he offered.

Cassie nodded. She was too overcome to talk. Jake slid his hands under the carcass and picked up the sheep as gently as he could. When he got to Puck, Cassie helped him guide the animal over Puck's back so they could tie the sheep behind her seat. The creak of wheels alerted Jake to the coming of the Castle wagon. He walked back to meet them to give Cassie time to compose herself.

"What's going on?" Jared asked. "Raymond Watkins just went by us on the trail without a word."

"Is Cassie all right?" Eden asked. She sat behind her parents with Hannah, who held a kitten on her lap. She looked beyond Jake to where Cassie stood with her face buried in Puck's neck.

"Is that a sheep?" Jared asked incredulously.

"It is," Jake admitted. "And there's a couple hundred more on her property."

"And that's why Watkins is having a bad day," Jared concluded.

"He found one of Cassie's sheep and killed it by dragging it," Jake said. "He was bringing it to town as evidence."

"That's horrible," Laurie exclaimed. Meanwhile, Eden got up from her seat. Jake knew, with her bad leg, that she would need help, so he placed his hands around her waist and put her on the ground.

"Thank you," Eden said shyly before she went, in her halting step, to where Cassie stood. Laurie followed her.

"Is Cassie's sheep dead?" Hannah, with her bright blue eyes, stared at Cassie.

"It is," Jared replied. "Stay in the wagon, sweetheart."

Jared and Jake walked behind the wagon, which was loaded down with supplies. Jake kept his eyes on Cassie, who seemed to be in good hands with Laurie and Eden.

"This is not good, Jake," Jared said. "Does she realize that this is going to cause trouble?"

"Cassie seems to think she can keep her sheep on her property," Jake said.

"Well if today is any indication . . ." Jared walked a few steps away, clearly agitated, and then he came back. "Did Watkins say where he found the sheep?"

"He just said by a stream," Jake replied. "He claimed the animal would foul up his water."

"Because his water comes across Cassie's land."

"Not all of it," Jake began.

"But enough of it that he does have a valid grievance."

"Only if he can prove it," Jake said.

"He won't have to prove anything," Jared said. "You know good and well that any mention of sheep in cattle country is enough to start a war."

"Maybe someone should have mentioned that to Cassie before she showed up here last fall," Jake said. He took a deep breath. He'd known this moment was coming as soon as he found out about her sheep. Maybe it was better that it was out in the open. At least now they could face it head-on. *They* . . . Since when had this become his fight? He looked over to where Cassie stood, with Laurie and Eden. Both women seemed to be commiserating with her. How quickly they had taken to her. Dang it, he'd taken to her pretty quick also. What was he getting into?

Dang it!

"She's been here that long?" Jared asked.

"That's what she said. And I'm pretty sure she knew she wouldn't be welcome. Why else would she have lain low for as long as she did?"

"Why do you think she brought them here of all places?"

Jake looked once more at where Cassie stood. She had her secrets, Jake was certain of it. Something had happened to her to drive her here with her odd little family. "To tell the truth, Jared, I don't think she had any place else to go."

"I know she's from Texas," Jared said. "She didn't say much more than that at lunch."

"Well at least I got it narrowed down to West Texas," Jake replied.

"I've got a good friend who does business in that part of Texas. I'll write him a letter and ask if he's ever heard of our Miss Parker," Jared said.

"Which means you'll find out if she had the same kind of problems down there that she's going to have up here?"

"That's one way of saying it." Jared looked at the ladies. "You know our new sheriff much better than I do. Which side do you think he'll land on?"

"He's already said that she has the right to do whatever she wants on her property."

"What if the sheep get off her property?"

"Then I'm thinking things are going to get ugly."

"Will he side with Watkins?"

"No," Jake said. "But that doesn't mean that he'll side with Cassie. I think he'll do what's best for everyone involved, while trying to keep to the law."

"I don't envy him his job," Jared said. "Because you're right. Where Watkins is concerned, things will get ugly."

"So what are we going to do?" Jake asked.

"You've already picked your side, haven't you, Jake?"

"I can't let Watkins run over her," Jake admitted. "She's stubborn enough to wind up killed."

"I agree with you on that," Jared said. "But you are the head of the Cattlemen's Association. Some might think you have a conflict of interest."

"Maybe I should resign," Jake said. "Dang, I don't know what to do."

"Just wait and see what happens at the meeting Thursday night," Jared advised. "Having to have a re-election might make things worse." Jared looked at Cassie. "Do you think you can get her there?"

"I can try," Jake said. "Whether or not she'll come is another thing altogether."

"Let's get the women home," Jared said. "That way I can have a look at these sheep myself. Cassie got a cat from the Martins while she was in town. We offered to deliver it for her."

"I wish the cat was the only critter of hers we had to worry about," Jake said as he and Jared went to the women.

TWELVE

Self-recrimination did nothing for one's peace of mind, and sitting on the porch with the new momma cat in her lap did nothing for the mouse problem in the barn. Yet here Cassie sat, petting the cat, while there was work to be done and problems to be solved and a meeting of the Cattlemen's Association to attend. That is if she could work up the courage to go. But what choice did she have? Hiding wouldn't change the fact that everyone now knew about the sheep.

What were her options? She could pack up and move again, but where would they go? And more importantly, would her mother survive it? She'd come to Angel's End to escape her past. Was that to be her life from now on? Running from one place to the next because things got too difficult?

"Running doesn't solve a thing," Cassie said to the cat, who meowed in agreement. "At least I've made one decision today. Your name is Suzie." She rubbed the calico's chin. "What do you think?" Suzie meowed again and followed it up with a rumbling purr. Cassie put her down and walked to the end of the porch. She leaned against a post and looked out across her valley.

"My valley," Cassie said. It really was beautiful, with the long grass rippling in the breeze and the sheltering pines below the majestic mountains with their snow-tipped peaks. The air was crisp and fresh. It made her feel alive, after two long years of feeling dead inside.

Jake Reece had a lot to do with that too. She couldn't deny it. She couldn't stop thinking about the man, despite all the other things she should be thinking about. He'd been kind to her, but more than that, he challenged her in a way that didn't make her feel uncomfortable. As if he wanted something, something that she was certain she couldn't give. Her scars were too deep for anything more. Still, it was pleasant to talk to him, and to tease him, and to see the look on his face as he watched for her reactions, much as she watched him. It was something to look forward to. But that too would be gone after tonight. After all, Jake was a cattle-man and cattlemen hated sheepherders. He was the head of the Cattlemen's Association on top of that. It was the way of the world and nothing could change it.

So should she hide here in her little valley and hope that everyone would just ignore her, or should she go and let them know that she was not going to be pushed around? Not anymore.

Max barked and Cassie looked up and was surprised to see a buggy coming up her drive. She didn't recognize the horse, but the driver looked very familiar. It was Jake. He'd said two days ago that he'd take her to the meeting, but she really hadn't expected him to do it. Not after what happened on the trail with the dead sheep.

Cassie was suddenly very conscious of how she looked. She dashed into the house. "Is something wrong?" Rosa asked her.

"I've got to change. I've got to go to the meeting. I need something to wear. I need some water to wash up with." She was babbling and she couldn't stop it.

"Shhh," Rosa said as she took Cassie's hands into hers. "It will be fine. I will heat you some water. You have the skirt you bought in town."

"Rosa?" Cassie asked. "Was this the right thing to do? Coming here?"

"You cannot spend your time looking back and second-guessing," Rosa said. "It is better spent looking forward."

"What if there is nothing to look forward to?" The sound of the wagon could be heard now as it approached the house.

"There is always something to look forward to," Rosa said. "Now go and get dressed for your meeting."

"I should go?"

"Hiding will not change a thing," Rosa advised. "You should go and let them know that Cassie Parker is here to stay."

"Cassie Parker is here to stay . . ." Cassie repeated. There was a knock on the door.

"Make him wait outside," Cassie said as she dashed to her room. A few seconds later she heard Rosa's voice and the answering rumble of Jake's.

"Let him have enough sense to stay outside," Cassie prayed as she opened the door of her wardrobe. She didn't want to answer questions about her mother's health.

Cassie jerked through her clothes. She had some decent

things. Things that hadn't been totally destroyed when her
stage was attacked, and she'd bought a skirt when she was
in town. It was nothing fancy, and the only appropriate gar-
ment small enough to fit her, but it was something. She
paired it with a shirt with a high collar and a tiny bit of lace
as trim. If she wanted to be treated as a respectable landowner, then she needed to dress the part.

She had a nice pair of boots that she hadn't worn in ages.
If it had been up to her, she would have gotten rid of everything from her past life before she came to Texas, but bless
Rosa, she was a wise woman and so she packed everything
away, knowing that someday Cassie would need it again.

Rosa came into the room with a pitcher of water. Heat
rose from the basin as she poured it in. "Mr. Reece has come
to take you to the meeting," she said. "And he is waiting on
the porch."

"Thank you," Cassie said to both Rosa and the good Lord
above. Cassie quickly stripped out of her clothes and grabbed
a cloth to wash up with before hastily dressing in the clothes
she'd laid out on the bed. Unfortunately there wasn't much
she could do about her hair, but a good brushing wouldn't
hurt it. She bent over at the waist and brushed it upside down
and then arranged it as best as she could with her fingers.
To her surprise it fluffed out and the ends curled up without
looking like it was going to fly off in every direction. Nonnie's potions obviously worked as she'd put them on her hair
after washing it the night before. Cassie added a gold brooch
that belonged to her grandmother to the neck of her blouse
and rubbed some of Nonnie's rose-scented cream on her
hands.

She was ready to go.

Cassie stopped to check on her mother before she left.
She still sat in her chair, staring at nothing as always.

Manuel came in through the back door. "Should I go with you?" he asked.

He was always there, ready to help, ready to support her, ever since the day he found her and her mother in the ruins of the stagecoach. Always faithful, that was Manuel; once he gave his heart, it was yours for life. It was a tragedy that he'd lost his only son. Every day Cassie thanked God that Rosa and Manuel loved her like their own daughter.

This was why she had to go to the meeting and let men like Watkins know that they would not be pushed around. Manuel and Rosa had risked everything when they took in Cassie and her mother. They had thumbed their noses at the most powerful man in West Texas until the only way they could survive was by leaving. They'd given up their home, because it was impossible for Cassie to stay there. Luckily, Cassie had a place for them. If they couldn't stay in Angel's End, they had no place else to go.

"I caused this problem Manuel. I'll take care of it."

"You don't have to fight all the battles by yourself."

"I don't consider this a battle," Cassie said with a smile that she hoped Manuel knew was genuine. "I consider this more of a scouting party."

"Good luck then," Manuel said with a smile. "At least you are not going into the breach alone."

"We'll see," Cassie said. "He might have ulterior motives."

Manuel grinned. "As you say, we shall see."

As Cassie opened the door, she couldn't help but think that Manuel was speaking of different motives than she was. What could Jake's motives be for helping her? Was it an obligation he felt to her grandfather? Or was there more to it? Maybe it was just a case of keeping a close eye on her, so he could tell the other ranchers what she was up to.

"I'm sorry if I kept you waiting," she said as she walked outside.

Jake leaned against the porch post looking out over her valley. He turned to her as she spoke and his eyes widened with something. Surprise?

"Er . . ." He cleared his throat. He waved his hand toward the barn. "I see you shored up your pens."

"Yes, Manuel and I worked on that all day yesterday." She studied him. Jake was dressed up. He wore a gray suit and a blue shirt that made his stormy eyes seem calm. Cassie was glad she'd taken time with her appearance.

It was nice to see the way Jake's eyes lingered on her.

"Shall we go?" Jake said. He held out his arm and Cassie took it. *That wasn't so hard.* What if he offered to pick her up to put her in the buggy? Would she be able to stand it? She shied away from most men, she didn't want to feel their touch, not after what had happened and the violence that came with it, but Jake . . . she could only hope he was different, because she was feeling things she'd never felt before. Whether or not she could act on those feelings was another thing altogether. She never imagined that she would want to feel this way, ever.

Jake didn't presume too much. He merely held her arm firmly as she gathered her skirt and stepped into the buggy. The seat shifted as he settled in beside her and picked up the reins.

"I really didn't expect this," Cassie began as he set the buggy in motion.

"I said I would take you, didn't I?" Jake said. "Two days ago when I left here."

"Yes, but . . ." Cassie huffed out a breath. "I thought you were just being polite. I didn't really think you wanted me to go. Won't my presence be counterproductive to the purpose of the meeting? It's a Cattlemen's Association. No mention of sheep at all."

"Oh, I'm sure there will be plenty of mention of sheep tonight," Jake assured her.

"As in I'm a lamb for the slaughter?"

Why did talking to him have to be so fun? "I still don't think I should be going," Cassie said.

"I didn't peg you for being a coward."

"What do you mean a coward?"

"I invited you to dinner and you didn't show up," Jake explained. "And the only reason you're going tonight is because I came to get you."

Cassie studied his profile as he expertly handled the reins. His jaw was smooth and he smelled like almonds. He must have used some of Nonnie's special soap. "But you came anyway." For some strange reason that made her very happy.

He looked at her and grinned. "Call me an optimist."

"Does that mean you don't expect any trouble tonight?"

"I'd like to think so." They turned south on the main road and he urged the horse into a trot. "I really don't know what's going to happen tonight." He looked at her once more, his eyes searching her face before dipping, just for an instant, to her chest before coming back to her face. "I do know that I'm happy that you didn't turn tail and run."

"But you do think it would be the best thing if I got rid of the sheep?" Cassie insisted. "You did make it clear how you felt about them the first time you were here."

"You took me by surprise," Jake confessed. "A couple of hundred sheep was the last thing I expected to see when I came over here."

He was being nice to her, yet she couldn't stop challenging him. "You think I should leave."

"I never said that," Jake insisted.

"But it's what you think."

Jake sighed in exasperation. "Let me get this straight. The things that I say, like me coming to pick you up tonight, you don't believe. The things I don't say, like you assuming that I think you should leave, you take as fact. Does that about sum it up?"

"I never said that," Cassie snapped back.

"Funny, I think I just said the very same words," Jake retorted. "And I know I never told you that I think you should leave."

Cassie looked at him in earnest. He must have sensed it because he turned to look at her in return. "But you did think it," she said. She couldn't stop pushing him. She didn't know why she couldn't stop, nor did she know what she expected him to say. Maybe she just needed someone to tell her things were going to be all right and that she had made the right decision. Maybe she just wanted him to say that he'd take care of everything. Wouldn't that be nice? To have someone take care of her instead of her having to take care of everyone.

"Hell, I think a lot of things." He grinned as she opened her mouth to say something about his colorful language. "Sorry," he said. "Sometimes it just slips out. Which goes along with what I was going to say. It's always best to think before you speak. That doesn't mean that I always do, but I give it a good try."

She smiled at him. Maybe he had given her what she was looking for. It was enough for now. She really wasn't sure what it was she wanted. She just knew she liked having him by her side. "It's nice to know that I'm not going into this lion's den totally alone."

"Not everyone is like Watkins," Jake said. He pointed to a turnoff in the trail. A sign hung on a post. "That's my place, by the way," he added.

"Not everyone is like you or the Castles either," Cassie replied as she observed the rocking *J* brand on the sign.

"You've seen a lot of the bad side of people, haven't you?" Jake asked.

"I have found that people's true colors usually show during a crisis. That you can quickly find out who your real friends are when something bad happens."

"Did something bad happen to you in West Texas?" His eyes searched her face once more. Cassie was suddenly cold. She'd forgotten her coat, which led to the realization that she'd gone out without her gun also. She never went anywhere without her gun. Not ever. What was she thinking? Or maybe it was that she wasn't thinking. Not clearly. Not where Jake Reece was concerned. Cassie wrapped her arms around herself at the sudden chill that shook her body.

Jake stopped the buggy. "You forgot your coat," he said. He took his off and put it over her shoulders. Cassie pulled it together in the front and lowered her chin into the folds. The smell of man, horses and almonds surrounded her. It wasn't such a bad thing, but his question still had her reeling. How did he know? Was it so obvious? Did she wear it like a sign around her neck that said *I was raped by the son of a rich man who bought his way out of his trial*?

"It's none of my business," Jake said when he had the buggy rolling again.

"Something bad did happen," Cassie said without knowing she was going to until the words came out. So much for taking Jake's advice about thinking before speaking. "It's something I'd rather not talk about," she continued. "And it made it impossible for us to stay there."

"*Us* being you, your mother and your man?"

"Manuel and Rosa. And he's not my man, he's my friend."

"A very good friend," Jake agreed. "Maybe you will find some friends here in Angel's End," he continued.

"That would be nice," Cassie agreed. "Maybe I'll find a whole bunch of them tonight," she said with a nervous smile.

"Well I reckon we won't know until we find out."

Cassie burst out laughing. "What is that supposed to mean?"

"It means worrying won't change a thing." They came to a rise in the road and the horse slowed as she pulled the buggy. "Things are what they are," Jake continued. "I used to worry about things all the time. But it doesn't change anything. So why waste your time?" He motioned to the beauty around them. "It's a beautiful afternoon. Why not enjoy it?"

They crested the hill and Cassie observed the beauty around them. The mountains rising up in the distance, the lovely aspens with their new leaves and the darker evergreens higher up behind them. The sound of the stream bubbling alongside the road. The bright blue sky behind the gathering clouds. It truly was a beautiful place. If only she could be sure that the atmosphere was as welcoming as the scenery.

The buggy picked up speed once more as they moved down the rise. A breeze kicked up and Cassie pulled Jake's coat closer around her.

"We might get a storm this evening," Jake observed. What was she thinking, going off without a coat and, more importantly, her gun? But it wasn't as if she could draw down on a meeting full of cattlemen. It was foolish to think that way. They weren't going to attack her, at least not because she was a woman. Still, it would be nice to have that security, and to know that they would have to think twice about attempting anything.

Suddenly the buggy lurched and Cassie was tossed into Jake. His arm went around her instinctively, to keep her from flying off the seat, and he used the other hand to expertly guide the buggy to a stop.

"We must have hit a rock," he said. He kept a hold on her as he looked at the road.

"More like a boulder," Cassie replied. She tried to sit up and couldn't because Jake's hold was so tight. He realized it and let go.

"Are you hurt?"

"I'm fine," she said as she rearranged her skirts and ran a nervous hand through her hair.

"I best check on Darby," he said.

"Darby?"

"The mare pulling the buggy," he replied. He quickly climbed down and walked around the buggy. "Yes, it was a rock," he said. "I guess I wasn't paying attention." Jake picked up a stone bigger than his fist and chucked it into the grass alongside the road. Then he went to the mare and ran expert hands over her flanks and down her legs.

Cassie watched him as he reassured the mare. She had taken a risk coming here, she knew that. She'd taken several more since she'd been here, without realizing it. She'd let people in. She'd relaxed her guard. There was nothing wrong with being cautious, but there was plenty wrong with letting caution rule your life. Maybe it was time she tried trust for a change.

Maybe she would trust Jake. She wasn't foolish enough

to think that the meeting tonight wasn't going to be difficult. But just maybe, she'd found a man she could trust.

"How is she?" Cassie asked as Jake once more climbed into the buggy.

"Fine and dandy," he said, and once more set the buggy in motion.

THIRTEEN

"You can't complain about the food," Cade said. He took a last bite of cake and sat his plate down on an end table.

"Nope," Ward agreed as he sipped his coffee. "The Castles always do things right."

"They're hoping that if everyone is full, then everyone will be happy, and Watkins won't cause a ruckus over the sheep," Jake said.

"Their plan would have worked out a lot better if Watkins had shown up for dinner," Ward observed. The three men stood by a window in the parlor of the Castles' sprawling stone and timber house, juggling plates and cups, as the house was full of people. Jake kept an eye on Cassie, who was deep in conversation with Eden Castle. He couldn't help but compare the two.

Eden was as beautiful as her mother, slim with waves of

golden blond hair that fell to her waist and the bright blue
eyes that all the Castles had. She had several inches on
Cassie and stood with her head tilted so she could catch
every word. What were they talking about? They seemed
to have become instant friends, as they had merged together
as soon as Cassie walked into the house. And as beautiful
as Eden was, Jake couldn't take his eyes off Cassie. There
was something about her that continually made him seek
her out.

"What's the story with the daughter?" Cade asked. "And
the granddaughter for that matter? If I'm not mistaken she's
got Indian blood in her."

"Jared's first wife was Indian," Ward said. "I'm not sure
what tribe."

"Sioux," Jake said.

"Sioux," Ward continued. "Jared had a son by her. The
little girl is his."

"Where is the son?" Cade asked.

"Leavenworth," Jake said. Cade arched an eyebrow.

"Jared won't talk about it much," Jake said. "Apparently
the little girl's mother was murdered and the son got caught
up in some trouble going after the killer."

"Believe me, I would be the last one to judge," Cade said.

"Laurie is Jared's second wife. Eden is their firstborn.
She was born with the limp. They have another son who's
in school back East." Ward finished the story of the Castles
for Cade.

"The man sure knows how to build a house," Cade said.

Jake had to agree. He'd often admired Jared's sprawling
house. "We caught you up on the Castles, now why don't
you catch us up on what happened with Watkins when he
showed up the other day," Jake asked.

"He said it was against the law to bring sheep into cattle

country," Cade began. "I asked him to show me the law on the books, because I'd never heard of it. He said he didn't need a book to know what was right and what was wrong. He figured bringing sheep into cattle country was right up there with being a horse thief, and both should be treated accordingly."

"Wait a minute," Jake asked incredulously, "are you saying he threatened to hang Cassie?"

"Not outright," Cade said. "He just spouted a lot of rhetoric about the way of the West and building something out of nothing. Which I pointed out to him was the same thing Cassie was trying to do."

"He was testing the waters," Ward said. "Trying to figure out if he could buy a sheriff and how much it was going to cost him."

"There isn't enough money in the world," Cade said. "I've lived that life and thank God every day I was able to leave it behind."

"How far do you think he'll go?" Jake asked.

"As far as we let him," Cade replied. "Which is why I'm here."

"And speak of the devil," Ward said as Raymond Watkins walked into Jared Castle's house as if he owned the place. Jake was happy to see that he was alone, but just to make sure, he checked out the window to see if any of Watkins's men were outside. There was no one loitering about except Jared's men, who were taking care of the horses and buggies of all those present at the meeting.

Laurie, always a gracious hostess, even to men like Watkins, came and greeted him. "Would you like something to eat before we get started?" she asked Watkins as she handed his hat and coat to a maid.

"No," Watkins said. "Where is Jared?"

"He's in the dining room," Laurie said.

"We need to get this meeting underway," Watkins said as he stared directly at Jake.

"I believe they were just waiting on you, Raymond," Laurie said, as easy and as smooth as could be, in the face of Watkins's bad manners. Watkins walked into the dining room without another word to Laurie.

Jake grinned at Ward, who raised his coffee cup in a toast to Laurie Castle. "A woman after my own heart," he said. "If only she wasn't married."

"As if she'd look twice at you," Jake said.

Ward put a hand over his heart. "I'm wounded."

"Go cry in your beer," Jake said.

"Nah," Ward said. "This is much more interesting."

"Worrying about it isn't going to make it go away," Jake said. "We might as well get on with it." His eyes found Cassie once more. She was trying to hide it, but he could tell she was scared. Her eyes held the look of someone going to their execution, even though she continued to chat with Eden. Somehow she'd managed to move both of them into a corner when Watkins came in, as if hiding from him would change his opinion. "Excuse me, gentlemen," Jake said to Ward and Cade. He put his dishes down on a table and went to join Cassie and Eden.

"I need to start the meeting," Jake said quietly to Cassie. "Do you want to step outside first?"

Cassie put a hand to her stomach and looked at the door as if she wanted to bolt through it. "No, I'm fine," she lied.

"Come with me," Jake said. "Eden, will you excuse us?"

"Certainly," Eden said with a quick smile at Cassie.

"You shouldn't do this, Jake," Cassie said.

"Do what?"

"Be seen with me," she hissed. "You're the head of the association. What will everyone think?"

"That I've got great taste in women?" Jake took Cassie's hand and put it through his arm. It felt like ice. "There's nothing to be afraid of," he murmured as he escorted her to the door.

"I know," Cassie said. "It's just nerves, that's all." Jake opened the door and they stepped outside and walked to the end of the porch. Several rocking chairs were strewn about and a swing hung at the end. It was cozy, with little pots of plants sitting around and a deep roof that was good at keeping out the weather. Everywhere he looked, Jake saw Laurie's touches that made the difference between the place being a house and a home.

"Everyone has been so nice," Cassie added. "And no one has mentioned the sheep at all."

Jake leaned against the porch railing while Cassie looked out over the lake that lay in the Castles' valley. Jake glanced out at the view before turning to Cassie once more. The sun had started its descent and sent its last warming rays dancing across the water. The breeze picked up the ends of Cassie's hair and she ran a hand over the flyaway ends to put them back in place. "That's probably because not everyone knows yet," Jake said.

"Thank you for making me feel *so* much better," Cassie said sarcastically as she turned to look at him. Jake laughed. "No seriously, I'm glad you brought me along for your entertainment."

He stopped laughing, but he couldn't stop grinning.

"What is so funny?" Cassie demanded. He was surprised she didn't stamp her foot as she looked at him with righteous indignation. Instead, she crossed her arms and glared at him.

"Nothing," Jake admitted. "You just make me laugh sometimes."

She rolled her eyes. "So what do you think is going to happen?" she asked.

"Nothing that you have to worry about."

"That's just like a man," she said. "Trying to placate a woman. Am I not supposed to worry my pretty little head?" Her words sound bitter. "This isn't about you, Jake, it's about me and my family and my sheep. So I do have something to worry about."

Jake instantly felt ashamed for the way he'd talked down to her. It wasn't that he meant anything by it; it was just that he felt a strange need to protect her. "You're right. I'm sorry," Jake said. "What I meant to say is that no one is going to attack you or force you to move or give up your sheep. I won't let them, and Cade is here to make sure Watkins stays in line. You haven't broken any laws or damaged any property. As long as you assure everyone that you'll keep your sheep on your property, no one should have an issue with them or you."

"I wonder if that goes both ways," Cassie said.

"What do you mean by that?"

"It means that I think Watkins got that sheep he killed off my property. Manuel found some tracks behind the house close to the road."

"Watkins and his men could have easily come across the sheep while they were looking for strays," Jake agreed. "But it will be hard to prove."

"Because he's a powerful rancher and I'm an interloper?" Cassie asked.

Jake had to agree with her. "I think it best you not say anything about it tonight. Let me speak to Cade about it." Cassie opened her mouth to protest. "I'm not trying to placate you, Cassie," Jake said. "I'm just hoping to avoid any trouble if at all possible. The last thing you want to do is make Watkins look bad in front of his peers. Can you trust me to talk to Cade? Or ask him to come out to your place tomorrow and have Manuel show him the tracks?"

She studied him for a long minute. Jake realized that his question was about more than trusting him to talk to Cade. It was about trusting him in general. She'd admitted something bad had happened in Texas. It was something so bad that she had issues with everyone. Her trust would be hard won.

"I trust you," she said finally.

Now he just had to show her he deserved it. "We best get inside," Jake said. "No need to keep them waiting any longer."

He offered her his arm and she took it, easily this time, without hesitation. He could only pray that he wasn't escorting her to her doom. All his lectures to her about worry came back to haunt him as they walked into the dining room where the members of the Cattlemen's Association were waiting to meet the woman who dared to bring sheep into cattle country.

"Now that wasn't so bad, was it?" Jake asked Cassie as they rode home. Full night was upon them and the sky threatened rain. Lanterns hung on both sides of the buggy to light the way. Cassie sat next to him, huddled up in his coat. Jake was feeling the cold himself but he'd never let on. Jake could only hope that he'd get Cassie home before the rain started. He seriously doubted if she'd invite him to stay over if they didn't. Tonight had been challenging enough without the added discomfort of wet clothes.

"Nobody got shot, if that's what you mean," Cassie replied.

He chuckled at her dry wit. She was right. The meeting hadn't been easy, but everyone was trying to be patient. Everyone but Watkins. Cassie had promised to keep her sheep in her valley and as long as they stayed put, there was nothing anyone could do or say. As Jake expected, the Castles had been the voice of reason and most of the other ranchers agreed. Only one other had sided with Watkins, and considering his place was on the other side of Angel's End, he'd just done it out off meanness. There wasn't any way Cassie's sheep could have an impact on his livestock.

After hearing the entire discussion, Jake wasn't so sure that sheep did have an impact on cattle. Not any more than the cattle had on the elk, deer, mustangs and other creatures that lived in these mountains. It was a fact that sheep tended to overgraze to the point of eating small trees, but Cassie's little flock wasn't enough to destroy every pasture in the area. Of course, there was always the chance that more sheep farmers would come and then there would be a problem, but that could also happen with cattle. Right now there was no reason why everyone couldn't get along, just as they had for the last several years.

"I don't trust Watkins," Cassie said. "He gave in too easy."

"I was thinking the same thing," Jake admitted. At the meeting, Watkins had argued against Cassie's right to keep the sheep, but eventually he'd agreed to let Cassie give it a try for the time being. His ready capitulation was surprising, especially on the heels of the threats Cade said he'd made in town. Because of those threats, Cade took the time to talk to Watkins after the meeting, time that allowed Jake to get Cassie safely home. That is if it didn't rain first.

"Feels like rain," Cassie said as she pulled his coat closer around her. She was nearly lost in it. The sleeves flopped over her hands and the hem came nearly to her knees. How could such a small package contain so much fight? What was it about her that made him want to protect her from all the evils in the world?

You are falling for her . . . The sudden realization struck Jake like the lightning that flashed in the distant clouds to the west. A few seconds later a rumble of thunder filled the valley.

"My grandmother used to tell me you could tell how close the storm was by counting the seconds in between the flash and the thunder," Cassie observed.

A burst of wind scurried around them and spooked Darby. The mare tossed her head and Jake calmed her and encouraged her to pick up the pace a bit.

"How far away is it?" Jake asked.

"Five miles," Cassie replied.

He was definitely going to get wet. Lightning flashed again and Jake automatically started counting. Before he got to three a loud bray sounded out from the road ahead and Libby charged up to the buggy.

"Is that my donkey?" Cassie asked as Jake pulled Darby to a stop.

"I'm afraid so," Jake said. Libby trotted to his side of the buggy and let out a panicked filled hee-haw.

Cassie clutched his arm. "Something's happened." Lightning flashed again, right above their heads, and the thunder rumbled immediately. Cassie's face showed pale in the flash and her eyes were round with fear.

Jake slapped the reins against Darby's back. The mare needed no more inspiration than that and she took off at a gallop. Jake braced his legs and Cassie hung on to the seat as the buggy bounced down the road with Libby braying and running behind them. Just as they turned up the road that led to Cassie's ranch, the sky broke open. They were both drenched within seconds. Jake couldn't see a thing, so he slowed Darby to a walk. Libby trotted beside him still braying her distress.

"Wait," Cassie practically yelled. The rain was so loud he could barely hear her. "Something's in the road." She stood up in the buggy. "Stop!"

Jake stopped the buggy and Cassie jumped off before it rolled to a stop. She disappeared into the curtain of rain and shrieked. Jake grabbed a lantern and followed her. They had stopped right before the sign that arched over the roadway. It was built of narrow pines with a split rail fading into the grass on either side. The double *P* had been branded years ago into a signboard that creaked back and forth in the wind.

Manuel was tied between the uprights. His entire body was slumped forward, supported only by the ropes that held his outstretched arms. Cassie knelt beside a lump in the road lying before Manuel that was Rosa. Jake went to Manuel and lifted his head. He'd been beaten, badly, but he was still alive.

"Rosa?" he gasped as Jake pulled out his knife and cut his bonds. Manuel slumped into Jake's arms and then staggered to his wife.

Libby moved behind Jake and nudged him with his nose. Jake patted her. "You did good, girl," he said, and knelt in the mud beside Cassie and Manuel. He held up the lantern. Rosa had a bruise on the side of her face and blood trickled from a cut. It looked like she'd been kicked or pistol-whipped.

"She's alive," Cassie said. "Just unconscious. They must

have hit her." She jumped to her feet. "Oh, God. Momma?" Cassie gathered up her skirts and took off up the drive.

"What happened here?" Jake asked Manuel, who was trying to pick up Rosa. He couldn't; he was barely conscious himself and struggling just to stay on his feet. Jake handed Manuel the lantern, picked up Rosa and placed her in the buggy. He had to help Manuel climb onto the back before he jumped in and sent Darby to the house. Manuel leaned over the seat and held on to Rosa as the buggy moved.

"Some men attacked the flock," Manuel began. "They killed some and the rest scattered. I tried to stop them . . ."

"There were more of them and they had guns," Jake said. "You're lucky you didn't end up dead."

"They said I would be next time," Manuel finished wearily.

"Did you get a good look at them?"

"No," Manuel confessed. "It was dark, they covered their faces." His voice broke. "I think they shot Max . . ."

"Damn . . ." Jake said and immediately chastised himself. It seemed as if Cassie was having an effect on him even when she wasn't there. "Did they hurt her mother?"

"I don't think so," Manuel said. "They left after they beat me. I could be wrong."

They arrived in front of the house. Light showed through the windows as if everything was fine. At least they hadn't tried to burn them out. Although it would probably be next on the list of whoever did this.

It had to be Watkins. Manuel was determined to carry Rosa himself, but he finally had to let Jake take her. Rosa was stirring, which was a good sign. Manuel led the way into the house with Jake following behind with Rosa in his arms.

"Please God, let her mother be all right," he said to himself as they walked through the open door.

Cassie knelt on a rug next to a chair that faced the fireplace. The fire had grown low; it was nothing more than embers. She talked quietly to the woman who sat in the chair. The woman didn't move or give any indication that she knew what was going on. He followed a limping Manuel to a room and placed Rosa on the bed. "I'll get some water," he said, and shook his head at the insanity of it. They were all drenched.

"Momma," Cassie said as he walked back into the main room of the cabin. "Can you just let me know you're not hurt?" Jake moved behind Cassie, so he could see her mother's face. She looked like a statue, just staring into the fire. She wasn't dead, he could see the slow rise and fall of her chest as she breathed, and still she seemed strange, like an empty shell. What had happened to her? Not tonight, but before? Was this the something horrible Cassie had mentioned? Jake knelt beside Cassie. She held her mother's hands in her own. Cassie's pale blond hair was plastered against her head and water dripped down her face, either from the rain or her tears, he couldn't tell.

"I don't think they came into the house," he said.

"I never should have come here." Cassie kept her eyes on her mother's face. "It's just more of the same thing we left behind."

Jake realized Cassie's mother was looking straight at him. The eyes that before had seemed dead brightened and her right hand trembled as if she wanted to move it.

"Frank," she said in a voice that was nothing more than a whisper. "You've come home."

FOURTEEN

Cassie stared at her mother. She'd been begging her to speak for two years and she finally did, as easy as you please, as soon as she laid eyes on Jake Reece. She was looking up at him now, with a sweet smile on her face.

"Who is Frank?" Jake asked.

"My father," Cassie replied. The smile disappeared off her mother's face and the vacant look came back. Her moment of lucidity was gone.

"Do I look like him?" Jake asked. "Is that why she's confused?"

"No, you don't look anything like him. His hair was the same color as mine and he'd lost most of it by the time he was your age."

"Sounds like Sam," Jake said. He held out his hand and Cassie took it as she climbed wearily to her feet.

"Manuel and Rosa?" she asked. "Should we send for a doctor?"

"Angel's End doesn't have a doctor," Jake said. "Rosa was stirring. I don't know how bad Manuel is. They beat on him but I'm pretty sure he'll survive."

Cassie went to the kitchen, found a large bowl and sat it in the sink. Jake joined her and pumped water while Cassie searched the hutch for towels and bandages.

"It was Watkins." The huge bundle of fear that had consumed her turned into anger. "And I know you're going to say there is no way to prove it."

"Manuel said he didn't see anything."

"And the rain washed all the tracks away." The words were bitter in her mouth. It was like she was living the nightmare of the rape all over again. There were no witnesses except for her mother, who could no longer speak after her stroke. All the tracks were washed away in a sudden rainstorm. It was her word against Paul Stacy's. And Paul Stacy could afford to hire the best lawyer around to defend him. The same lawyer that she had planned to study under.

It was another case of life isn't fair and Cassie was tired of being on the receiving end of it. She slammed the hutch door shut and tried the next one. It didn't have what she was looking for. She couldn't even remember what it was she needed. She slammed it shut too, and in frustration she swung her arm across the counter and sent Rosa's basket full of yarn and knitting flying. The knitting needles clattered onto the wood floor and rolled in every direction and her mother didn't even notice the noise. Cassie wanted, no, she needed to hit something. She clenched her hands into fists and swung out at the air as frustrated tears blinded her.

Strong arms grabbed her from behind and she shrieked in fear. It was just like before, when Paul Stacy had grabbed her, after the trial. Only he'd used her long braid to capture her, and pulled her to him like a fish on a line. That was why she cut it off. So it couldn't be used against her.

Cassie fought against the arms, but he was too big and too strong, just like before. And she didn't have her gun. Why oh why didn't she have her gun?

"I got you." Gentle words murmured against her ear. Somewhere in her brain the words registered differently than they had before. He didn't mean *I got you trapped*. He meant *I got your back. I'm here for you. I will help you*. Still, it took a moment for her body to stop its wild jerking and clawing. A very long moment where Jake held on to her, not too tight, just enough so that she wouldn't hurt herself, until finally the fight went out of her and she collapsed like a rag doll.

How easily he picked her up, as if she didn't weigh a thing. "You're freezing," he said. She hadn't even noticed it until he said it. Her body shook violently and she realized they were both still wearing their soaking wet clothes. Jake had to be colder than she was as she still had on his coat. He looked around for a moment and must have realized where her room was, as he started in that direction with Cassie in his arms.

"Why are you here?" Cassie asked. She felt weak and boneless. She didn't want to move. Yet she had to. Manuel and Rosa were hurt. The sheep were scattered. She'd promised to keep them on her land. God only knew where they were, or if there were any left.

"Did you think I'd just leave?"

"Some people would."

"You've been hanging around with the wrong type of people." Jake lowered her so her feet touched the floor but he kept a hold on her. "Can you stand?"

Cassie nodded.

"I'm going to get Darby out of the weather and check on the rest of your stock while you put on some dry clothes."

Cassie sniffed.

"May I have my coat back?"

She didn't answer, but instead just shrugged out of his coat. She stuck her arm out to hand it to him without looking him in the face.

"Cassie," he said. "Look at me." Her head seemed to turn of its own volition. Jake's short-cropped hair glistened with moisture and his white shirt was plastered to his shoulders and chest, showing the well-defined muscles beneath it. The skin of his neck was covered with goose bumps, yet he didn't shiver, he just stood there, calmly talking to her. "I'm just going down to the barn. I'll be back. Can you find me a dry shirt to put on when I get back?"

Once more she nodded, because speech was just too hard at the moment. Jake stood there for a few seconds, seconds when she really wasn't sure what he was going to do, then he ran a hand through his dripping hair and left.

She had to do something. Manuel and Rosa needed her. Her mother needed her. It was too much to expect from her. Why did she have to take care of everyone and everything? It was just too hard. She just wanted to take off her wet clothes and climb into her bed and pull the blankets up over her head and sleep.

Cassie took a deep breath. There was work to be done. First she needed to change clothes and then she'd take the rest as it came. It was the same thing she'd been doing for the past two years. Why should anything be any different now?

The rain still pounded on the roof. Whoever had done this, and Cassie knew beyond a shadow of a doubt that it was Watkins's men, was long gone. It would be impossible to see how much damage was done until daylight. How many sheep were dead, and how many were scattered to the hills?

Cassie changed into her everyday clothes and hung her wet things on the pegs. She ran her fingers through her hair and picked up a towel, dropped in her earlier haste, to dry it.

"Max!" Cassie just realized she hadn't seen Manuel's dog since they discovered Manuel and Rosa on the road. If those bastards had killed Max . . . Her gun was still in the pocket of her jacket, which hung by the door. Never again would she be without it. Not that it would have changed anything tonight, but if they'd come home earlier and caught them in the act . . .

Was she ready to take that step? Was she ready to kill someone? To actually pull the trigger and end someone's life? Cassie finished drying her hair and looked in the mirror as she tossed the towel aside. Her skin was a ghostly white and her eyes huge in her face. The tip of her upturned nose was red with cold. Could she actually shoot someone after all the time she'd spent shooting at targets? She had always hoped she'd never have to find out, but now, to protect those she loved, she might just have to.

Cassie checked on her mother again before she went to the kitchen to once more search for what she needed to tend Manuel and Rosa. Her mother was the same as always, it was as if she hadn't spoken at all, and this time she found what she needed on her first pass through the hutch. The scattered things on the floor would have to wait.

The scene she walked in on was intimate. Manuel sat on the side of the bed. Rosa, thank God, was awake and had her hands on Manuel's bruised and bleeding face. Tears streamed from Rosa's eyes, tears of gratitude, Cassie was certain, because both of them were still alive.

"What happened, Manuel?" Cassie asked. She sat the bowl of water and towels on the bedside table. Manuel gingerly moved aside so Cassie could see the spreading bruise on the side of Rosa's face. Cassie knew Manuel's injuries were probably more serious, but also knew that he would not let her help him until he was certain Rosa was fine. Cassie wiped the blood from Rosa's face as Manuel began.

"We were just finishing up dinner when the donkey started braying," Manuel said. "I thought it might be a coyote, so I turned Max out. Then we heard gunshots. I took my rifle and went out. Three men were shooting the sheep. I shot at them but one of them roped me and dragged me to the place where you found me. The others tied me up and beat me until I passed out."

"I tried to stop them," Rosa added. "One of them kicked me here." She pointed to the side of her face where the skin was broken. "That is all I know until I woke up here."

"I think they shot Max," Manuel said. He covered his face with his hand. Max was the last link they had to their only child, a son, who'd died four years ago in the south of Mexico while trying to help the beleaguered plantation workers. "I heard him cry out, and have not seen him since."

Cassie didn't know what to say to comfort him. If Max was able, he'd be beside Manuel. He would have died to protect him; he might be dead already. "We'll find him," she said, but she didn't hold out much hope.

"I am fine," Rosa said. "Manuel is the one who is hurt the worst."

"I think I agree with you," Cassie said as Manuel protested his injuries. They slipped into Spanish, gently chiding each other over the risks they each had taken this night. Cassie, satisfied that Manuel's injuries weren't life threatening, although he would be laid up for a few days, left him to Rosa's tender care.

Her mother still sat in her chair. Cassie put her to bed,

which consumed the next half hour, and then she picked up the mess she'd made earlier. The rain still pounded against the roof, although the earlier thunder and lightning had moved on. Jake had been gone a long while. A good long while. Cassie looked at the small windup clock that sat on the mantel. Maybe an hour?

He must have left. Why shouldn't he? Why would he want to get caught up in her problems? He'd made it plain he didn't want her here, and he certainly didn't want her sheep here, as he'd said many times since the day they'd met.

You're not being fair . . . Jake said he was going to put Darby in the barn and check on her stock. That wouldn't take an hour. Not unless something else had happened.

Sitting around worrying about it wouldn't change it, if it had. Cassie put on her coat and hat, picked up her rifle and went outside. The air had changed. Where before there'd been a chill in the air, now it was balmy and heavy with the rain that still poured from the skies. Cassie squinted against the thick curtain of water and made out the darker shadows of the barn and outbuildings that lay below the cabin, but no light shone from any of them.

He's gone . . . Why did she believe him when he said he would stay? Why should he stay? Cassie grabbed the lantern that hung by the door and went down to the barn. Water chased her down the slope as she went; the ground was saturated and couldn't hold any more. The water kept on rolling, past the barn and on down the path and into the stream that bisected her land. Would it flood?

Cassie slipped into the barn. Suzie the cat ran to meet her with a questioning meow. The buggy sat in the aisle and Darby was in the stall next to Puck. Both turned their heads in her direction. Libby was in a stall also and wheezed a greeting.

"Jake?" Cassie called out. The only answer was the rain pounding on the roof. She walked through the barn and out the door on the opposite side. Cassie leaned the rifle against the door and lifted the lantern. The fence that they'd worked on so hard was trampled and the white patches scattered across the pasture were dead sheep. At least twenty, and probably many more that she couldn't see. So much waste. And where were the rest of them? Scattered who knows where, after all her promises to keep them home. Watkins had to be behind this. He'd sent his men to attack Manuel while he was at the meeting being cooperative.

Cassie called out again. "Jake?" In the distance she saw a light bobbing up and down. It had to be Jake; if Watkins wanted to do any more damage, he had plenty of opportunity and he definitely wouldn't be walking around her pasture with a lantern. Still, she kept her hand on her pistol until she was sure.

"Cassie!" he called back. "Is something wrong?" He trotted into the circle of light cast by her lantern. Water streamed from his head and his clothes. He couldn't have been any more wet if he'd fallen into a tub full of water. *He's still here* . . . His gun belt was strapped around his waist. He was prepared for trouble, but there was none to be found. Not now. Only a fool would be out in this weather. Or someone who thought he could help a fool.

"No, I was just worried," she admitted. "You were gone so long."

"I was looking for Max," Jake said. He wiped his hand across his face. Raindrops still hung on his lashes and his eyes were as stormy as the night.

Cassie was afraid to ask but she had to know. "Did . . . Did you find him?"

"No. No sign of him. I kept walking bigger and bigger

circles. I counted thirty-seven dead sheep, but no sign of your dog."

"I hate to think of him out there somewhere, especially if he's hurt."

"There's nothing more we can do tonight."

Cassie didn't know why she was standing in the rain looking at him. Just looking at him. At the way the water sluiced into the hollows of his jaw and around the cords of his neck. The way the raindrops hung to his hair and lashes. "You've done more than anyone could expect," she said. He was close enough that she could touch him if she wanted to. Did she want to?

"Without doing anything at all," Jake finished for her.

"No," Cassie started, but words failed her. How could she tell him what it meant to her that he was here, and that he had stayed, that she hadn't had to face this alone. Instead, she just stood in the rain looking at him.

He took another step. A step that brought him so close to her. Close enough that she could feel the chill off his skin. He had to be cold. He would probably be sick. Yet here they stood with the rain pouring over them. He placed his hand on her cheek and the place he touched instantly warmed.

"I'm sorry this happened," he said. "Life isn't fair sometimes. That's not an excuse; it's just the way it is."

"I know."

"I have a feeling you've had more than your share of unfair."

She made a noise, something between a laugh and a sob. He looked at her for a long moment, a moment when she really wasn't sure what was going to happen. A moment filled with anticipation. Then he dropped his hand and wrapped his arms around his body. "Can we get out of the rain? I'm freezing."

Without a word Cassie went back into the barn and Jake followed her. He picked up her rifle and trimmed the wick on his lantern before hanging it on the hook on his buggy. Suzie met them and trailed after them. Steam rose from Jake's body as they quickly passed through, and Libby brayed as he walked by her stall. As they came to the opposite door, Cassie handed Jake the lamp, scooped up Suzie and put her inside her jacket. They took off at a run up the slope to her house. As if they could suddenly stay dry.

It wasn't until they reached the porch that Cassie realized Jake would be spending the night. And she had no place for him to sleep.

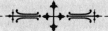

FIFTEEN

I t was in the wee hours of the morning that Jake decided
he'd much rather sleep outside on the ground than on a
cold hard floor. The ground seemed to be more giving, or
maybe using his saddle as a pillow made the positioning
that much more comfortable. The coons scratching and chattering beneath the floorboards didn't help either. All in all
it was a miserable night. The fact that Cassie was right on
the other side of the wall didn't help much either.

Dang it, she'd gotten under his skin. He should be at home
right now, lying in his big bed with Josie chewing on his arm,
and thinking about *his* day on *his* ranch doing *his* work.

But Cassie needed help. There were dead sheep scattered
around her pasture, a missing flock and a dog that could be
hurt or dead, and Manuel would be hard-pressed to do anything after the beating he took.

He really should let Cade know what was going on too.

Not that they'd be able to prove anything. But he should
know, just so he could let Watkins know that this would not
be tolerated. Jake decided he'd had enough suffering on the
floor. He got up, folded up the quilt Cassie had given him
the night before, stretched his sore muscles and pulled on
his pants that he'd left hanging by the fire to dry. They were
still damp, but that wasn't surprising considering how wet
he'd been. Jake went out the back door to relieve himself.
The sky was still gray and threatening but the rain had
stopped for a while. That was a good thing. Rains like the
one they had last night were bothersome, especially when
warm air came with them. The mountain peaks were still
covered with snow, and with the quick melt and sudden rush
of water there was a chance of a flash flood washing down
from the ridges that surrounded them.

Manuel was up when Jake went back in. He was putting
wood in the stove, and Jake went to help him. "How are you
feeling?" Jake asked.

Manuel tested his jaw. "Lucky to be alive?" he replied
with a painful smile. His face was heavily bruised and he
rubbed his side before filling the coffeepot with water. He
must have taken some punches to his body also.

"Do you think you cracked a rib?" Jake asked. "I got
thrown one time and busted a couple of them. It sure was
hard to breath."

"I am breathing," Manuel assured him. "It is not that difficult at the moment."

Jake found his shirt and boots and put both on. The murmur of women's voices came from the room where Cassie
and her mother slept. That was something else that was
strange, how Cassie's mother had thought he was her husband.
The woman had obviously had something go wrong with
her at some time. It looked to Jake to be a miracle that

she survived it. Not him, he'd rather be dead than left in such a state. He had no one to care for him anyway.

Now that was a sad thought.

"I looked for Max last night," Jake said to Manuel. "There was no sign of him."

Hope filled Manuel's dark eyes. "That is good to know. Thank you."

"From what I saw, over thirty sheep are dead," he added. "I'll help you gather them up before I head into town."

Manuel almost sighed in relief. "That would be most helpful," he said. Jake was glad to help; it would give him a chance to find out more about this strange little group that had settled in Angel's End.

Cassie and Rosa came in with Cassie's mother between them. They guided her to the same chair she was in the night before. Jake suddenly felt very much in the way as they settled her for the day. "I'll just go out and get started," he said as Cassie walked out the back door without a word.

"No," Rosa protested. "I will fix breakfast first." She pulled out a chair at the table for him. "Please sit and tell us about the meeting last night so we might better understand what to expect." The side of Rosa's face was swollen and had a strange greenish cast. Jake felt himself getting angry all over again. What if Cassie had been here when it happened? What if she was the one they kicked aside and left lying in the rain? He had to do something to make sure this didn't happen again. Because if it did, he knew the outcome would be worse, much much worse.

Rosa put cups of steaming coffee in front of Jake and Manuel as Cassie came back into the house. She was wearing those confounded boys' clothes again. The ones that she liked to hide behind. There was no denying she was a woman, so why was she trying to hide it?

As Jake stirred milk into his coffee, the sudden realization of what happened to Cassie struck him. She admitted it was something bad. She didn't like to be touched, although she tolerated him somewhat. She dressed like a boy. She carried a gun everywhere she went. She'd gone crazy when he came up behind her last night; at the time he thought it was because she was so angry, but it could have something to do with what troubled her.

It made sense. He couldn't outright ask her, but he knew in his heart that she'd been raped at some time. And her mother had more than likely witnessed it, which is what led to her sorry condition. It had to be the reason why she came here. The letter with the promise of land must have seemed like a godsend at the time, although now, after last night, not so much.

Right now he wanted to kill someone in the worst way. He wanted to kill the bastards who'd attacked Manuel last night and he wanted to kill whoever hurt Cassie so badly in the first place. Hell, he even wanted to kill her grandfather, Sam, who was already dead, for going off and deserting her when she was just a girl. *You got it bad, Jake.*

Jake took a drink of his coffee. It was hot and strong, just the way he liked it, and he gave Rosa a nod and a smile. Yeah, he was in it, and he wasn't sure he wanted to be. Just a few short months ago he'd been mourning the loss of Leah to Cade Gentry. He wasn't looking to fall in love with a pixie mix of stubborn and sweetness with a side of sass.

Love? Now where did that come from? He needed to get away from Cassie Parker and her problems. He needed to think things through. Jake was a planner and he was always very careful about the decisions he made. Cassie Parker was not something he'd seen coming. Jake studied her as she fixed a plate of food and took it to her mother. She sat down next to her to feed her.

"Can you tell us what happened last night at the meeting?" Manuel asked.

Rosa sat a plate of eggs with a huge piece of ham down before him. She went back for a pan of biscuits and joined the two men at the table.

Jake gave them the details of the meeting and summed up the conclusions for the couple. "Most everyone was nice, a few were not," Jake said. "Cassie agreed to keep her sheep on her property and everyone else agreed to wait and see if she could."

"And now they'll know that I can't," Cassie said.

"No one is going to blame you considering the circumstances," Jake said. Cassie put her mother's plate in the sink and fixed one for herself. She didn't sit down, instead just leaned against the cabinet and ate.

"Oh I know they won't blame me," she agreed. "They'll just say it's too much responsibility for me. That I'm a woman, all alone. That I don't have any business trying this on my own, much less with sheep. They'll find lots of reasons not to blame me, but the fact of the matter is, our sheep are out there somewhere and I'm responsible for them."

"We'll get them back."

"It's not your problem, Jake, it's mine. You've got your own place to run. You've spent enough time on my problems. You need to go take care of your own." Cassie scraped her plate into a bowl and then looked at it, stricken for a moment.

Max . . . Lord, let that dog be alive.

Cassie went to the door and put on her coat. "I'm going out to find the sheep."

"Wait," Jake said as he jumped up from the table. "You can't just take off by yourself without a plan."

"Like I said, Jake, it's not your problem. I appreciate all your help." She wouldn't look at him. And short of picking her up and locking her in her room there wasn't a thing he could do to stop her. What had got into her? Last night he'd thought that there could be something between them. Dang, he'd even thought about kissing her, but something held him back. Maybe it was the fear that seemed to be hiding in her pale blue eyes. "I'm serious, Jake. Don't try to stop me," she threatened, and Jake couldn't help but recall the first time he met her on the trail. Cassie shut the door in his face.

"Give her time, Mr. Reece," Rosa said. "She needs time to work things out in her mind. A lot of unexpected things have happened."

Rosa was right about that. "Let's see to those dead sheep," Jake said. He had his own chores to do. The sooner he was done here, the sooner he could get back to his own.

"What will you do with them?" Jake asked Manuel later when they had hitched the wagon to the two mules and gone out into the pasture. Cassie was long gone, off on Puck, searching for the rest of her flock.

"Save what wool we can," Manuel said. "Burn the bodies."

"Why do you raise sheep?" Jake asked. "I don't mean that as in it's not the thing to do, I mean, how do you make a profit? I can't imagine there's a call for the meat like there is with cattle."

"For the wool," Manuel explained. "Rosa spins it and we sell it."

Jake recalled seeing a spinning wheel in the main room of the house. He hadn't thought much about why it was there.

"She also does the dyes," Manuel explained. "We've

always made a good profit. Of course, now we'll have to find new buyers since we no longer have our contacts in Texas."

"Why did you leave Texas?" Jake asked. They'd come to the first body and together they heaved it into the back of the wagon.

"Cassie had the land," Manuel said.

"Come on, Manuel," Jake said. "I know something bad happened in Texas. Cassie told me that much. And since I'm knee-deep in your trouble I'd appreciate knowing some of the reasons why."

"Some things are for Cassie to tell you," Manuel said as they picked up the next body.

The words were bitter in his mouth, but he had to say them. He had to understand why she acted the way she did. "She was raped," Jake said.

Manuel's ruddy skin turned pale beneath his bruises. They heaved the next sheep into the wagon and Manuel leaned against the side. He pulled a bandana from his pocket and wiped his face. The air was muggy, heavy with the promise of more rain, and the two men had already worked up a sweat.

"She was," Manuel said finally. "She was with her mother on a stage when it was attacked. Loretta's heart gave out when she saw it."

"That's what I figured," Jake said.

"I found the both of them in the wreckage of the stage and took them home to Rosa. Cassie recovered and her mother didn't. They'd lost everything they had in the robbery."

"What were they doing there? What made them come to Texas from Illinois?"

"Cassie wanted to study the law. There was a lawyer in Amarillo who said she could study with him."

"She wanted to be a lawyer?" Jake asked. Her tenacity amazed him. "I don't think I've ever heard of a woman being a lawyer."

"As you saw this morning, she doesn't like to be told what she can't do," Manuel said. "I don't know what she was like before the attack, but after, she was afraid of things. She wanted to learn how to protect herself, so I showed her how to shoot. Finally, when she felt confident enough to work, she took a job doing filing and bookkeeping for the lawyer. She wasn't ready to study yet. She was still trying to get back to normal. To trust again."

"She trusted you," Jake pointed out.

"I'd seen her at her weakest," Manuel said. "When I found her. If I had wanted to hurt her I could have done it then."

The story was making Jake sick to his stomach, but he had to hear it all. "Go on," Jake said. "What happened to make you leave?"

"One day she was walking down the street and Cassie saw the man who raped her. His name was Paul Stacy and his father owned the biggest spread around."

"Like Watkins."

"Like Watkins," Manuel agreed.

"I'd reported the robbery to the marshal," Manuel continued. "He didn't care much because I wasn't considered to be a citizen, as we had only been in America for a few years. But he did follow up with Cassie. So she filed charges against Stacy."

"Whose rich daddy hired the best lawyer to defend him?"

"The same lawyer that she worked for."

"And it was her word against Stacy's. She was betrayed twice," Jake concluded. "Once by the law and again by the man who she thought was her friend."

"After the trial, Stacy tried to attack her again. He thought he was untouchable. Her hair was long, down to her waist. She wore it in a braid," Manuel said. "He grabbed her by her braid and Cassie cut it off with a knife so she could get away. She wouldn't go to town after that."

Jake could see her doing it. Pride and stubbornness were as good weapons as any when you were outmatched. "Is that why you left?"

"Stacy's father made it impossible for us to stay."

"Because you helped Cassie and you had sheep," Jake said. "The same thing is happening here that happened in Texas."

"She feels responsible for Rosa and me," Manuel said. "Because we helped her."

"What did you do before you started herding sheep?" Jake asked. "You don't talk like a farmer." Jake grimaced at the words he'd just said. "I didn't mean it like that. What I mean is, you sound as if you're educated."

"I taught at the university in Mexico City," Manuel said. "Our son was killed in the union riots in the south of the country. We thought it best to leave after that. There was nothing to keep us there."

"Was there ever justice for Cassie?"

Manuel shook his head. "Paul Stacy is a spoiled boy who never had to take responsibility for his actions. He and his men robbed the stage as a lark. They killed two men and left Cassie and her mother for dead and later laughed about it, and then laughed some more when the trial was over. He considers himself to be above the law."

"Someone needs to put a bullet in him," Jake said. He couldn't see the man's face, but he could well imagine the satisfaction he'd feel at pulling the trigger.

"I will leave that to God's discretion," Manuel said.

Jake found himself looking at Manuel with a newfound respect. He knew from personal experience about life beating you down. His first response had always been anger and the determination to prove life wrong. It seemed that Manuel had that same determination, but he responded with patience and kindness.

"I have one more question," Jake said.

"I don't know what else I can tell you," Manuel said. "I fear I have told you too much."

Jake shook his head and smiled. "This one is about Libby, the donkey. Why did you buy her?"

Manuel laughed. "I have wondered that myself ever since I brought her home," he said as he shook his head. "A donkey will protect the sheep as well as a dog, sometimes better. They will fight the coyotes and wolves."

"Now that's something I'd like to see," Jake said. "Knowing Libby the way I do, I'm fairly certain she'd give them a good fight."

"We have visitors," Manuel said, and he picked up his rifle that lay in the seat of the wagon.

Jake touched the handle of his pistol and relaxed when he recognized the horses. "It's the sheriff," he said. "And Ward Phillips. They must have spent the night at the Castles' when the rain started." Manuel still looked wary. "You can trust them," Jake assured him.

They had time to collect another carcass before the two men rode out to where they worked. "How bad is it?" Cade asked as soon as they were in earshot. "Anyone hurt?"

"Manuel took the worst of it," Jake said as the two men dismounted. Jake introduced them.

"Can you identify the attackers?" Cade asked Manuel.

"Sorry, I cannot," Manuel replied.

"How did you know something had happened here?"

Jake asked. If someone had said something, then maybe there was a way to trace it back to Watkins.

"We didn't," Ward said. "We were just on our way home from the Castles' and Cade decided to pay Cassie a visit to talk to her about what you said last night. That she thought Watkins had taken the sheep from her land. It wasn't hard to figure out what happened when we saw the dead sheep." Ward looked around. "Where is our lovely Miss Parker?"

"Out rounding up her sheep," Jake said.

"By herself?" Ward asked incredulously.

"Couldn't stop her," Jake said.

"She is one determined woman." Ward shook his head in disbelief. Jake walked to the closest carcass, shaking his head also. Ward didn't know the half of it.

"You best tell me all of it," Cade said to Manuel.

"His wife was attacked too," Jake said.

"We should go to the house," Manuel offered.

"Go ahead, I'll help Jake," Ward said. Manuel and Cade headed to the house, and Ward took off his coat and rolled up his sleeves. "The sheriff is in a hurry to get home to his wife," he said.

Jake knew Ward was watching him for a reaction. "Can't blame him," he said. "What with Leah being pregnant and all. I know it didn't break your heart to spend the night at the Castles'."

"The only thing better than the food was the view," Ward said. "Whichever way you turned you saw a beautiful woman."

"Be careful what you say my friend," Jake said with a grin. "That's Jared's wife and daughter you're lusting after."

Ward laughed. "I guess you got stranded in the storm also?" The two men bent to pick up the sheep.

"Yeah, the storm and Watkins's mess. I couldn't just leave

Cassie alone after we found Manuel and Rosa in the middle of the road. They tied him to the gateposts and beat him. One of them kicked Rosa in the side of the head."

"Whoever did it ought to be horsewhipped," Wade said. "Any way to prove who it was?"

"Neither one saw anything that would identify anyone. It was dark and they wore bandanas over their faces. All the tracks were washed away in the storm. There's not a chance in hell of proving a thing."

They put the body in the wagon. "You're getting in pretty deep here, aren't you?" Ward asked.

"It's starting to feel that way," Jake admitted.

Ward grinned. "Is she driving you crazy?"

"Absolutely."

"Just like Shakespeare," Ward said.

"What is that supposed to mean?" Jake asked.

"Just remembering a talk we had a few days ago."

Jake wasn't ready to admit anything to Ward. He wasn't even sure of his feelings. "How about we have less talking and more working," he said.

Ward ignored him of course. "She took off by herself?"

"That's what I said."

"Why didn't you stop her?"

"Because I was pretty sure she wanted to shoot me."

"Why didn't you go with her?"

"Because I couldn't leave this for Manuel to do on his own. He's all busted up." They picked up another sheep. "Besides, I've got my own place to take care of. I can guarantee you my hands are more than likely lying about the bunkhouse instead of out there working like they're supposed to be."

"Maybe you should send some of them over here to help."

"Maybe I should," Jake said. "Or maybe I'll just mind my own business from now on and you can mind yours."

"You got it that bad?" Ward asked.

"I'm afraid so," Jake said finally. He wiped his forehead with his sleeve. "And to tell you the truth, Ward, I don't know what to do about it. I'm think one of the reasons she's out there looking for her sheep is because she's scared."

Ward put a comforting hand on Jake's shoulder. "Don't worry my friend, you'll figure it out."

"I hope so," Jake said. He looked around the pasture. "Let's move the wagon. We've still got a lot of work to do."

SIXTEEN

"Now what?" Ward asked Cade as they left the Parker ranch. Ward was as impatient to get back as the sheriff. Except he was missing a dog instead of a wife. There was something kind of sad about his situation, and it was something he didn't want to think about at the moment, which is why he asked Cade the question.

"Right now all I can think about is getting home to Leah and Banks," Cade said. "But I reckon I should swing by Watkins's place, just to let him know that he's not getting away with anything."

"You best tread easy," Ward said.

Cade laughed. "I'm guessing that means I can't just shoot them."

"While it's tempting, I wouldn't recommend it. You are impressive with that gun, but I'm pretty sure Watkins will have more men than even you can handle."

"I could deputize you," Cade threatened.

Ward raised his hands in mock surrender. "I am nothing if not a man of peace."

"Yeah, I really believe that," Cade said.

"How about you tread easy, because I don't want to have to tell Leah that her second husband got shot in the line of duty."

"I can live with that," Cade said.

"You better, because she would kill me and I'm much too young and good-looking to die." They crossed the main road and cut back to the drive that led to the Watkins place. The heavy skies finally came through with their promise of more rain and a light drizzle started.

"We're going to have some flooding if we get another downpour like last night," Ward observed. "When the snow turns loose of the mountain peaks it gets pretty bad."

They were moving down a gentle slope. "I've seen it run right through here," he said, pointing to the stream that bubbled down from Cassie's land, "and then run into the bigger stream that runs behind Watkins's spread."

"What about the town?" Cade asked. "Is there ever much water through there?"

"I've seen it get up to your shed," Ward said. "Without much more rain than this. We had an exceptional amount of snow last year. I'd be wary if I were you."

The valley opened up before them as they rounded a bend. A lot was going on, in spite of the drizzle. Several cows milled about in a large corral. Some cowboys were inside with ropes, and others were around a small pen. A few were on horseback, watching the others work.

"Oh great," Ward said. "It's castration day."

"What, are you afraid someone will slip up and tie you down?"

"Just don't like the noise," Ward admitted. "The way those poor fellas cry."

Watkins saw their approach and rode up to meet them. "Sherriff," he said. "Phillips. What brings you back out my way so soon?"

"Actually we never made it home last night," Cade said. "The rain started and the Castles asked us to spend the night."

"Isn't it nice when everyone is so neighborly," Ward added. "Welcoming and all that."

"Some people are just that way," Watkins said. "Others aren't."

"And you're in the 'aren't' category?" Cade asked.

"I've seen more people come and go than you'll ever know, Sheriff," Watkins said. Ward got the feeling there was a hidden meaning in Watkins's statement. As in there were bodies buried and they would never find out where.

Cade must have been tired of messing around because he got right to the point real quick. "We just came from the Parker spread," he said. "People are hurt and livestock are either dead or missing. I *am* going to find out who did it."

Watkins made a noise deep in his throat and spat in the dust in front of Cade's horse. "Are you threatening me, Sheriff?"

"Nope." Cade casually leaned across his saddle horn. "Just assuring you that I'm determined to make sure that everyone in this valley is safe. In case someone comes and does the same to your place."

"Don't worry about us," Watkins assured him. "We can protect ourselves from anyone who decides to pay us the visit."

"Just as long as you know that others are inclined to do the same," Cade said.

"I'll keep that in mind," Watkins said, and without another word turned his horse and went back to his work.

"What do you think?" Cade asked as they also turned their horses and started the trip back to the main road.

"I think he could care less what you or anyone else thinks," Ward said. "Which is pretty much the norm for him."

"I'm all for living your life the way you see fit," Cade said. "As long as you don't hurt other people when you're doing it."

"Live and let live?" The rain came down harder as they made the turn to town. Both men hunkered down in their slickers. Ward knew Cade was deep in thought. This was his first real test as sheriff. Most of his work since taking the job last December had been making sure the drunks at Ward's bar didn't shoot up the town. They rode the rest of the way in silence, not even talking when they got to Martin's livery beyond a "See you later," after they'd taken care of their horses.

Lady greeted Ward as if he'd been gone for a month instead of a night. She whined and jumped and licked his cheek before flopping over on her back for a belly rub and then scrambling up again before he could touch her.

"That dog has grieved the entire time you were gone," Pris said as she came down the stairs. She stretched and yawned and retied the belt on her robe. It was pretty early for Pris to be up and about.

"She loves me; I have no doubt about that." Ward hung his slicker on the coat stand, knelt down next to Lady and hugged her. "We missed breakfast this morning," he said. "But don't worry, I'll make it up to you at lunch."

Pris giggled. "I'm sure Dusty will love that."

"He'll get over it soon enough," Ward said. "Did I miss anything last night?"

"Just some wet cowboys is all," Pris said. "Bob can fill you in. I went upstairs as soon as I saw them. I can't stand that Baxter guy from the Bar W. He gives me the creeps."

Now that was an interesting turn of events. Cowboys didn't usually come to town during the week. Not unless they'd been out doing something and wanted to celebrate afterward. And these guys were from the Bar W, which was Watkins's place. "They didn't bother you, did they?" Ward asked her.

"No, sir. You put a good lock on my door and I know how to use it."

"Good," Ward said. He looked around the Heaven's Gate. Everything was as it should be. His clothes were a bit damp, but they'd dry soon enough. As was his habit, he went to his piano. He had some thinking to do and he always did his best thinking when he played. Lady lay down beside the bench, content that he was home, and the rain beat a steady accompaniment on the roof.

SEVENTEEN

Cassie huddled down inside her coat. Water poured over the brim of her hat and onto her legs where they hung on either side of the saddle. She was chilled to the bone and soaked besides. She'd been foolish when she'd left, not taking any supplies and even leaving her slicker behind.

To tell the truth, her fear of Jake had been more instrumental in her desire to get away from the house than her desire to find the sheep. Right now she could care less about the sheep, although she was worried about Max. If he was hurt and hiding someplace, then they would never find him. There were too many nooks and crannies to hide in.

If only she could crawl in one and hide too. She should get out of the rain, but she had come so far, farther up into the canyons that fed into her property than she ever had before. Yet she wasn't accomplishing a thing. It was raining so hard that she could barely see in front of her, and the way

Puck kept tossing his head let her know he was having difficulty also. She needed to find shelter until this deluge blew over. She really didn't have a clue if she was still on her land as she'd yet to ride all the boundaries. First there'd been the winter weather, and then all the work when spring finally arrived. She should have been ready in case something like this happened. She should have explored her land already, instead of waiting for a disaster to send her out with no more signs to follow than a swath of trampled grass next to the stream that led into the mountains. Surely the sheep would all be together, somewhere. She could only hope that they hadn't all just followed one another off the nearest mountain face to their death. It sure would make life easier if they had.

"Stop it," Cassie told herself. "What will you do then?" Without the sheep they had no income. The partnership she'd formed with Manuel was her responsibility. The circumstances they were in, the beating Manuel and Rosa had taken, were all her fault. If not for her they'd still be back in Texas, living peacefully without notice. She had to find the sheep. She had to keep them on her property. She had people depending on her.

The trail was rockier now as the canyon walls rose up around her. Surely the sheep hadn't come this direction. There was no place for them to go, as the way was getting narrower. Behind the pounding of the rain Cassie heard the roar of the stream as the water tumbled down its path. She began to look for a cave or an overhang, or someplace where they could take shelter until the rain let up. Puck tossed his head nervously and Cassie gave his neck a reassuring pat. "Find us some shelter, boy," she said encouragingly. Forget about the sheep. Finding shelter was now her biggest problem.

No, Cassie had to admit to herself, Jake was the biggest problem. And it wasn't Jake specifically; it was her feelings for Jake that were causing her dilemma. She'd spent the night tossing and turning because she couldn't stop thinking about him. She didn't want to think about him. She didn't want to think about any man. She didn't want to feel these things she was feeling. She was scared out of her mind.

Feeling these things meant she might be expected to act on them and that was one thing she was certain she could not do. The memories of what happened were too close, so close that she never knew when they were going to creep up on her. There were nights when she closed her eyes when she would still see Paul Stacy's face above her. Still feel his hands clawing at her. Still feel the pain of his attack.

Suddenly Puck reared. Cassie felt her seat give way and she tumbled backward over Puck's hindquarters. She hadn't been paying attention and she'd paid for it. She landed on her hip with her leg twisted beneath it. A pain shot up her side as she rolled to get away from Puck's flailing hooves. Puck reared again and kicked out. Cassie realized why when she saw the rattler coiled on the trail. Puck jumped backward as the snake tried to strike and then disappeared into the curtain of rain. Cassie backpedaled away as the rattler shook its tail in anger. She pulled her gun from her pocket, aimed down the barrel and pulled the trigger. She was rewarded with the sight of the rattler's head exploding with blood. Cassie kept her gun in her hand as she searched the area for another snake. All she saw was the rain splattering off the rocks and soaking the ground beneath her.

She dropped her head onto the ground and lay flat on her back, looking up at the gray skies. She had to get up, yet the pain in her leg told her it wasn't going to be easy. What if she'd broken something? What if she couldn't move? What if she just laid here until she died? That had to be easier than getting up. She was so tired of fighting. She was sick of everything being so hard.

"Get up," she said. "You've got to get up." Cassie managed to roll onto her uninjured side and push herself up into a sitting position. She whistled for Puck and heard nothing. She whistled again, louder this time. He was gone, she hoped on his way back to the ranch and his warm, dry stall. Meanwhile, she was getting wetter, if that was possible. Cassie struggled to get to her knees and pushed herself up. Her leg instantly buckled and she teetered for a moment before regaining her balance. She hobbled as best she could as she cursed herself for every kind of fool.

Jake was right. She shouldn't have gone off on her own, but at the time she was more worried about getting away from him than anything else. His kindness, his patience, and the way he looked at her, as if he wanted to kiss her . . . it was her own fault she was in this mess. And she would just have to figure a way out of it.

Her first need was shelter. She couldn't walk home, so she had to find a place to wait out the storm until Manuel came looking for her. He would come looking, when Puck showed up without her. That is if Puck showed up. Cassie could only pray that the snake hadn't bitten him before he got away. She turned in the direction that led out of the canyon and took a hobbling step.

Even if Puck didn't show up, Manuel would come looking for her. Even with his injuries . . . Guilt consumed her once more. Manuel would suffer for her foolishness, just as he had before. Cassie kept on hobbling until she was close to the canyon wall. "Surely there has to be a cave or something here." She wrapped her arms around her body against the chill that permeated her bones and kept on, limping heavily as she shivered with cold.

It was amazing what a hot bath and clean clothes could do to make a fellow feel better on the outside. And Fu's bowl of soup should have made him feel better on the inside. It was filling, but it did nothing to belay the worry that gnawed at Jake's insides.

Cassie hadn't come back; at least she hadn't by the time he left. The rain had started again before he got home. Surely she had enough sense to turn back when it started. He finished his soup, picked up his cup of coffee and wandered through his house with Josie chasing his heels. Jake always loved his house, the big rooms with the high-peaked ceiling and the stone fireplaces, but today it felt cold and empty. He walked into the front room that held his office and looked out the window.

He'd been right; his guys had taken advantage of the dreary weather and stayed in the bunkhouse today. He didn't mind, though. Only a fool would be out in this weather. The chances were pretty good that there would be flooding in the low-lying areas too.

"It's not like she's going to find anything," Jake said to the rain trickling down the glass panes. He put down his coffee cup and picked up Josie, who'd been chewing on the toe of his boot. She looked up at him with her two different-colored eyes, gave him a doggy smile and then went to work on the button of his shirt while Jake rubbed her head. "Of course, as stubborn as she is . . ."

He should have known. It was bound to happen. Libby came charging up the road and didn't stop until she was on the porch that stretched across the front of his house. She raised a leg and struck her hoof against the door. The noise startled Josie, who barked and wiggled until Jake put her down so she could run barking to the door.

"Company, Mr. Jake?" Fu asked as he came out of the kitchen.

"Just that crazy donkey again." Jake sighed. "I reckon I'll be taking her home."

"Donkey wants to live here," Fu said. "Be better for all if you let her."

"I'll take it under advisement," Jake said. "Can you pack some food for me? I have a feeling I might be gone for a while."

Libby's hooves still pounded on the door. "Will you let her in?" Fu asked.

"No, but I will send her down to the barn," Jake said. He opened the door and Josie charged out, and then ran back in with a startled yelp when Libby drew her lips back and brayed loud and long. The wooden door was scarred from her barrage, but that was the least of Jake's worries at the moment.

"I know, I know," Jake said. He shoved Libby aside so she wouldn't come in the house, and closed the door behind him as he stepped outside. Dan and Randy had come out on the porch of the bunkhouse after hearing all the ruckus and Jake waved them up.

"More trouble on the Parker spread?" Dan asked. He bent to pet Josie, who was trying to decide if Libby was going to eat her.

"It seems that way," Jake said. His guys knew about the sheep and the attack. Gossip spread between the ranches, the same way it spread in town. Jake made sure they knew the facts as soon as he got back. Dan took Libby's halter and led her down the two steps of the porch so she was on the ground, yet still protected from the rain by the roof. Josie tumbled down after him and quickly piddled. She attacked the steps like she was climbing a mountain and Jake scooped her up. "Good girl," he said.

"I'm not that fond of sheep," Randy confessed. "But there are things that are worse. Baxter being one of them. That man is lower than a snake's belly in a wagon rut."

"Is there something you want to tell me, Randy?" Jake asked. "Do you know anything?"

"No, sir," Randy replied. "But we all have our suspicions."

"And we hate to see bad things happen to good people," Dan added. "Whether there's sheep involved or not."

"There's a bunkhouse on the Parker place, isn't there?" Randy asked.

"Yes," Jake said. "But I'm not sure what kind of shape it's in."

"We thought we might go on over there and have a look at it," Dan said. "Maybe hang around, in case some uninvited guests show up."

"I think it would be much appreciated by everyone if you were to do just that," Jake said. He might curse his men for being lazy sometimes, but when it came down to it, they were good men, with hearts as big as the sky.

"I reckon you're heading that way?" Randy asked.

"I am, just as soon as I collect my gear," Jake said.

"We'll bring this troublemaker along with us," Dan said. "Why do they want this donkey?" he asked. "It seems to me like she's more trouble than she's worth."

"Apparently donkeys are pretty vicious when coyotes and such come around the flock," Jake explained. "And will fight them off."

Randy shook his head in wonder. "Don't that beat all," he said. "I reckon a fella can learn something new every day if he tries hard enough." The two men left, with Libby between them.

Jake went inside to change, with Josie trailing after him. He could only imagine what had happened at the Parker place, and all of it was bad. He threw an extra shirt and socks into his saddlebags, which Josie was attacking with great gusto, and went back through the kitchen to collect the food Fu put together for him.

"I don't know how long I'll be gone," Jake told the cook. Fu picked up Josie, who wanted to chase Jake out the back door. Jake gave her a good-bye pat. "Spoiled rotten, aren't you?"

"She misses you when you are gone," Fu agreed. "Hopefully Mr. Jake not run into any more problems like last night."

"I hope so," Jake said wearily. He put on his coat, and his slicker over it, and dashed down to the barn.

Skip was already saddled, thanks to Randy, who was saddling his own horse when Jake arrived. "Is herding sheep like herding cattle?" he asked.

"From what I saw, it's more like herding cats," Jake said.

"That ought to be a nice change," Randy said dryly. Dan joined them with supplies for both the men and tied a lead to Libby's halter. The men went to mount up and Libby brayed loud and long.

"Just give her to me." Jake sighed, and taking Libby's lead, they rode out into the rain. There was no time to waste on a crazy donkey. Cassie needed him. Whether she liked it or not, he was going to help her.

EIGHTEEN

Jake hoped to discover Cassie on her way out to find Libby. Instead, he found Manuel on the back of one of the mules just coming out of the barn.

"Where's Cassie?" he asked.

"Lost," Manuel said. "Puck came home without her. Libby got out when I was putting him up."

"This is Dan and Randy," Jake said as he dismounted. "They've come to help."

"Thank you," Manuel said as he shook hands with the men. He took Libby from Jake and followed him into the barn. Jake went to Puck's stall. The horse was spooked over something, Jake could tell by the way the gelding tossed his head and rolled its eyes.

"Any signs of a wound on him?" Jake asked. "Is he lame?"

"I checked him," Manuel said. "Something scared him."

"If only we knew what," Jake said. "Any idea where to start looking?"

"None," Manuel said.

"Let's get a move on," Jake said. "It will be dark soon, and if this rain doesn't stop we're going to need a boat instead of horses."

The men mounted up again. Dan and Randy had stashed their stuff in the bunkhouse. They took off across the narrow bridge in the direction Cassie had gone earlier that morning. The stream beneath the bridge was running high and fast, and Jake knew the flooding would be worse once they went up into the canyons.

"Watch the ground for signs," he said. "See if you can figure out from which direction Puck came in."

The four men spread out and kept their eyes on the ground. It was churned up from the sheep the night before and the deluge of rain hadn't helped a bit. It was impossible to see anything.

"Come on," Jake said. "Lord, give me something." He was concentrating so hard on the ground that it took him a moment to realize there was a sound beyond the rain.

"What is it?" he asked when he saw Manuel stop his mule. The three men converged on Manuel to see what had his attention.

"The sheep," Manuel said, pointing. The men pulled up their horses and watched as a gray and soggy cloud of sheep swarmed out of a canyon and into the valley.

"Max," Manuel called out. Sure enough the dog was bringing up the rear, dashing from one side of the flock to the other and nipping at the heels of the laggards.

"Well I'll be danged," Dan said.

"Let them come to us," Jake said. "We don't want to spook them." Sure enough the flock came right at them. The horses laid their ears back at the strange creatures, but they were well trained and held their ground. Manuel got off his mule and embraced Max, who joyfully jumped into his arms and gave his face a thorough washing with his tongue. Manuel guided him to the ground and rubbed his sides. Then he put his hands on the dog's face and looked into his eyes.

"He was hit with a bullet," Max announced. "See his ear?" Jake looked and the tip of the dog's pointed ear was gone.

"You were lucky," Jake said. "Both of you." He'd been watching, beyond the sheep, hoping beyond hope that Cassie would be with them, that she'd found the flock and brought it home. How proud she would have felt, and how sassy she would have been.

Would have?

"Help Manuel get them settled," he said to Dan and Randy.

"Are you sure, boss?" Randy asked.

"I'm not coming back until I find her," Jake said. "Take care of things here, and if I'm not back by this time tomorrow, send for the sheriff."

"Will do," they assured him. Jake set Skip into a ground-eating gallop the way the sheep had come. There was no need looking for tracks now, they were obliterated. He'd search around the many ridges and cutaways that led into the mountains. There were only a couple of hours of daylight left. Jake couldn't afford to waste any time. He had to get it right the first time. Once he went up a canyon, he'd be committed.

The visibility was so bad that Jake thought he was seeing things. Or maybe he just wanted to see something. After what felt like hours of looking, he dismounted and ran his hand over the ground. The earth was churned up, and there was the distinct imprint of a horseshoe. The grass was lying flat also, as if it had been trampled, and closer inspection showed the imprint of sheep tracks in the soft dirt beneath the grass, heading along the edge of the pasture, not into the canyon before him. Cassie went up the canyon thinking the sheep would be there. That had to be where Puck came from. With a hastily said prayer, Jake urged his horse up the canyon.

"I will not cry," Cassie told herself as she took another halting step. "I will not cry," she said again. It became her litany as she hobbled down the trail. She looked for a tree branch to use as a crutch but there was nothing about, just rocks, grass, some scrubby brush and a stream that kept getting higher and higher as the rain continued pounding down from the heavy skies. She was soaked to the skin. "I couldn't be any wetter if I was a fish in the sea," she said, and then laughed at her silliness because being wet didn't bother fish at all. But it sure did bother her.

If only she wasn't so cold. If only she wasn't so foolish. If only she'd stayed home like Jake asked her to. If only she'd stayed in Illinois instead of going to Texas. If only her father hadn't gone off to the war. There wasn't any room in her mind for *if onlys*. There was only put one foot in front of the other and don't fall, because if you fall you will not get up and you will die here, cold and alone.

Cassie didn't want to die. But she wasn't sure if living was much better. At least not the way she'd been living. Alone and afraid. Even with the company of Manuel and Rosa, and her mother, who was hollow inside and nothing more than a shell that erased all the happy memories. The funny thing was, Cassie felt the same. She might not have suffered a stroke, but her attack had shattered her soul enough, so that she never thought she'd feel normal again. She let it rule and ruin her life and that was worse than the physical part of it. The violation. She couldn't even stand to say the word.

Rape. She was raped. And the bastard that did it got away with it and would probably do it again, given the chance. And there wasn't a thing she could do about it. Learning how to shoot and cutting off her hair and running to Colorado wouldn't change it. Being fearful and hiding from people, hiding from life, wouldn't change it. Nothing would change it and she was in this mess because she was trying to run from something that would never leave her. Tears mingled with the raindrops on her cheeks and she wiped them away. So much for telling herself she wasn't going to cry.

The ground was so wet that her feet felt like they were sinking. Then there were the rocks that she had to go around and over, while her left leg wouldn't really support her and every step was agony, from her knee all the way up her spine. It would be dark soon, the sky was grayer and gloomier than ever, and the rain felt like it would never end. The water sloshed around her ankles.

"My ankles," Cassie said. She looked down and realized she was standing in water. The creek was over its banks. "Oh, this is not good," she said. "Not good at all." She looked around. She needed to get to high ground, higher than where she stood. The walls of the canyon were steep and with her bad leg . . .

There was nothing to do but try. Cassie got as far away from the creek as she could and kept on hobbling, upward and onward.

"I'm not going to cry . . ."

Jake was getting worried. How far had she gone? If he was wrong about where she'd gone . . . For all he knew, she could have headed north instead of south. He wasn't a tracker; he didn't know what he was doing. Jake urged Skip onward. He was in it now. It was too late to try anywhere else. Night would soon be upon him.

"Cassie!" he yelled again. His voice was nearly gone, he'd yelled so much. The water was rising fast, but that didn't concern him as much as what was happening on the ridges above him. Beavers loved to build dams and the water backed up, but with the melting snow and all this rain the dams couldn't hold much more. Jake would have bet money there was a beaver dam somewhere above them.

"Cassie!" What if she was unconscious? What if she'd hit her head when Puck threw her. Something drastic had to have happened to unseat her. He'd seen her ride, she was good. He urged Skip up a rise and looked upstream to where the canyon curved east. If he didn't find her when he reached the bend, he'd turn around and try somewhere else. "Cassie!"

"Jake!" He heard her yell and turned to the sound. She looked so small, minuscule compared to the vista around her. Like a pixie, a drenched pixie that was far away from home. Her body lurched toward him, she was hurt, and then she disappeared behind a rise. She had fallen.

He kicked Skip toward where Cassie had disappeared. She appeared again and stumbled in his direction, dragging her left leg behind her. Right now, all Jake cared about was that she was alive.

A noise startled him. A huge crack, like a gunshot, only much louder and much longer. Skip, always dependable, shied suddenly and turned away from Cassie, shaking his head as if to say, no, I'm not going. Jake pulled up on the reins and Skip circled as Jake fought against the horse's natural instincts to bolt. A huge rumbling sound followed, like thunder, only it kept on rumbling, long after it should have given out. A chill washed through Jake, and it had nothing to do with the rain. He knew without seeing it, that a wall of water was heading their way, hidden behind the curve in the canyon.

He gave Skip a kick that meant business and the horse, who knew his life was at risk, just like his rider's, jumped forward. Cassie stood frozen in place as she looked upstream. She sensed what was coming too.

"Cassie," Jake yelled again as Skip nimbly hopped over rocks and dodged boulders in his haste. He didn't know if she heard him, as the roar of the coming water was so loud. She must have recognized his intent as she managed to pull herself up onto an outcropping of rocks where she stood, balanced on one leg. Jake put out his arm, grabbed her as Skip went by and slung her onto the saddle behind him. He flung her so hard that she landed with a thump, but it took her no time at all to wrap her arms around his waist.

Debris filled the stream that had quickly overflowed its banks. There was no time to outrun the wall of water that was still out of sight but coming fast. The only place to go was up and Skip knew it. He gave it his all, scrambling up the steep incline. Jake bent over his neck and Cassie clung to his back like a tick. The water roared around the bend, and tree limbs and rocks crashed against the opposite wall of the canyon. There was too much water for the confines, and it rose fast, nipping at Skip's heels as he powered up and up until he found a level place to stop. Skip stood with his head down, blowing hard as Jake watched the canyon below fill with water. He placed his hand over Cassie's. She was clutching his coat so hard that her fist felt like a rock, and he could feel her trembling behind him.

"We made it," he said, just in case she didn't believe it. He felt her head move against his back. Jake twisted around to look at her. She was huddled up against him and hanging on like a burr. She'd lost her hat in their escape and her hair lay flat against her skull like a gold cap. "Cassie?"

"I don't want to die," she said.

"Neither do I," Jake said. "So let's not do it today."

There was no going back the way he'd come. The canyon was flooded and the water swirled dangerously beneath them. Entire trees floated by and Jake was pretty sure he saw the antlers of an elk tangled in one, which meant the body was probably beneath it. The only way out was up and it was going to be too dark to see anything soon. They needed shelter from the rain. He scanned the ridges above them and spotted what he thought was a likely place. The way was steep, though.

"I'm guessing by the way I saw you limping that you're not able to climb," he said to Cassie.

"I did something to my leg when Puck threw me."

"What happened?"

"A rattler," Cassie said. "I don't know if it got him or not . . ."

"He's safe back in your barn. That's how I knew to come looking."

"Thank you," Cassie said.

"I'm going to dismount and lead Skip up to that overhang," Jake said.

"I understand," Cassie said.

Jake squeezed her hand. "You're going to have to let go." She slowly unclenched her hands. "That's my girl," Jake said encouragingly. He swung his leg over Skip's neck and dismounted so Cassie could slide forward into the saddle. She looked so small sitting up there. Like a bedraggled kitten that had been dunked in a washtub. Jake smiled wistfully at her and her chin quivered.

"Just a little bit more, Skip," he said encouragingly to his mount as he took hold of his bridle. Skip gallantly leapt forward with Jake by his side. The climb was slick and treacherous, and Jake slide backward a number of times, staying upright only because of Skip's endurance, but finally they reached the overhang, just as the dim gray sky darkened on them. He plucked Cassie off Skip's back and once again marveled at how light she was. She felt like nothing in his arms. He ducked under the overhang.

"Let's just hope this place isn't occupied," he said. But he didn't add, *Because things couldn't possibly get any worse.*

NINETEEN

Warmth was just a memory as far as Cassie was concerned. She stood where Jake left her, with her hurt leg bent so she wouldn't put any pressure on it and her arms wrapped tightly around her body, as if they could erase the desperate chill that sunk into her soaking wet body. She felt strange, as if she wasn't in her body, but hovering somewhere above and watching everything that was happening to her. The rain still pounded outside and the darkness was heavy, so everything around her was nothing more than shadows. Luckily, Jake had a box of matches in his pocket and he lit one to explore the overhang they'd sheltered in. She watched the tiny point of light as he raised it and lowered it around the stone walls until it fizzled and went out. Only a few seconds passed until he lit another one, and she was hypnotized by it until she blinked and realized Jake was standing right in front of her.

"We're alone," he said. Cassie heard the words but her mind didn't understand them. All she felt was the cold and the wet. Her ears rang with a sudden silence even though she knew the rain still fell and Jake's voice echoed around her. "No one is at home," he continued. Jake bent down to look at her. "Cassie?" He touched her cheek. "Dang, you feel like a block of ice. We got to get you warm."

Warm . . .What did warm feel like? She couldn't remember. She felt Jake's hands on her. He pulled off her coat and it fell to the ground with a plop. He rubbed her arms and her body jerked back and forth with the motion. She was still balanced on one foot with just her toe touching the ground on her left. She staggered and he caught her.

"Hang on," Jake said. What was she supposed to hang on to? She needed something solid, and even though she was surrounded by stone walls, there was no place to grip. Jake went out into the rain. A moment passed, or it could have been days for all Cassie knew. He tossed his rig inside. She heard him talk to Skip and then somehow he got the horse inside the cave. He went to the back of the cave again and returned with his arms full of something . . .

"We aren't the first to take shelter here," he said. "Believe it or not there was some wood back there. It's older than dirt but I think it's enough for a small fire." He dropped the wood at the opening and pushed Skip to the back of the cave.

"Fi-fire . . ." Cassie said through her chattering teeth.

Jake knelt down and had a fire going before she could blink. "It's going to be smoky in here but we can tolerate it." Once more he was before her and took her upper arms into his hands. "Cassie. We got to get these wet clothes off you. Do you understand?"

Somewhere deep inside her, fear coiled like a snake. A

man was touching her. He pulled at her clothes. His hands were on her.

"No!" Cassie said, and slapped his hands away. She staggered back against the wall. Where was her gun? She'd lost it. It was in her coat pocket. Where was her coat? Why didn't she wear it on her hip in a holster? Because she'd never found one that fit. And now, when she needed it, she couldn't get to it.

"Cassie, I'm not going to hurt you." He had a gun. The man who was touching her. The man who wanted to take her clothes off. "You're freezing," he said. "I've got a blanket and some spare clothes." He held his hands up and away and Cassie's eyes darted to the gun that hung on his hip. "You can put those on."

Cassie lunged for his gun. Her leg gave way and she crashed into him. He wrapped his arms around her and she struggled against him. Once more she was too weak and too small. It couldn't happen again. She wouldn't let it happen again. She would rather die first.

I almost died . . . If not for Jake . . . Somewhere in her addled brain she realized what had almost happened to her. She would have drowned in the flood if he had not been there. Jake came after her. He saved her. He was the man in the cave with her. He wasn't going to hurt her. Where his arms wrapped around her, she felt the warmth of his body. She was so tired of being cold. She was so weary of being alone.

"I got you," he said against her ear. He'd said those words before. Just last night, when she was so angry after the attack. She was tucked up beneath his chin with his arms wrapped securely around her waist. Her feet were still on the ground, but he supported all of her weight. "I'm not going to hurt you, Cassie. I know what happened."

Her stomach flipped over and shame filled her. "You know?" The thought that he knew her secret was more than she could stand. There was no place to go, she couldn't get away, and she couldn't hide it. She couldn't pretend like it hadn't happened and she couldn't make it go away.

"Can we get you warm and dry first?" Jake asked. "Before we talk?"

All she could do was nod in agreement.

"Can you do it yourself?"

Cassie looked down at the small fire. There wasn't much wood and it wouldn't last until dawn, but it offered something. A spark, or was it a ray of hope, perhaps? Things didn't have to be the way they were. But it was entirely up to her to change them. She heard Skip shifting around at the back of the cave. There wasn't much room; another body and certainly another horse would have made things crowded. But it was shelter from the storm. Shelter was something she'd been seeking for a long, long time.

"You might have to help." Was that her voice that sounded so shaky? "My leg won't hold me."

"Yeah, I noticed that too," Jake said. "Would you believe me if I said I'll keep my eyes closed?"

"Nope," Cassie said with a nervous laugh that made her feel strangely better. It felt good to laugh. It felt natural. It felt right.

"I'm glad to see that you know the real me," Jake said in reply. She felt his smile above her head. "There's a spare shirt in my saddlebag. How about you put that on and get undressed beneath it. Then you can wrap up in the blanket."

"Is it dry?" she asked.

"I wrapped it up in oil skin. It should be."

"You think of everything, don't you?"

"I'm a planner, Cassie. But I wasn't planning on you."

She tried to see his face in the darkness, but it was nothing but planes and shadows from the small light of the fire. "What's that supposed to mean?"

"Never mind," he said. "Let me get that shirt for you."

She balanced on one leg again while Jake rummaged through his saddlebags. He came back with a shirt and a thick pair of socks. Cassie unbuttoned her flannel and dropped it to the ground. Her long-sleeved undershirt was wet also but she waited until Jake threw his shirt around her shoulders. Then she turned around. Jake put his hands on her waist to balance her, and she buttoned up his shirt and then pulled off her undershirt from beneath his. She wore another undershirt beneath that was light muslin and sleeveless. She felt the heat of Jake's hands on her skin through the thin fabric.

Cassie longed to be warm all over. Jake moved his hands as she put her arms through the sleeves of his shirt and it swallowed her, falling down to her knees. She shivered again, so hard that her teeth chattered. Jake steadied her by putting his hands on her waist again. They felt nice there, comforting and oh so very warm. Cassie reached underneath the shirt to unbutton her pants and slid them down her hips.

"Don't you want to take your boots off first?" Jake asked. "Hang on." He kept one hand on her waist and picked up the blanket with the other one. He shook it loose and dropped it on the ground beside her. "Sit down," he directed and he helped Cassie to the ground. Another pain shot up her spine as she sat, and she grimaced. The light was so dim that Jake didn't see it.

"I'll take care of these," Jake said. He knelt before her and pulled off her boots and then her socks.

Cassie pushed herself up on her hands and another pain

shot down her leg. This time she wasn't able to hide it so well.

"Just sit," Jake said. "I hope nothing is broke."

Cassie obeyed because the more she moved the more her hip hurt. Jake reached up beneath the shirt tail and Cassie froze. "Shhh," he said like he was gentling a horse. He looked at her. His face was lost in the shadows, his eyes dark as the night, but she saw the flash of his smile and it was gentle. "Just relax," he encouraged. "We're almost done." He tugged her pants down her legs and threw them aside. He picked up her feet and placed them on his knees. "Like ice." He grinned, and he placed his hands over her toes and squeezed.

It felt so good that Cassie sighed. Jake laughed. "If I'd known the way to shut you up was to rub your feet, I would have done it days ago."

"Just shut up and keep rubbing," Cassie said. It was wondrous how relaxing his touch was. The fact that he touched her and she had no fear. She'd been terrified before because she'd come so close to death. Funny how she'd been thinking about dying, how it would be so much easier than the everyday struggle that was living, and yet when faced with it, she realized that she very much wanted to live.

Live. Not just exist, marking time and counting down the days until her life was finally over. She wanted to live and she wanted to feel alive.

Jake quit rubbing her feet and put the socks on her. She didn't want him to stop, but she wasn't brave enough to ask for more. He pulled the edges of the blanket around her body and tucked it up under her chin. "Get warm," he said, and turned to put more wood on the fire. "This fire won't last all night, so you've got to get over this chill." He picked up her clothes and spread them out close to the fire and then rummaged in his saddlebags again. He unwrapped a sandwich from some brown paper and handed it to her.

"You do plan ahead, don't you," Cassie said as she took a bite. It was ham, and it was very tender and juicy, and held a taste of molasses. Since she hadn't eaten all day, it was heaven. Jake sat on the other side of the fire. He must have the patience of a saint. He'd seen her at her worst, time and time again, yet here he was.

And he knew what had happened to her. Manuel had to have told him. Yet he didn't treat her any different, that she could tell. She always felt as if she should be ashamed, as if it was a failing on her part. It was foolish, she knew, but that didn't make it any easier to accept. If Manuel trusted him enough to tell him, then he thought Jake was a stand-up guy. Shoot, she thought Jake was a stand-up guy, but that didn't mean he was supposed to take care of her and her problems.

Jake started on his sandwich. "For every possibility," he said.

The food was helping. Cassie felt solid now, where before she felt like she would dissolve in the rain. "I know you said Puck came back to the barn, but why were you still there?" She felt like she'd been gone a year instead of hours. "Did something else happen?"

"Libby showed up at my place again," Jake said. "She might as well wear a sign that says *Trouble follows wherever I go*.

"The first time I saw Libby, she was standing in my yard braying loud enough to wake the dead," Jake said. "It was last October and the weather had just cleared from an early blizzard. I'd never seen her before, and the way she was acting had me worried. So I saddled up and decided to see if I could find out where she came from. She led me straight to this mining camp on the other side of town. Everyone there was dead from the measles." Jake poked at the fire. "Men, women and children, twenty-seven people, all dead."

"Libby was from the camp?" Cassie asked.

"She had to be," Jake said. "We think Ward's dog came from there too. And the cat you got from the Martins."

"Suzie," Cassie said.

"Suzie," Jake said. "So now whenever Libby shows up, I think there's trouble."

"There wasn't any trouble the night we met."

Jake laughed. "Maybe not for you. But I recall having someone point a gun at me and accuse me of being a thief."

Cassie was grateful Jake couldn't see her blush. "Maybe I should apologize for that," she said.

Jake pointed a finger at her. "Maybe you should."

"Didn't your mother ever tell you it's not polite to point?" Cassie asked, hoping he didn't see her joy at his teasing. She didn't want him to treat her any differently because he knew about the rape.

"My mother didn't have time to tell me much of anything, because she was always working to support us," Jake said.

"Where was your father?"

Jake shrugged. "Beats me. I never laid eyes on him. And as far as I know, my mother only laid eyes on him the one time."

"I'm sorry," Cassie said as a vision of a sad and lonely little boy replaced the actual presence of Jake across from the fire.

"It's nothing for you to feel sorry about. It's just the way things were. My mother was very practical," Jake said. "She knew nobody was going to hand you a thing, and if you wanted something you had to work for it, so she worked two jobs. During the day she was a maid and in the evenings she worked in a pub. We rented a room above the same. She wanted better for me, so she enrolled me in a private school so I'd have a decent education. Work was what eventually killed her. She died when I was seventeen."

"What happened then?"

Jake shrugged. "I took off. We had no family and I couldn't pay the tuition anymore. So I headed west and took whatever job I could find. And continued to learn as much as I could about the world around me. I probably had worked twenty jobs by the time I was twenty, in every different trade you could imagine. I'd figured out pretty fast that showing up to ask for a job in clean clothes while being polite as possible would get me hired in a hurry."

He put the last of the wood on the fire. "All the while I was moving west. I finally signed on with a rancher down around Abilene. He liked my work ethic and took me under his wing. Taught me everything he knew. He didn't have much close family either. I was with him five years until he died. When his brother showed up to claim the property, I took the money I'd saved up all those years working for him and moved to Colorado. When I found a pretty little valley in the mountains, I made it mine. That was seven years ago. Awhile after your grandfather got here."

"So this is home?" Cassie asked.

"It is now," Jake said.

"I've always wanted a place to call home," Cassie said, suddenly sad because the hope that had filled her so quickly had disappeared. "And now I have no place to go."

"Who says you're going anywhere?" Jake asked.

"What else am I supposed to do? The sheep are gone. Without them we have no way to make a living. Yes, I have the money from my grandfather, but that won't last forever."

"The sheep aren't gone," Jake informed her. "They're home."

"They are?"

"Yes, Max brought them back."

It was more than she'd dared to hope for. "Max is alive?"

"He is." Jake tugged on his ear. "He's missing part of his ear, but he was alive and well last time I saw him."

"Thank God," Cassie said. "Manuel loves that dog so much. Max belonged to his son."

"He told me about his son," Jake said. "And why you left Texas."

Cassie didn't know what to say; shame once more washed over her. She was a bundle of conflicting emotions and nerves. She'd almost died. She was exhausted and once more she felt like she was floating around the ceiling of the cave instead of sitting safely on the ground. She was still cold yet her skin felt hot. It was all so very strange.

"None of it was your fault, Cassie. Just like none of this mess is."

If only it were true. Jake would never understand the guilt she carried. No one would. Because of what the incident did to her mother, she would always feel guilty. "I'm just a victim of wrong place at the wrong time?" she asked because she wanted to hear his justifications.

"You're a victim of somebody else's cruelty," Jake explained. "With what happened before and what is happening now."

She didn't want to talk about the rape. She never wanted to talk about it. "We should get back. If Watkins finds out the sheep survived, he might attack the ranch again."

"We're not going anywhere tonight and probably not tomorrow either." The fire dimmed and Jake pulled a stick from the fire and stirred it up before tossing it back on the flames. "It will take awhile for the water to subside. It might even be jammed up again with all the stuff that washed down with it. And your ranch will be fine. A couple of my men are there."

"Why are you doing this, Jake? Why are you helping me?"

He didn't answer; instead, he just stared at the flames that were getting lower and lower. "I don't know," he finally said. "I just feel like it's the right thing to do."

It was a safe answer. At least it made her feel safe. It didn't put any pressure on her. And pressure was something she didn't need right now. She'd taken a few small steps and she was still scared that if she took any more someone would find a way to knock her down again. It had taken her too long to take them.

And she was cold. So very cold. Her insides were shaking. Cassie yawned and her teeth chattered loudly.

"The fire is almost gone," Jake said. "But I can help keep you warm, if you want."

He said it so quietly, so matter-of-fact, that Cassie didn't even think about what it meant. She just knew that she was cold, that her hip hurt, that she was so very tired, and she was so alone. And she wanted it all to go away.

"I'm tired of being cold," she said. Jake shifted from the opposite wall and crept over to where Cassie sat. He leaned against the cave wall, stretched his legs out, and then scooped her up as if she weighed nothing. Cassie's bare legs flashed and she was terrified, but only for a moment, as he carefully settled her in his lap and secured the blanket tightly around her, making sure that her feet were covered too.

"Try to get some sleep," he said. "The rain should be over soon."

Every muscle in her body clenched with tension. She

needed to relax. Cassie looked at the dying embers of the fire and told herself over and over again that nothing was going to happen. Jake wouldn't hurt her. He'd proven himself. If he'd wanted to hurt her, he'd had ample opportunity. Her body and mind battled each other until her mind finally won and precious warmth filled her bones. She felt Jake's cheek against the top of her head, listened to the steady thump-thump of his heart and then finally, she slept.

TWENTY

Why are you doing this? Jake repeated Cassie's question to himself as he waited for her to fall asleep, willing himself not to disturb her.

Now if he could just will his own body to relax. Cassie was scared and hurt and all he could think about was how soft her skin was when he touched her legs, how small her waist when he held her up, and how much he wanted to kiss her.

But he knew Cassie wasn't ready for kissing yet.

Rape . . . it was such a horrible word, not one that was fit for any conversation, polite or otherwise. One associated it with evil and war, and it made delicate woman back East swoon into their teacups. Jake didn't even want to say it, much less think about it. He just knew that if he ever laid eyes on the bastard who did it, he'd kill him and wouldn't think twice about it.

It had to be incredibly frustrating to be under someone's control like that. To be smaller and weaker and powerless to do anything to stop them. It had to be the worst feeling in the world to have all that anger and rage afterward, and to want justice and to know that no matter what you did, there wouldn't be any.

No wonder she was so stubborn. Jake looked down at the pale cap of her hair, which was now a tangled mess, and understood why she cut it off. He understood everything about her now. The only thing he didn't understand was the feelings he had for her. Where had they come from? Why Cassie Parker, of all the women in the world?

Jake's mind drifted back to last fall, and one of the many conversations he had with Leah. He'd wanted to marry her and she told him over and over again that she didn't love him. Then she fell in love with Cade Gentry, who'd been an outlaw before he became sheriff. Leah wouldn't settle for anything less than love. Jake had thought her foolish, but now, now that he had an inkling of what love was . . . what it could be . . . he realized just how right she was.

Was he in love with Cassie Parker? He could be, given the right circumstances. She certainly wasn't what he imagined when he thought about the rest of his life. He'd always pictured a peaceful life and a quiet and mostly agreeable wife, neither of which was Cassie. What he'd imagined sounded boring now that he knew Cassie.

Cassie shifted in her sleep and by the light of the embers he saw the wince of pain from her hip. She'd probably be black-and-blue come morning. He hoped that wouldn't be the least of her problems. No, *their* problems, because he was in it now, up to his eyeballs in sheep of all things.

Cassie shifted again and mumbled something. Jake's legs tingled; they'd fallen asleep and he desperately needed to move, yet he didn't want to disturb her. Holding her all night long wouldn't prove anything, though, and it certainly wouldn't change anything. And she was warm now.

Jake laid Cassie down on the ground next to him and rose. At the cave entrance he lit another match to get his bearings. The rain had stopped but the water was still swirling below. He didn't need a light to see it; the noise was threat enough.

He thanked God that this canyon was adjacent to his land and there was a pass over the mountain he could take to get them to safety. Cassie's valley was more than likely flooded, but her house, barn and other buildings were high enough that they shouldn't be hurt. Dan and Randy knew enough to make sure the stock was safe. Thank God the two men had volunteered to help out. He'd reward them for it too, come payday.

Jake took a moment to check on Skip. He rubbed him down with a cloth he kept in his saddlebag and bid him good night with a pat to his neck. He checked on Cassie's clothes. They were still soaking wet, so he spread them out as best as he could. His saddle blanket was damp on one side but dry beneath, so he laid it out on the floor next to Cassie. She was shivering again, so Jake slowly eased her body next to his. He curled his body around hers and pulled her tight against his chest. Her body felt hot, even though she shivered. She had a fever, but like everything else there was nothing he could do about it at the moment. Soon she settled in between his knees and his chin and her shaking subsided. He only hoped that was a good sign for the future.

Jake woke to find someone was playing with his ear. He was stiff and sore from a second night of sleeping on an unforgiving surface, but the soft little bundle curled up against him was worth the aches and pains he felt. A good stretch would take care of most of them.

Skip. Cassie. Cave. It only took a moment for Jake to realize where he was and who he was with. If not for Skip nuzzling his ear, he might have kept right on sleeping, enjoying being cuddled up with Cassie. He rolled away from her with a groan.

He heard her rustling around and turned to look at her. Cassie had propelled herself to the cave wall and had the blanket pulled close around her. Her pale blue eyes were huge in her pale face as she looked frantically around the cave. Her will-o'-the-wisp hair flew out in every direction and she raised a shaky hand to push it out of her eyes.

"I'll . . . er . . . check to see if the water has gone down," Jake said and hastily left the cave. Skip followed him out. The rain had subsided, leaving behind crisp blue skies and a fresh wind, and much to Jake's relief the water in the valley wasn't as high as it might have been. That was a good sign. Maybe they'd be able to pass through the valley instead of going farther up into the mountains. It would take them all day to go over the mountains to his place and Jake wasn't sure how much longer he could stand to be in Cassie's company without kissing her.

Jake willed his body into submission. This was getting ridiculous. Cassie Parker had him so twisted up he didn't know what he was doing. He was missing work at his place to take care of her. He had his men camped out on her property protecting her sheep. He was spending more time on her sheep than he was on his cows. And for what? She wasn't interested in him and he refused to fall for another woman who didn't want him. As soon as he got her back to her place, he was done with her.

Skip nudged him with his nose and Jake put his arm

around the horse's neck and gave him a good rub. "I know you're hungry, boy," he said. "You've worked hard and I'm standing around feeling sorry for myself, because I'm no better than a stud after a mare in season." Skip rubbed his head against Jake. "Don't pretend like you know what I'm talking about," he teased the gelding.

His saddle sat right inside the cavern, so it was easy enough to grab it and get Skip ready for the trip down the mountain. With luck he could have Cassie home before breakfast. And after that . . . well, it was Saturday, so he might as well go to town.

Jake stepped back into the cave once Skip was ready to go. "The way is clear," he said. Cassie was dressed in her clothes and struggling with her boots. Jake quickly moved to help her.

"Let me," he said.

"I can do it," she said, and hobbled a few steps away from him.

"You are stubborn beyond words."

She huffed in indignation. Jake tilted his head sideways to get a better look at her in the dim light. She was pale as a ghost and her skin was covered with perspiration. He touched her forehead and Cassie jerked away from him.

"Settle down," Jake said. "I think you have a fever."

"I know I have one," Cassie said wearily. "I'm burning up and I feel dizzy."

"Yet you won't let me help you put your boots on."

She looked at him in exasperation.

"The sooner you get your boots on, the sooner you can go home," Jake said.

"Do you take pleasure in always being right?" Cassie said, and handed him a boot.

"Only when it is you admitting it," Jake said with a laugh.

"Lean against me and I'll pull them on." Cassie lifted a dubious eyebrow in his direction. "Cassie." Jake sighed. "If I wanted to take advantage of you, I'd have had plenty of opportunity last night."

"Hmph."

"Don't flatter yourself too much," Jake warned. He spread his arms. "I've got all day if you want to dillydally."

Cassie gave in, albeit not gracefully, and leaned against him. She didn't seem any bigger than Josie. Jake braced her against his leg, put his arms around her and when she lifted her foot, he yanked her boot on. "That wasn't so bad, was it?" he asked.

"You're not done yet," Cassie said, and handed him the other boot. He did the same and put his arms on her shoulders to stand her upright when he was done.

"Your clothes are still wet," he observed.

"Tell me something I don't know."

"Are you always this cranky in the morning?" Jake asked.

"Are you always this cheerful?" Cassie replied.

"At this rate I won't be for long." Jake picked up the blanket, along with his shirt and socks. He quickly got the gear together and tied it onto the back of his saddle. Cassie stood by the entrance of the cave, watching him. "Ready?" he asked when he was done.

Cassie nodded and hobbled to Skip.

Jake sighed. He would grow old watching her wrestle with her pride. "Don't shoot me," he said, and picked her up and put her on Skip's back. She made a face and settled gingerly into the saddle.

"I can't," Cassie said. "I lost my gun somewhere in our climb yesterday."

"Does that mean you would?"

"I'm tempted."

Jake grabbed the reins and led Skip down the way they'd come. "Why don't you wear a holster?"

"I can't find one that fits."

"Have Gus take a measurement next time you're in town. He can order one."

"I'll think about it."

"How's your hip?"

"Sore."

"A good soak will take care of it."

"I hope so," Cassie said. Jake glanced over his shoulder at her. She didn't look good at all, but she wasn't complaining. The slope was treacherous from the rain and the going was steep. All Jake could do was let Skip have his head and hope that Cassie could hang on. Skip passed him by, as Jake tried his best to stay upright until they got down to a gentle slope.

"It should be easier from here," Jake said. He swung up behind Cassie. "Slide forward and then sit on my lap," he said. "It should be much easier on that bruised hip."

The fact that she agreed so readily let Jake know how bad she really felt. A compliant Cassie was much more worrisome than a sassy Cassie.

"Talk to me, Cassie."

"What do you want to talk about?" She was tired and it showed in her voice. He needed her alert in case the way became more treacherous than it already was.

"Let's talk about you," Jake said. "You heard all about me last night. I think it's only fair that you return the favor."

"You telling me about your past was a favor?" Cassie said. "I'm surprised Skip can carry you, with that big head of yours. However do you find a hat to fit it?"

Jake grinned. "Hey, you're the one that asked."

"So I did," Cassie agreed. He couldn't see her face as it

was below his chin, and he was concentrating on the path, on the lookout for sinkholes and random tree stumps, but he could easily imagine the look on her face and the way she stuck her nose in the air when they were sparring with words.

He liked their verbal sparring. The challenge of keeping up with her kept things interesting.

"You came from Illinois," he prompted.

"We had a farm. We lived on my grandparents' farm in Illinois. My father was a doctor and he was killed in the war. My grandmother died soon after and that's when my grandfather took off and came here."

"I know that part. What happened then?"

"My mother was a teacher. She took a job at a private school for girls in Chicago. One of the benefits was I was able to go to school there also. We lived in a small cottage on the grounds."

Before she'd been short, reciting to him instead of telling him, but as she talked her voice grew softer and more melodious, as if she were telling him a story.

"It was quite lovely there. I felt like the entire world was at my fingertips because of the extensive library. My mother made me believe there wasn't anything I couldn't do, if I wanted it badly enough and I worked hard enough. After all, my father was a farmer's son and he became a doctor. My mother's family immigrated to America when she was ten years old and she became a teacher. The world was full of possibilities, and I decided I wanted to be a lawyer."

Manuel had told him that much, but he wanted to hear about it from her point of view. Jake wanted to know why she came to that decision over all others. "That's an ambitious undertaking," he said.

"Because I'm a woman?"

"Because it requires a lot of studying. I don't know if I'd have the patience to do it."

"I used to think I had all the time in the world for things like studying," Cassie said with a yawn.

Jake wanted to hear more, especially since she was being so agreeable. "Go on," he said.

"I started writing letters. I had the required schooling, the same as any man, but I needed an attorney that would let me study under him as an apprentice. I read every newspaper I could find for stories about court trials, and I learned the names of judges and college professors, and I kept on writing letters. Finally, after two years I received an answer from a man in El Paso named Arthur Gleason. He said he admired my spunk and wanted me to clerk for him. He even wired me the money for a train ticket and the stage. It was like a dream come true."

"El Paso is a long way from Chicago," Jake observed.

"Which is why my mother decided to come with me," Cassie said. "We only had each other. She said I had followed her dreams of being a teacher long enough, now it was her turn to follow mine. And she was certain she could get a teaching position somewhere in town. So we packed up and we moved to El Paso."

She got quiet then for a long time and when she spoke again, her tone held a forced nonchalance.

"Manuel told you what happened on the trip to El Paso. You know the rest of the story."

Manuel had, and Jake did. The details were something he could only imagine, and she didn't need to share them. "I'm sorry for what happened," he said.

"I don't want to talk about it anymore," she said. "I'm tired."

"Try to rest if you can. We should be home soon." In a

matter of minutes, her head lolled beneath his chin and he knew she was asleep.

Jake understood more about her now. He knew where her stubbornness came from, and her tenacity, along with her fear. It was a sad thing that happened to her. But what was even sadder is that she let it continue to rule her life.

If only there was a way to get her past it.

The ground was a mess and the footing treacherous, but Skip, bless him, made it through, even when he had to slosh through water up to his knees. The sun was high in the sky, and Cassie felt as hot as the rays that shone down on his back when they came into her valley. In the distance Jake saw the sheep huddled up next to the barn and recognized Dan and Randy on horseback, with one of them dragging a large tree behind them. He kicked Skip into a ground-eating canter and his men saw him and came to meet him.

"Is she all right?" Dan asked.

"She's fine," Jake said as he shifted Cassie in his arms. She kept her head buried against his chest and squeezed his jacket into her fist. "A bit bruised and running a fever. How are things here?"

"Peaceful," Randy said. "It was kind of scary for a bit when the water came through, but everyone was more worried about you two than what was happening here."

"We're just cleaning up the mess," Dan said.

"Remind me to give you boys a bonus come payday," Jake said.

"You can count on it, boss." Randy grinned.

Manuel, Max and Rosa were waiting on the front porch when Jake rode up with Cassie. "Thank God," they said when they saw that she was alive. Cassie blinked as Jake lowered her to the porch from Skip's back. Rosa immediately put an arm around Cassie's waist.

"Thank you so much," Manuel said. Rosa already had Cassie through the door. Manuel shook Jake's hand and followed them inside.

"I'll come by and check on her tomorrow," Jake said to his retreating back. The door closed behind Manuel and just like that, he was alone. Jake stared at the door for a minute and then sighed. "I need a drink," he told Skip and turned his horse toward home.

TWENTY-ONE

Another Saturday night at the Heaven's Gate Saloon. Every table was full, which was good for his pockets. Ward looked out over the crowd of cowboys and miners that gathered around the tables. Pris flitted between them like a butterfly, serving drinks and playfully smacking away wandering hands. Spirits were high. Most of the heavy lifting of spring was done and the flooding had been minimal for most everyone, the worst of it being at the Parker place, if what Ward heard from the gossip among the tables was true.

He'd like to get close to the table where Watkins's men were gathered. Just in case they decided to talk about what they were up to a few days past. But since they were in the corner it would be a bit obvious. His only hope was to get them in a card game and hope they'd become distracted enough to let something slip.

Lady looked at the door and wagged her tail. Ward

touched her head as the door swung open. Jake entered, followed by Cade and Jim Martin. Ward walked around behind the bar to serve his friends.

"You look a bit rough," he said to Jake as he poured four shots of the good stuff. Jake had dark circles beneath his eyes and at least two days' growth of beard.

"A couple of nights without sleep will do that to you," Jake said.

"Something else happen at the Parker place?" Cade asked.

"Nothing beyond Cassie being stubborn," Jake said. Jake told them about his recent adventure with the very stubborn Cassie Parker. Ward could tell there was more to the story, but Jake shared all he was going to share. Something must have happened between those two. Whether it was good or bad remained to be seen.

"And you're saying Libby showed up to let you know that something was wrong again?" Jim asked.

"She sure did," Jake said. "Came right up to my front door this time."

"Maybe I oughtta hire that donkey as a deputy," Cade said.

"She does have a nose for trouble," Ward agreed.

"But Cassie's all right," Jim said. "That's the important thing."

"She's bruised up from the fall and sick from being wet for so long, but for the most part, she's fine," Jake said. He tossed his shot back and turned his glass over. Ward watched as his eyes searched the patrons reflected in the mirror over the bar. "Busy night," Jake said.

"I noticed a couple of your guys are missing," Ward said. "Something going on?"

"Dan and Randy volunteered to keep an eye on the Parker

spread, for which I was very grateful and will have to pay them extra come the first of the month."

"You can't buy a good heart," Jim said. "But they are worth every penny you pay them."

"But you can buy bad deeds," Jake said. "And there are many willing to do them. Any word from Watkins?" he asked.

"Nary a peep," Cade said. "But I'm keeping an eye out."

"I'd bet money the guilty ones are sitting at that corner table," Ward said.

"Well how about we go have a chat with them," Jake said, and pushed away from the bar.

"Wait a minute, Jake," Ward said. Jake ignored him of course.

"Let him go," Cade said. "He might get them to do something stupid enough so that I can throw them in jail."

"Works for me," Jim said.

"You just want the entertainment," Ward said.

"Well there is that," Jim said. He shook his glass and Ward poured him another shot. Jake stopped off at a table that held some of his men to talk with them. Ward would have bet money it was to tell them that there might be a fight, not that any of them would mind. A good fight was often a highlight of a Saturday night in town, as long as they kept the breakage to a minimum.

"I'm a bit worried about him," Ward confessed. "I think he's got a thing for Miss Parker."

"Why is that a problem?" Jim asked.

"Sounds like a good idea to me," Cade added. "I highly recommend it."

"Once Jake sets his mind on something, he has a hard time letting go. For example, your wife," Wade reminded Cade. "Jake made up his mind that he was going to marry her and even though Leah told him time and time again that she didn't love him, Jake just kept on telling her that she would eventually come to her senses and that it was the best for all concerned if she'd just marry him."

"She said as much." Cade nodded his head. Ward was glad to know Cade bore no ill will toward Jake. Why should he? It was obvious that Leah loved her husband, even with all the problems his coming had caused. "But that doesn't explain why Jake having feelings for Cassie is a problem."

"Jake discounted Leah's excuse about not loving him time and time again. He scoffed at it. Jake's a practical man and, for him, love is just another word. So what if he suddenly finds himself in love after all these years of never knowing what it is? Might make him do something foolish."

"Like take off in the middle of a rainstorm to look for Cassie?" Jim said.

"And side with her against the Watkinses, even if it means defending her sheep," Ward said. "A few weeks ago Jake would have been the first one to say that sheep didn't belong here. But now he's their biggest defender. Yeah, Jake's falling in love with Cassie, but he's not ready to admit it yet. But when he does . . . well let's just hope Cassie Parker is open to the idea."

"I don't know," Cade said. "She seems kind of standoffish where men are concerned."

"There's some sort of history there," Ward said. "Something that happened in Texas, I'm sure. But Jake's just stubborn enough to not let that stand in his way."

"Just as stubborn as she is?" Jim asked.

"Time will only tell." Ward raised his glass as Jake stopped to talk to some of Jared Castle's men. "Here's hoping for a happy ending."

Jim and Cade touched their glasses to his. "For a cynic, you sure are romantic," Cade said after they'd downed their shots.

"I have my moments," Ward confessed. But that was all he was going to say on the matter. He put down his glass and came out from behind the bar. He wanted to be ready if something was going to happen. And it was a sure bet that something was going to happen, because Jake was on his way to Watkins's table right now.

"Just checking to see if you boys had any flooding at your place," Jake said to the men gathered around the table. He recognized Baxter and the other man from the run-in on the trail. The rest looked about the same. Average men who followed where they were led, whether it was good or bad. Occasionally one would stand up against wrong, but in a crowd like this, that man was wise to move on to greener pastures. They'd all gotten quiet when he approached, which Jake expected. It meant they were talking about something they didn't want him to hear. Another raid at Cassie's place, perhaps?

Baxter drained his beer and looked up at Jake. He smiled at his companions and tilted his chair back so that he was balanced on only two legs. As Jake expected, Baxter was the spokesman for the group. "When you say flooding, do you mean water? Or stinking sheep shit?"

"Well I was being neighborly and asking about water," Jake said, although he knew they knew good and well why he was there. The thought of burying his fist into Baxter's face, and having a good enough excuse to do it, was tempting. "Can you not tell the difference?"

"Oh, I know the difference between sheep shit and water,"

Baxter drawled. "Just like I know the difference between sheep and cows. But here's a question for you . . ."

Say something, anything, that will let me pound that smug expression off you face. Jake was so full of pent-up frustration that he was about to bust. And he knew it wasn't Baxter's fault that Cassie had him tied up into knots. But he was pretty sure Baxter was the one who had attacked Manuel, and he knew for certain Baxter was the sadistic bastard who'd killed the sheep by dragging it. The man deserved a beat down, and Jake was hoping he'd be the one to give it. But he couldn't just hit the man for no reason.

Baxter leaned his head back and scratched his neck. "Do you know the difference, Jake? Because from where we sit, it seems like you've got a fondness for sheep." He looked around at his friends. "Or maybe it's just for the shepherd."

Jake leaned hard on the table and put his face close to Baxter's. The man reeked. Obviously he'd skipped the annual Saturday afternoon bath in his haste to get to town. "What I have a fondness for is none of your dang business."

"Does she baa when you stick it in her?" Baxter asked and the rest of the table started baaing.

Thank you! Jake grinned dangerously, stuck his boot under the back leg of Baxter's chair with a flourish and scooped the chair out from under the man. Baxter landed on his back and the rest of the gang jumped up from the table with a crashing of chairs. Jake heard more chairs hit the floor behind him and knew, without looking, that his men, along with Jared Castle's, were staring the bunch down.

Jake put his boot on Baxter's chest. "It looks like you need a lesson in manners."

Baxter grabbed Jake's boot with both hands and tried to push it off. "Are you the one who's going to give it to me?"

"Yes I am." Jake backed off.

"Jake, you paying the damages?" Ward asked.

"Just put it on my tab," Jake said with a grin. Baxter climbed to his feet, put his head down and charged into him. Jake braced himself and the two crashed into a table and then rolled to the floor.

Jake lost the next few moments to a haze of punching and being punched. Wood broke, glass shattered and Lady barked. Jake couldn't remember the last time he'd had so much fun. He relished in it. Every bit of the frustration that he felt over Cassie he poured into his fists. He was aware that there was fighting going on around him, and part of his mind winced at the money he was going to owe Ward, but it was worth it. Every time his fist landed on Baxter's face he felt satisfaction. He hit him because he'd dared to attack Cassie's land. He kept hitting him to let him know he wasn't going to tolerate it again.

Finally the sound of a shot at close range brought him back to his senses. His hand was clenched in Baxter's shirt and he released it. Baxter dropped to the ground like a stone.

"Party's over, boys," Cade said. "Anyone who wants to continue is welcome to do it over at the sheriff's office. And for those of you who are too dense to think right now, it means that the next one who throws a punch is spending the night in jail. Got it?"

Jake tested his jaw and wiped the blood from the corner of his mouth. His left eye felt tender also, where Baxter had landed a solid punch. Was it worth it? Yes, it was. He checked on his men. They all were okay, with black eyes and sore fists. They went to work, picking up chairs, turning tables right side up and kicking broken glass out of the way. Bob walked from behind the bar with a broom and immediately started sweeping behind Cade, who stood in the middle of the room.

The sheriff nudged Baxter with the toe of his boot and the man grunted. "Yeah, you like it when they can't fight back, don't you?" Cade said as he poured a beer in Baxter's face. Baxter came up sputtering but wisely kept his hand off his gun. Cade jerked his head at the Watkins bunch. "Your night is over, boys. You can hightail it back to your ranch, or you can spend the night at my luxury hotel. The choice is yours."

"What about the rest of 'em?" one of them asked. "You running them off too?"

"That's my business," Cade said. "But if you want to make it yours, I'm more than willing to talk with you."

Jake was mighty glad that he was on Cade Gentry's side, because he sure as hell didn't want to go up against him. Just the look in the sheriff's eye was enough to send shivers down his spine. Watkins's men quickly lost their sass, and two of them picked up Baxter between them and hustled him out the door. Jake went to the bar while Cade made sure everyone else was done for the night also.

"I waited until I figured you owed my about a hundred dollars," Wade said. "Then I told Cade to stop it."

"Thanks a lot," Jake said. He downed the beer that Ward put in front of him.

Jim grinned. "Well that made my night," he said. "How about you, you feeling better?"

Jake flexed his fist. "A mite," he said. He touched his lip and winced. "I'll let you know about the rest in the morning."

Pris walked up with a bowl of water and a towel. "Want me to fix you up, Jake?" she asked with a flirtatious bat of her eyes.

Jake took the cloth from her. "I'm good," he said. "But thank you anyway."

Pris shook her shoulders, which brought her abundant breasts into better view. "Your loss," she said. "Just remember, I've got all kinds of remedies for what ails you." She gave his crotch a long look and then sauntered away.

"That girl has a heart of gold," Jim said. "And is hot after you," he added.

"No thanks," Jake said. "I've got my eyes set elsewhere."

"And how does she feel about it?" Ward asked.

"I couldn't begin to tell you," Jake said. He pointed to his glass. "Pour me another one." Ward was more than happy to oblige.

TWENTY-TWO

Cassie needed to get up, but the thought of moving from the comfortable bed was more than she could stand. She was stiff and she was sore and the past few days were nothing but a blur. The smell of bacon frying and coffee boiling was comforting and familiar, which made her feel very grateful. She was home. She could have been dead.

Ever since the rape, Cassie had wondered if she'd be better off dead. After the last few days she knew alive was better, but dead sure would have been easier this morning. She also knew that lying in bed for another day wouldn't change anything. Cassie stretched and then gasped as a pain shot through her hip. Suzie, who'd spent the past day cuddled up beside her instead of in the barn chasing mice like she was supposed to, let out a questioning mew. Cassie rolled over on her side, threw the blankets back and pulled up her gown. She was black-and-blue from her waist down to mid thigh.

She was lucky she hadn't broken anything. Lucky to be alive. Lucky to be in Colorado instead of Texas. Lucky. Lucky. Lucky.

"Get up," she told herself, and because she said it out loud she had to do it. Suzie stretched and yawned and followed after her on silent feet.

Her mother sat in her chair as usual, with the same blank expression on her face. Would she have even noticed if Cassie hadn't come home? Would she have grieved if her daughter had died in the canyon, caught up in the flood? Would she even realize it? There was no way to ever know. The only sign she'd shown of life was when Jake walked through the door. And dang it all! Cassie could relate to that; she felt more alive in Jake's presence too.

Rosa called to her from the kitchen. "You feeling better?"

"Just grateful to be alive," Cassie said. "Where's Manuel?"

"He's fine," Rosa said, not answering the question. "Eat." She sat a plate at Cassie's customary chair, and her stomach growled in gratitude. She couldn't remember the last time she'd eaten. So much had happened in such a short time.

Jake had happened. And she didn't know what she was going to do about it.

If only he wasn't so dag-gone wonderful. If only he'd quit helping, quit showing up every time she needed him. If only he wasn't so handsome and funny and didn't make her feel so alive. She didn't want to feel alive. She didn't want to feel anything at all.

Suzie jumped into Manuel's chair and put a white paw on the table to see if anything was within her reach.

"Aren't you supposed to be eating mice?" Cassie asked the cat. She broke off a piece of bacon and put it on the table. Suzie's head popped up; she caught the bacon in her paw and ate it from the chair seat.

"She is more of a house cat than a barn cat, I think," Rosa said. "She thinks it is her job to keep Max in line. And he lets her."

"I'm so glad Max wasn't hurt," Cassie said. "And I'm sorry you were."

"It is not your fault," Rosa said. "The world is made up of good and bad people. And they all must learn to live together. The men who attacked us are bad. But there are plenty of good folks around to balance it out."

"You're talking about Jake," Cassie said. Why couldn't she escape the man? He was always around, in the flesh and in her dreams, and now he had Rosa carrying on about him.

"Yes. He is a good man. I think the ones who carried Suzie home are good too. The ladies came around yesterday asking about you."

"The Castles?" Cassie asked. "Laurie and Eden?"

"And the little girl."

"Hannah."

"Yes, she is very sweet."

"Did they come inside the house?" Cassie asked.

"I thought it rude to leave them outside," Rosa said. "Especially since you were ill and they could not visit with you." Cassie glanced back at her mother. "They were very nice and understanding," Rosa said. She sat a jar down on the table. "They brought this grape jelly also."

Cassie looked at the gift. And then at Rosa, who was busy at the sink. She hadn't been fair to the woman, who was so kind and gave her mother such good care. Rosa was an educated woman and she now lived a lonely life. Of course she would want some company, especially when she was caring for Cassie too. She knew Rosa was waiting for her to say something to her about letting the Castles in. Instead, she got a spoonful of jelly and spread it on her biscuit.

"I'm sorry I missed them," Cassie said. "Maybe we can go visit them someday. Their house is beautiful. You would love it."

"I would like that very much," Rosa said with a sweet smile. Cassie felt like sighing in relief. It shouldn't be that difficult to open herself up to people. Not everyone was out to get her, even though it had seemed that way at one time. Maybe it was difficult because she made it so. "The lambs are coming," Rosa said. "Manuel is in the barn with the cowboys, showing them what to do."

"Why didn't you tell me?" Cassie asked. She took a big gulp of coffee and immediately regretted it because it was still piping hot. "I should be helping," she said as she fanned her mouth. She jumped up from her chair.

"I didn't tell you because you wouldn't have eaten breakfast. And you wouldn't be any help to him at all if you pass out."

Rosa was right. If she'd known about the lambing she would have dashed right down to the barn in her haste to help and would have just caused more trouble. Just like she did when she took off to look for the sheep. Of course, she deserved what happened to her. She hadn't dashed off to look for the sheep. She'd left because she was scared of being around Jake. Cassie quickly put on her clothes and left the house to go to the barn. Suzie trailed after her.

Jake . . . The man had her twisted in knots inside. She couldn't go on this way. Yes, she liked talking to him, and he had this knack for showing up whenever there was trouble, but was it worth it? Was it worth this restlessness she'd felt since she'd met him?

He wanted more from her. Yesterday morning in the cave was proof of that. And there'd been times when she was certain he wanted to kiss her. She just wasn't sure if she wanted to kiss him back. She couldn't kiss him back. She had to stop things before he wanted something she couldn't give. It would be hard, but it was for the best.

Jake made her feel vulnerable. He knew things about her that she didn't want to share. She couldn't love him. Loving someone meant opening yourself up to more hurt. She clearly remembered how devastated her mother and her grandparents had been when her father died. She would never forget how her grandfather grieved after his wife died. And the love her mother felt for her was the cause of her condition now. Cassie knew she wouldn't survive it if she opened herself up to Jake and he pushed her away. Life was much safer when you lived it defensively. There was less chance of suffering, less chance of hurt.

She couldn't love Jake, so she wouldn't. It was that simple, wasn't it? Cassie, her mind made up, would make sure it stayed that way. And speak of the devil; there he was coming up her drive. It must be providence. It was time to tell Jake not to come around anymore.

Cassie must be feeling better. She walked down her drive with a purpose, even with the slight limp. Her cat followed along behind with her bushy tail up in a question mark. He was glad to see Cassie had quickly recovered from her escapades. Now if he could just convince her not to do anything else foolish. *Like get in a fight in a saloon?* Jake tested his jaw another time. It was sore, and the skin around his left eye was a bit green, a predecessor to turning black-and-blue he was sure. But it was worth it to give Baxter the beating he deserved. Not to mention he'd slept like the dead last night in his room at Ward's. Jake felt darn good this morning.

Jake stopped Bright and propped his arms on the saddle horn as Cassie got closer. The weather was perfect after all the storms, not too hot, a nice breeze blowing, one of those days that you really enjoyed being outside. "Nice day for a stroll," he said when she was close enough that he wouldn't have to raise his voice.

"I really didn't notice," she said, and she kept on walking with a noticeable limp.

"Where are you off to?" Jake asked.

"The barn," she said. "There's work to be done."

"Well wait a minute. I've got something for you."

She gave him an exasperated look, but she stopped. Jake dug a crumpled paper bag from his pocket and handed it to her. She opened the bag and a slight smile chased across her lips before she closed the bag and put it in her pocket.

"I noticed that you like peppermint," Jake said. "That first day we rode back from town."

"I do," Cassie said. "Thank you." She took off again.

"So what kind of work has you in such a hurry to get it done?"

"Lambing."

"Lambing?"

"Yes, lambing. You know what lambs are, don't you, Jake?"

"Baby sheep?" he said with a grin. "I was just discussing the merits of sheep with someone last night."

"I take it from looking at your face that the discussion didn't go your way."

"That's because you haven't seen the other guy's face."

Jake got off Bright and fell in beside her as Cassie did not seem inclined to stop. "So tell me about lambing."

"It's busy."

"What, they all give birth at the same time?"

"Pretty much."

"That's convenient."

"Don't cows do the same?"

"It all depends on when the bull got to them." Jake decided he like the turn the conversation had taken and grinned.

"I guess that makes it easy for you," Cassie said.

"I reckon it does," Jake replied. She seemed snippy, almost bitter. There was an edge to her comments that was different from before. "I'm glad to see you're feeling better," he gently offered.

"Thank you," Cassie said. She had her nose in the air again.

"I'd say dang near back to normal except for that rod up your backside."

"I beg your pardon?" Cassie rounded on him. The cat twirled around her ankles and then his before rubbing against his pant leg.

"You heard me," Jake challenged her. "I find it hard to believe that after everything we've been through the past few days you're acting like this."

"Acting like what?" she asked indignantly.

"A petulant child," Jake stated.

Cassie sighed. "I can't do this, Jake."

"Do what?"

"This dance of yours . . ." She looked away from him for a moment and then turned back. "I really appreciate everything you've done. You saved my life. That's something I can never repay. Ever," she said with finality and started walking again.

"Wait just a dang minute." He went after Cassie and grabbed her arm. She jerked him off in a hurry.

Jake moved his arm back, took off his hat and ran his hand through his hair. "I'm sorry," he said. He should know better than to grab her like that. He wasn't thinking. Or maybe he'd thought after what they'd been through, she wouldn't mind it so much.

"I wish I hadn't lost my gun," Cassie said, and started walking again.

Yeah, she minded. Jake planted his hat back on his head. "Why, are you planning on shooting someone?"

"I might." She looked at him sideways from beneath her long, lush lashes. Her hair was all over the place again and some of it hung in her eyes. Jake laughed. "It's not funny, Jake."

"Yes it is." He sure had missed her sass these past few days. "What have I done to deserve being shot? Besides bringing you a sack full of peppermint?"

"What haven't you done?" Cassie retorted.

"If this is how you treat your friends, then I'm glad I'm not your enemy."

"Is that what we are, Jake?" She stopped and put her hands on her hips as she looked at him. "Friends?"

"That's what I thought, and I did buy you candy. I guess I thought wrong."

Cassie started walking again. "What's the news from town? Do I have anything else to worry about?"

"I don't know anyone's intent right now," Jake said. "There's no proof as to who attacked your place even though we're all pretty certain it was Watkins's men. As long as Dan and Randy are here you should be safe."

"They can't stay here forever," Cassie said. "They work for you, not me. But I will pay them for their time while they're here."

"No you won't pay them," Jake argued. They came to the barn. "They work for me. I'm the one who pays them."

Cassie stood beside the door with her arms crossed once more. "I'll pay you then."

"No you won't," Jake said as he opened the door. The cat dashed in before them.

"Damn it, Jake," Cassie spouted as she went in. "You can't keep doing things for me. It's just not right."

"Ha!" he said with glee. "You just cursed."

She stopped abruptly. "Because you drove me to it," Cassie grumbled. She drug the toe of her boot through the hard-packed dirt. Jake was glad to hear her admit that he got to her. Because she sure had been getting to him since he met her.

"Why isn't it right if I help you?" he asked. He was conscious of the fact that Manuel, Dan and Randy were in the largest pen in the barn. He could hear them talking and laughing over the quieter baaing of the sheep, but he didn't care at the moment. Because figuring out what was up with Cassie was more important than anything they could be doing.

Cassie sighed. "Because I can't be beholden to you."

"Beholden to me?" Jake asked incredulously. "What the hell is that supposed to mean?"

"It means that I can't see you anymore, Jake," Cassie said. "You can't come around anymore. You've got to stop helping me. I can't live my life expecting you to show up every time there's trouble."

Jake shook his head in disgust. "Then maybe you should stop doing stupid things."

"Like what?"

"Like taking off by yourself to hunt sheep." Jake suddenly found himself angry at her foolishness. "What made you think you could find them anyway? Are you a tracker too?"

"Maybe I wasn't trying to find the sheep." Cassie's voice rose to match his. "Maybe I was just trying to get away from you. Did you ever stop to think that maybe I don't want you around?"

"Well, you're not the most pleasant person in the world either," Jake said.

"Maybe it's because you bring out the worst in me," Cassie said.

"No, it's not because I bring out the worst in you. It's because you're scared."

"Scared of what?" Cassie sputtered.

"Scared of feeling something. Because if you feel something you might have to act on it. And you are terrified because of what happened to you."

"I'm not scared," Cassie protested weakly.

"Prove it," Jake said, and he took her face between his hands and kissed her. He meant to do it to prove a point, but the moment his lips touched hers he completely forgot the reasons why and just experienced it.

Her lips trembled beneath his, but they were soft and they were pliable and they hesitantly followed his lead. Jake felt her hands clenching the lapels of his jacket as he held her face steady in his hands.

You shouldn't push her . . . But he couldn't stop himself. Once he'd tasted her he wanted more and he didn't pull away until they were both panting for breath.

Cassie looked at him with eyes that were full of fear. "You are right," she said. "I am scared." She turned and ran out of the barn, only limping slightly.

"Dang it, Cassie," Jake started.

"Let her go," Manuel said. Jake turned at the sound of

his voice and saw all three men standing there watching him. They'd seen everything. Dan and Randy looked like they were about to bust out laughing and Jake gave them a murderous look. They both covered their mouths with their hands and made a production of looking at the barn rafters, at the empty stalls across from them and at the cat, which was sitting on a bale of straw.

"If you push her too hard, she will only run farther," Manuel explained.

Dang it, he was right. Jake took off his hat and ran his hand through his hair. "What do you suggest I do?" he asked Manuel.

"Give her time," he advised. "She is like a wild horse that is afraid of all men. She must be gentled. You can't accomplish it in a day."

Gentling horses he could do, but Cassie, he wasn't so sure.

"Hey, boss, you need to see this," Dan said. "There's lambs. And dang if they ain't the cutest things I've ever seen."

"Cute, huh?"

"Yeah, cute," Dan said.

With a sigh Jake went to look in the pen. To his surprise Dan was right. Lambs were pretty cute. The only thing cuter would be Cassie sitting right in the middle of them.

TWENTY-THREE

Jake knew the expression *misery loves company*. For the life of him he couldn't figure out why. He wasn't fit company for anyone. It would be a week tomorrow morning since he'd kissed Cassie. A week in which he worked his men like they'd never been worked before, and not given them a reason to complain about it, as he'd been right there alongside them. He pushed himself hard so he'd fall into bed exhausted every night. But he'd still lie awake at night, with Josie sleeping beside him, staring at the ceiling of his bedroom thinking about Cassie Parker. After all the years of carefully laid plans. After years of knowing exactly what he wanted and how to get it, he didn't have a clue what to do next.

He made sure to check in with Dan and Randy every evening in hopes of catching a glimpse of Cassie, but she stayed out of sight. He was pretty sure that she knew he was coming around every night, but she never came out, or even waved through a window. And he couldn't figure out an excuse to go to the house, beyond apologizing for the kiss, and he dang sure wasn't going to do that.

Meanwhile, Dan and Randy were pretty antsy, as nothing had happened. They missed their friends and they'd sacrificed the past Saturday night in town to keep watch. There was no sign of trouble and no indication there'd be any. As a result, Jake had given them tonight off. They should be able to enjoy a Saturday night in town.

Jake might even join them for a bit, he thought, as he rode into town. But first he had to talk to Ward. He needed a plan to help him woo Cassie, and as much as he hated to admit it, Ward could help him with that. Lord knows he couldn't come up with anything to do or say to make Cassie come around to his way of thinking.

As he rode into Angel's End, he noticed Leah and Cade standing in the street. Banks, Leah's son, and his dog, Dodger, were playing a came of tag around the couple. Cade waved at Jake and he walked over to join them.

"It's good to see you, Jake," Leah said.

"You too," Jake said. Banks threw himself at his leg and Jake ruffled the boy's blond hair. "And it's good to see you also, young man," he said. "How's school? Are you keeping those grades up?"

"Yes, sir," Banks said. "Cade said he'd bring me out to your place when you take the cows up to summer pasture."

"We thought we'd look into getting him a mount," Cade said. "If the offer still stands."

"It does," Jake said. "Come anytime." Banks let out a whoop and went off to chase Dodger again. The three watched him for a moment, and Jake smiled as he imagined his own son chasing Josie around in the same manner while he and Cassie watched. The past week had clarified exactly what he wanted from Cassie. Now he just had to convince her.

"Has there been any trouble down your way?" Cade asked.

"Nary a thing," Jake replied. "Dan and Randy have had their fill of sheep, so I gave them the night off. I don't know how much longer I can expect them to hang around the Parker place. Have you seen anything out of Watkins?"

"I dropped by one day last week. He said I was interrupting his work and that was the high point of the visit. Does the man have any family? I can't imagine anyone wanting to live with him."

"His wife died around the time I got here," Jake said. "He has a son the same age as Jared Castle's youngest, back East in school. He comes for a couple of weeks every summer to visit. I think he lives with his grandparents in New York."

"Good to know," Cade said. "I wonder if he holds himself accountable to anyone."

"You two talk like Watkins is the one responsible for everything," Leah said. "Maybe his men acted without his knowledge."

"I don't think so," Jake said. "Remember we caught him dragging that dead sheep to town. So even if he wasn't there when Baxter killed it, he condoned the act."

"Leah always sees the best in everyone," Cade said. "For which I am very grateful."

Unfortunately, it was just the opposite with Cassie. With good reason, she saw the worst in everyone.

"So, Jake," Leah said. "Will you have a date for the dance? It's only a few weeks away."

"I'm working on it," Jake lied. He'd actually forgotten about the Cattlemen's Association's annual dance. It was held every year at the Castles' barn on the third Saturday in May. Everyone looked forward to it and he hadn't given it a second thought until now. And he was the head of the association. Dang if Cassie Parker didn't have him twisted up inside.

"I'm looking forward to it," Leah said. "If Cade doesn't mind dancing with two," she added, and put a hand on her belly.

"I don't mind at all," Cade said, and slipped his arm around his wife.

"I'll see you then," Jake said, and left the happy couple. He couldn't help smiling as he walked away. Maybe the dance was just what he needed to gentle Cassie, as Manuel said. He'd show her that he could be the perfect gentleman. It was as good a place to start as any. He whistled a happy tune as he walked into the Heaven's Gate Saloon. Coming to town had been a good idea.

Another Saturday night at the Heaven's Gate. Ward hoped that this one wouldn't be as damaging as the last. Some of his chairs were in sorry shape after the fight last week and one table was completely out of commission. When he looked out over the crowd, he noticed Dan and Randy from Jake's ranch were here, but the cowboys from Watkins's place were missing. That didn't bode well in Ward's mind. From the gossip he'd heard, there hadn't been any more problems at Cassie's place, but that didn't mean there wouldn't be. Ward sat down at his piano and Lady lay down beside the bench as Ward began to play.

Jake walked in with a grin on his face, went to the bar to get a beer from Bob and came over to the piano. "What's got you in such a good mood?" Ward asked as he continued to play.

"Making plans," Jake replied.

"And do any of them involve our sweet Miss Parker?"

"They do," Jake said. "I'm going to ask her to the dance."

"Ah yes, the dance," Ward said with a smile. "That's as good a place to start as any."

"She might need some convincing," Jake added.

"I believe you're the man to do it," Ward said.

"Just got to figure out the best time to do the asking," Jake said. "Considering she'd just as soon shoot me as look at me."

"And what did you do to deserve shooting?"

"Well according to her, just my being alive is enough to make her want to shoot me. But considering I kissed her good and proper, with an audience watching, I'm fairly certain that will be the excuse."

"You kissed her?" Ward stopped in the middle of his nocturne.

"Right in the middle of the barn."

"Good for you."

"I knew you'd be proud." Jake grinned.

"Are you serious about this woman, Jake?" Ward started playing again, a sonata this time. "Because I get the feeling there's something in her past that might complicate things a bit."

"You're right, there is, and I know what it is. As far as getting serious, I know I'd like to, but that's entirely up to her. She's got a lot of walls to get past."

"And asking her to the dance is part of your plan to get past those walls?"

"It's a start. Manuel advised me to act like I'm gentling

a horse. And to give her some time. Well I've given her a week to think that kiss over."

"I believe Sunday morning is the perfect time to ask someone to a dance. She won't be able to use work as an excuse not to talk to you."

"Ward, I believe you're right," Jake said. He looked at the crowd. "Things look pretty quiet tonight."

"I thought so too. Do you notice anyone missing?"

"Yeah, Watkins's men." Jake put down his mug. "And I let Dan and Randy have the night off."

"There's no way they could have known that in advance, is there?"

"No, I told them on my way here. They rode on ahead. We didn't pass anyone on the road."

"It's probably nothing then," Ward said. "Watkins probably is punishing them for getting into a fight last week."

Jake put his mug on top of the piano. "I think I'll pay Cassie a visit tonight."

"Do you want any company?" Ward asked.

"Nope, but thanks for the offer. I'm sure if there's a problem Libby will come looking for me. I'll just send her on to you."

"I'll keep an eye out," Ward said as Jake left.

Lady whined and Ward stopped to look at her. "What?" he asked. Lady sighed and put her head down on her crossed legs once more.

Jake felt a sense of urgency as he left the outskirts of Angel's End. There could be a lot of reasons why Watkins's men weren't in town on a Saturday night. He urged Bright into a canter. Cassie told him she couldn't live her life expecting him to rescue her every time there was trouble. But dang it, she couldn't fight off a bunch of men alone. She needed to accept the fact that there were things she could not do on her own.

And what if there wasn't a reason for him to show up? What if he was just charging in to save the day in hopes that Cassie would just fall into his arms? Then he'd just ask her to the dance and he wouldn't take no for an answer. He'd make her see reason.

A group of riders were headed his way. Jake slowed Bright down and rubbed his arched neck to soothe him when the horse protested. It was Watkins's bunch. Eight of them and Baxter in the middle. So he was overreacting. Jake guided Bright to the side of the road and let the group pass. Baxter and a couple of his buddies gave Jake a hard stare as they went by, but no words were exchanged, which was fine with Jake. Once they were passed, he started up again at a much slower pace. He needed time to think about what to say to Cassie.

Minutes passed. Minutes during which he thought out every argument Cassie could throw at him and every counter he could offer. Bright suddenly shied, and danced sideways on the road, which curved to the left around a rock slide that happened years ago. Jake searched the road for a rattler and heard a rustling above him. A cougar perhaps? Just as he turned he was hit in the side by someone throwing themselves at him from the rocks. He was rolled off Bright before he had time to react. Bright reared and kicked and reared again as Jake struggled with the man who was on top of him. He wore a bandana over the bottom part of his face, but Jake recognized the eyes as Baxter's. Baxter raised his gun.

"Don't kill him, you fool," someone said as Baxter swung the handle of the gun at Jake's face. He tried to block it but he couldn't. He heard rather than felt the crack and darkness filled his vision and then all went black.

Cassie stood on the porch and looked out over her valley. It was a peaceful evening after a peaceful week of nothing but blue skies and sunshine. The moon hung bright and low in the sky, so low that it felt like if she reached far enough, she could touch it. The sheep were gathered together in a tight group to protect the week-old lambs and even Libby seemed content as she grazed alongside them. Puck and Manuel's mules browsed in the corral by the barn and Suzie snoozed in one of the rocking chairs that graced the porch, while Max lay at the end of the porch, enjoying the cool breeze. Yes, everything was at peace.

Except for Cassie. The last thing she felt was peace. Ever since Jake kissed her, her mind had been a swirl of emotions, and her dreams had left her yearning for something more. Something that she was too afraid to want.

Suddenly, Max jumped off the porch and ran down the drive. He stood a moment with his ears pricked, and then he started barking. The glow of torches coming over the rise and around the bend sickened Cassie, and she ran into the house to get her rifle.

"Someone is coming," she said to Manuel before she ran outside again. She heard the scramble behind her, and Manuel appeared beside her with his rifle. "This can't be good," Cassie said.

"Agreed." Manuel's eyes never left the approaching group.

The riders came on, four of them and all heading straight for the barn. Cassie took off at a run down the drive with Manuel beside her. Max bravely charged at the riders and there was a yelp as he got caught up beneath a horse. Cassie stopped, raised her rifle and pulled the trigger, but missed as they rode around the barn. A torch flared upward and landed on the roof and another one went into the open door of the loft. Flames quickly shot up and licked at the top of the barn, lighting up the sky.

"No!" Cassie yelled. Luckily Puck and the mules were outside, but the milk cow was inside.

"Get them as they come back around," Manuel said. Cassie crouched behind a fence post and Manuel took cover behind the oak tree.

"We got to get the cow out," Cassie yelled. They could hear the poor animal bellowing now, and Puck and the mules joined in. They were dangerously close to the flames.

Two of the riders came around the barn and the other two set out across the valley to where the sheep huddled. Max, recovered from his fall, charged after them. Soon Libby joined into the cacophony of noise; braying, barking, baaing and the plaintive mooing of the cow accompanied by the nervous calls of Puck and the mules. Cassie and Manuel shot at the two riders heading toward them and Cassie watched in satisfaction as her shot knocked one of the men off his horse.

She took off at a run for the barn.

"Wake up, Jake." Water sloshed in his face and Jake sputtered. He rubbed water out of his eyes and looked up at Ward, his face illuminated by the moon.

"What happened?" he asked. His mind felt like it was wrapped in a blanket and stuffed in a box, and his head throbbed at the temple. He touched the side of his head and felt blood.

"You tell us," Ward said. He held out a hand and Ward and Cade hauled him to his feet.

"Someone attacked me on the trail."

"And left you for dead by the looks of it," Cade added. "Your horse turned up in town."

"Thank God," Jake said. "He could have just as easily gone home and no one would have noticed him until tomorrow morning. It was Baxter, it had to be. I passed him on the way."

"He wasn't in the group that showed up at my place," Ward said.

"He's at Cassie's," Jake said. He took a step toward Bright, staggered and quickly righted himself. The world tilted as he swung onto Bright's back and he felt the contents of his stomach heave upward, but he quickly swallowed it back down and kicked Bright into a run with Ward and Cade by his side.

This wasn't good. It wasn't good at all.

Cassie flinched every time she heard a shot. From the sounds of it Manuel was keeping them busy. She couldn't worry about that now; she had to get the poor cow out. The heat was unbelievable and it felt as if her skin was blistering. When she opened the pen, the cow charged out into the night. Cassie ran on through the barn to the corral and undid the gate. Puck trotted through but the mules needed encouragement. She finally got them headed in the right direction and followed after them.

Her entire valley was bright as day with the moonlight streaming down and the firelight behind her. Several dead sheep lay in the valley and she heard Libby braying loudly in the distance. Max's barks sounded close to the house, so she headed in that direction. Lord help all of them if the house was on fire.

It was. Cold fear gripped Cassie's heart. She picked up her pace. The riders were headed back down the drive but she didn't care. Her mother and Rosa were inside; Manuel fired a few parting shots and followed her.

"Mother!" Cassie screamed as she got to the porch. Suzie dashed out from beneath it, and Cassie heard the panicked chattering of the coon family along with the pops and cracks of the fire.

"Rosa!" Manuel called out.

"Go around back," Cassie yelled. "See if they got out that way. I'll meet you in the middle."

The heat was like a wall. Cassie dashed through the door where flames licked around the frame. "Rosa?" The ceiling was on fire and flames poured down the ladder that led to the loft. "Rosa!" Cassie called again. Manuel came through the back door and shook his head. They heard a crash from Cassie's room.

"Help us!" Rosa cried out.

Manuel and Cassie both ran to the bedroom. A timber had fallen and Rosa and her mother were trapped against the back wall of the cabin. Rosa held her mother upright and was shielding her from the fire with her body.

"Oh God, what do we do?" Cassie cried out. The flames were getting higher and the heat was unbearable. They only had minutes, if that.

"Rosa, can you come to us?" Manuel said. "You're going to have to jump."

"Mother can't jump," Cassie said. It was hard to breathe; her lungs felt scorched and she buried her nose and mouth in her sleeve.

"Maybe we can pull them to us," Manuel said.

Rosa put her arm around Loretta and half drug her closer to the door. Cassie watched in shock as the bed caught on fire where the timber lay across it.

Her mother whimpered.

"Cassie!"

It was Jake.

"In here!" she screamed. She felt the smoke in her throat. She couldn't breathe and she started coughing violently. Manuel did the same. Jake crashed in, followed by Cade and Ward. It only took them a few seconds to figure out what to do. Jake pushed himself against the door jam and propelled himself over the timber, and Cade did the same. There was a large popping sound.

"The roof's going to go," Ward said. Cade scooped up Rosa and jumped back across the timber. Ward grabbed Manuel and shoved him out the door after Cade and Rosa. Jake picked up Cassie's mother, and Cassie looked in horror as her mother's dress caught on fire.

"Oh God, oh God, oh God," she prayed, but her voice was nothing more than a croak.

Jake beat at the material with one hand as the flames around them shot up higher. "Get her out of here, Ward," he said.

Ward grabbed Cassie around the waist and pulled her back. "No!" she tried to scream, but the words could barely form in her raw throat. "Let me go! Jake! Mother!"

She heard another crash as Ward dragged her into the main room of the house. The walls were on fire around them, but still she fought against Ward's strong hold until miraculously, Jake was behind them with her mother thrown over his shoulder. They made it outside just as the entire roof fell into the house. They kept moving until they were at the bottom of the hill. Jake lay her mother on the ground beneath the huge oak tree. They were all coughing violently and Ward went to the trough for water. Cassie noticed three men sitting on the ground with their hands tied behind them by the corral and Dan and Randy standing guard over them.

Cassie knelt down. "Mother?" Her hair was singed, and there was a huge burn on her hip where her gown had caught on fire. Cassie touched her mother's soot smeared face. She saw a spark in her mother's eyes, something she hadn't seen in the past two years.

Her mother lifted a trembling right hand to Cassie's face. Her mouth moved and Cassie leaned close. "Cassie," she whispered, and Cassie sobbed because her mother knew who she was. "Be happy," she said. "Just look ahead . . ." Her voice trailed off and the breath rattled in her chest.

"Mother?" Cassie put a hand on her mother's chest. It wasn't moving. "Mother?" she asked again and gently shook her.

Jake knelt beside her. "I'm sorry, Cassie," he said. "She's gone." Rosa knelt on the other side and closed her mother's eyes, made the sign of the cross and put her hand to the silver cross she wore around her neck and said a prayer.

"Not like this," Cassie said. She staggered to her feet. "Not because of more violence," she whispered, because her throat was so raw from the smoke and the flames.

"Cassie?" Jake was behind her. She knew that he wanted to comfort her, to hold her and tell her everything was going to be all right. She couldn't let that happen. If she did, she might just dissolve into tears. She had to hold on. She had to keep going. She had to be strong.

She was so tired of being strong. Cassie wrapped her arms around herself. Why should she be strong when there was nothing left? Her mother was gone. The sheep were gone. Her home and the barn were gone, and Manuel and Rosa would be better off without her.

Jake put his arms around her from behind. She held herself rigid. She couldn't accept his comfort, because she had nothing to offer in return. Her emotional strength was spent. She couldn't give him herself, because her capacity to feel was gone.

"You're not alone," he said. "You'll never be alone again."

Cassie stood, stiff and unresponsive. He didn't know. How could she believe him, how could he say these things? He didn't know. But he did . . .

Jake bent his head next to her ear. "As long as it takes, Cassie, I'll be here waiting."

His body was so warm and she felt his heat enveloping her. She nodded in agreement and let her body relax against him. And then she cried.

TWENTY-FOUR

Riders were coming. Jake wasn't surprised. The flames and the smoke had to be visible for miles. Cade and Ward both took up a position on the road, ready for whoever it was. Ward with his pistol out in case of trouble, and Cade in a deceptively easy stance that belied his ability to draw quickly if necessary.

Cassie's tears had finally subsided. They'd been heart wrenching and he'd never felt as helpless in his life. If only he'd gotten here sooner. Was it worth the few minutes it took to catch Baxter and the others? If he'd arrived earlier, would they have been able to save Cassie's mother?

The barn was gone, nothing but a pile of burning timbers. He could only pray that Puck and the rest of the stock weren't inside. The cat sat on the lowest limb of the oak tree with her tail twitching. Manuel had covered Cassie's mother with a blanket.

"Someone is approaching, Cassie," Jake said. "We need to be prepared, in case . . ." He couldn't imagine anything else bad happening tonight, but if Watkins and the rest of his men showed up and there was a shoot-out . . .

Cassie wiped her eyes. Her rifle leaned against the tree where Cade had put it after retrieving it from the burning house on their way out. She checked the load, found it empty and sighed.

"There are cartridges in my saddlebags," Jake said. "Here's hoping we don't need them." She and Manuel found the ammunition while Jake pulled his gun and went to stand with Cade and Ward. His palms and face stung with burns. Within a minute Cassie and Manuel joined them, along with Dan and Randy. There wasn't much left to protect, but dang it, they were going to fight for it.

The riders came over the rise. Watkins and his men.

"Let me do the talking," Cade said. "I've dealt with his type before."

"You're the sheriff," Ward drawled.

Watkins and his riders halted when they saw the group standing in the road with their guns ready. "Looks like you had some trouble here, Sheriff," he said.

"Just a bit," Cade said. "You looking to cause some more?"

"Just looking for my men," Watkins said.

Cade jerked a thumb in the direction of Baxter and the others. "These men?" Cade asked. "I'm afraid they are under arrest."

"For?"

Cade ticked the charges off on his fingers. "Arson, attempted murder and murder, for now. I'm pretty sure I'll think of some more come morning."

"Baxter! Are you boys guilty?" Watkins called out.

"No, sir," Baxter said.

"They're not guilty," Watkins said. "Let them go."

Cade laughed. "It doesn't work that way. You're not the judge around here. Nor are you the jury. We'll have an official trial and let a jury decide."

"You got any witnesses?" Watkins asked. "And I mean someone that isn't a dirty sheep lover."

"I got Jake," Cade said.

"Jake wasn't here," Baxter said. "We left him on the trail."

Jake grinned at Ward. Baxter's cockiness had cost him. "And that would be the attempted murder charge," Cade said.

"Since he's alive, what's the murder charge?" Watkins asked.

"The fire killed my mother, you son of a bitch," Cassie said.

"Easy . . ." Jake said. Her grip on the rifle was tight and he wasn't entirely sure that she wouldn't start shooting at any minute. While he knew Cade was deadly with a gun, and he and Ward were handy, they were still outnumbered and he didn't want to lose Cassie in a gun battle after everything else that had happened.

"Miss Parker's mother died in the fire," Cade said. "Which makes it murder."

"You idiot," Watkins yelled at Baxter. "I told you to make sure nobody died. I just wanted them gone."

Cade laughed.

"That sounded like a confession to me," Ward said.

"To me too," Cade said with a satisfied grin. "Raymond Watkins, you are under arrest."

"The hell I am," Watkins said, and reached for his gun.

If Jake had not seen it, he wouldn't have believed it. Cade

drew his gun and shot Watkins before the man's fingers touched the handle of his gun. He flopped over the back of his horse and landed in the dust. The rest of his men looked at the body in shock. Jake and Ward kept their guns leveled on the group that was still trying to figure out what had happened to their leader.

"Was he a boss worth dying for?" Cade asked the men. A few of them raised their hands in surrender. Jake kept his gun steady. Cassie stood beside him, only half his size, but the hold she had on her rifle was steady.

"Why don't you go on home now," Cade continued. "I heard Watkins has a son. Take care of the place until he can get here."

One of them spoke up. "Just as long as it's clear to you we were only following orders, being here tonight."

"It's clear," Cade said. "Just as long as it's clear to you that if I hear of any more trouble coming from your direction, I will put a whole lot of hurt on all of you. Got it?"

"Yes, sir," the man responded.

"You the foreman?" Cade asked.

"Yes, sir."

"You seem like a smart man. I'll trust you to keep the rest in line."

As one the men turned on their horses and rode away. Jake hadn't even realized he was holding his breath until Cassie lowered her rifle. He reached out his arm and pulled her to him. "It's over now," he said.

"No it's not," Cassie said. "I've still got to bury my mother."

Cassie thought that burying her mother would be the end of it, but it was only the beginning. The beginning of what to do next. Except she didn't know the next step. She'd let herself be carried along on the tide of caring and concern that came their way when the community found out what had happened.

Raymond Watkins was dead and had been buried on his land. The men who attacked her place were in jail in town. The one she'd shot was only wounded and Cade said he'd survive. Cassie was grateful. When it came down to it, she didn't want to be responsible for someone's death. She'd seen the look in Cade's eyes after he'd killed Watkins. She didn't want to carry any more guilt. She had quite enough to last her for a lifetime.

Luckily the bunkhouse on Cassie's property had escaped notice by Baxter and his friends and it was livable, but there wasn't any privacy. She felt like an intruder with Rosa and Manuel, even though they did nothing to make her feel unwelcome. They'd lost another twenty-five sheep in the attack, including some of the precious lambs, but the rest of the stock, including Libby, was fine.

They'd spent the Sunday after the attack sifting through the ruins. Leah and the Martins came from town, and the Castles were there, and Jake of course, and his two men, Dan and Randy, who apologized over and over again for not being there when the attack happened. Jake's cook, Fu, showed up at lunchtime with a wagon full of food and Jake's puppy, Josie, who kept everyone entertained while they ate. The Gentrys, the Castles and the Martins had all brought furniture and supplies from their own households to help replace everything lost in the fire, and Cassie felt overwhelmed by their generosity.

So much had happened that she couldn't comprehend it all. It seemed she had just closed her eyes to go to sleep and the next thing she knew she found herself standing in a borrowed dress with a pinned-up hem by her mother's grave listening to Ward Phillips read from the Bible with his dog sitting by his side.

The cemetery really was in a pretty spot. Tucked behind the freshly painted white church at the end of Main Street, the graveyard had a stream running through it and a field of wildflowers just beyond it. Someone had gathered a bouquet from the field, tied it up with a piece of blue ribbon and laid it on the coffin that had been hastily made by Jim and Cade.

How wonderful it would be just to sink into the field of flowers and lie on her back and watch the clouds float across the sky. How wonderful it would be to lean on Jake, who stood behind her as Ward read the Twenty-third Psalm. Yet she couldn't. Cassie knew it wasn't because she didn't want to. She did. She just couldn't bring herself to cross that bridge. She couldn't let go, she couldn't take that final step, and she had no one to blame but herself.

Someone started singing a hymn, "Blessed Be the Tide that Binds," and other voices joined in. Cassie mouthed the words; her throat still hurt too badly to sing. Jake croaked out a few words behind her and tried to clear his throat. His voice seemed like it would be nice given other circumstances.

The song was over and everyone stood patiently, waiting on Cassie. She knew what she was supposed to do. It was time for her to say good-bye. Cassie scooped up a handful of dirt and looked down into the grave that held her mother's coffin. She dropped the dirt and heard the chunk-chunk as it hit the wood. "Good-bye, Mother," she said, but it was only words. Two years was a long time to say good-bye to someone.

Was it wrong that what she felt was a sense of relief that

her mother's suffering was over? That she was glad she was gone because the alternative was only a living hell?

Jake took her arm, and she let him because it was easier than saying no. She was only going through the motions now. Doing what was expected because it was just too dang hard to do anything else. Everyone followed as Jake led her to the Devil's Table where a luncheon was ready for them. Cassie almost laughed as they walked up the steps and into the café. All this time of trying to keep the devil at bay and here she was, walking into his place plain as day.

"We want you to come stay with us for a while." Laurie Castle slid into the chair across from her when Jake got up to refill her glass with tea.

"Please do," Eden begged as she stood beside her mother's chair.

"You need time to heal, Cassie, time to relax, time to just be," Laurie continued.

"I would love to have someone close to my age to talk to," Eden said.

"Let us take care of you," Laurie said.

Cassie looked at Jake. He stood at a table talking to the Martins. There was a red streak on the side of his face where he'd been burned, and he held two glasses in his hand, one for her and one for him. He must have felt her eyes on him, because he looked up and gave her a sweet smile.

She wasn't ready to be with him. She didn't know if she'd ever be ready. So she looked at Laurie and Eden and said, "I'd love to."

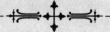

TWENTY-FIVE

Cassie going to the Castles' to stay was not something he expected, and once again Jake didn't know what to do. Just when he thought he had it figured out, that he would give her time to get over her mother's death, yet be there for her to lean on, she went and pulled a fast one on him. So just like every other Saturday night, he was at the Heaven's Gate Saloon listening to Ward instead of spending time with Cassie, which is what he'd much rather be doing.

"What you need is a plan," Ward said. They sat at a table off to the side of the bar. Jake gave Ward a look.

"No, I'm serious," Ward said. "So far your plan for getting Cassie has consisted of hanging around and hoping there's trouble so you can ride in for the rescue. Not very well thought out, if you ask me."

"I haven't hoped there was trouble," Jake groused. "I've

been hoping there won't be trouble so she can see that I'm not there just to help her."

"How's that working out for you so far?" Ward asked.

"What do you mean? I haven't seen her since she went off with the Castles."

"And why is that?" Ward said. "Because you can't think of a reason to go out there? Isn't the Cattlemen's Association dance next Saturday night? Aren't you the head of the association? Shouldn't you make sure that everything is going as planned? Weren't you going to ask Cassie to the dance?"

"Well I was," Jake said. He didn't bother responding to the rest of Ward's questions as he had no response. "But that was before."

"Before her entire world went to hell?"

"Pretty much," Jake admitted. "Now I'm not so sure it's a good idea."

"Why not?"

"Because it would be disrespectful to her mother's death."

"Her mother is going to stay dead forever," Ward said. "But Cassie might not hang around that long."

"Dang, Ward, it's only been a week."

"I'm just being realistic here. I'm sorry her mother died, but what's done is done and there's no changing it. Besides, from what I heard from Dan and Randy, it was a good thing that her mother finally died."

"Well I'll have to agree," Jake said. "I only saw her the one time, but it wasn't much of an existence. Not that you'll ever catch me admitting it to Cassie."

"If it's the thing that's in her past that's holding you back, then you need to get over it and you need to help her get over it too."

"Once I figure out what you said, I'll think on it," Jake said.

"You might not know what I said but you know what I meant," Ward growled.

"I know what you mean, Ward. The problem is how do I get Cassie to accept it?"

"You show her that the future is going to be a lot better than the past," Ward replied. "I watched you for three years with Leah. You had no problem telling her the way things should be."

"And she had no problem telling me to go pound sand," Jake replied.

"Yet you hung in there."

"And it turned out she was right. But what if Cassie tells me to go away? She's not as kind as Leah. And she's a might more stubborn, if that's possible. Once she makes her mind up . . ." Jake's voice trailed off. He didn't want to think about the alternative to life without Cassie.

"So," Ward said. "Convince her to see things your way."

"And how exactly do I do that?"

"Tell her how you feel."

"That's something I'm trying to figure out for myself."

"Talk about stubborn," Ward said. "You could win a prize."

"What's that supposed to mean?"

"You're in love with Cassie Parker," Ward said and he sat back to wait for a reaction.

Jake didn't move. He had feelings for Cassie, but love? Love was something he scoffed at when Leah told him she didn't love him. It was something Leah was so certain about when she decided to forgive Cade.

Was love not being able to live without someone? The panicked thought that if you lost them your life would be incomplete? The idea that you wanted to do whatever it took to make them happy, that you would do anything in the world to make sure they were happy.

"You know something, Ward?" Jake said. "I reckon I am in love with Cassie Parker."

"So, what you going to do about it?" Ward asked.

"Go tell her."

"That's my boy," Ward said with a self-satisfied grin. "Now you have a plan."

"Why hello, Jake, what brings you out our way?" Laurie said as she opened the door.

Cassie scrunched down in her overstuffed armchair at the mention of Jake's name. She was in the Castles' very comfortable parlor, reading a book. Eden sat in the chair opposite her, working on a piece of needlepoint. Hannah was trying to put a doll's dress on one of two black and white puppies that tumbled on the rug between them. While Cassie was trying to become invisible, Eden put her sewing aside and looked to the hallway where the deep rumbling of Jake's voice could be heard.

"I just came to make sure everything was ready for the dance next Saturday night," Jake said. "And thought I might pay Cassie a visit if she's available."

"She's in the parlor with Eden," Laurie said. "Can I get you something?"

"No thanks," Jake said. "Fu keeps me well fed."

Eden grinned at her and Cassie made a face. There was no place for her to escape. Her week of hiding was over. She should have known it was too good to last. But she also had to admit to herself that she was glad Jake was here. She had spent the better part of a week wondering if he was going to show up, and the rest of the time torn between what she would do if he did and what she would do if he didn't. And now that he was here, Cassie had no idea what to do or say.

"How nice to see you, Jake," Eden said.

"Eden," Jake said. He crouched down. "Hi, Hannah." The little girl giggled. Finally he turned to her. "Hello, Cassie."

She'd missed him. The realization hit her in the stomach like a punch. The strong jaw, the stormy eyes and the way he looked at her. There was no denying that she missed having him around. "Hi, Jake."

"I brought you some candy," he said and handed her a sack. Hannah instantly snapped to attention, her bright blue eyes wide as she looked at the bag.

"You keep bringing me candy, Jake." She opened it up. It looked like there was at least one of everything from the Swansons' store.

"And you keep eating it."

"Don't want it to go to waste," Cassie said. She offered the bag to Hannah, who pulled out a peppermint stick, and then to Eden, who pulled out a piece of hard candy.

"No, we wouldn't want that," Jake said with a grin. "Want to go for a ride? I brought Puck over. I thought you might miss him."

"I do miss Puck," Cassie said. "You didn't happen to bring Suzie too, did you?"

"Nope. Didn't want to press my luck."

Eden giggled.

"Would you like to come along?" Jake asked her.

"Oh no, I have things to do," Eden said. "I need to finish up my dress for the dance."

The dance . . . Eden and Laurie had been talking about the dance all week and they expected Cassie to go. But how could she? She was a beggar in hand-me-down clothes, and it was just too soon after her mother's death.

Jake knelt down to pet the puppies. "I heard you got two of them," he said as Lucky and Lucy alternated between wiggling and wagging. "Do they chew things up as much as my Josie? I swear she'd eat the house if we'd let her." Hannah laughed at the thought of a puppy eating a house. Cassie couldn't help but smile as she watched him. He was so gentle with Hannah and the puppies, so loving. He would be a wonderful father. She imagined a little boy with hair as pale as the sun, then she shook her head. Why was she thinking about Jake and children together?

"We keep them well supplied with bones," Eden said. "And they have each other to chew on when the bones are gone."

"That might make the difference," Jake said. "Maybe I ought to look for a friend for Josie to play with. I'll give it a thought when we take the cattle to market."

"Hannah, we should take the puppies out before they wet the rug," Eden said. "Enjoy your ride." The puppies followed her halting step as she and Hannah went to the back of the house.

"Shall we go?" Jake turned to Cassie and offered her his arm. She rolled her eyes at his gallantry, but she took it anyway and he escorted her to the front door.

It *was* good to see Puck. Cassie hadn't realized how much she missed him, along with Suzie and Libby and Rosa and Manuel. And her mother. The mother she'd lost two years ago. The vibrant, supportive mother.

She'd come to the Castles' because she wanted to escape her life. Now that she saw Puck, she realized that her life, as it was, really wasn't that bad. And her mother wouldn't suffer anymore, even if her death was tragic. She rubbed her horse behind his left ear in greeting and he nibbled at her pocket where she'd stuffed the bag of candy.

"Give him a piece of peppermint," Jake said. "He'll love it."

"You think?"

"Try it and see." She offered the treat to Puck, who lipped it delicately from her palm. Bright swung his head up and down. "Hey, don't leave him out," Jake said, and with a laugh Cassie gave the other horse a piece too. Suddenly the day seemed fairer, brighter and happier as Jake stood by her side and they fussed over the horses.

"It's a pretty day," Jake said.

"Yes it is," Cassie replied.

"Want some help?"

"Sure." Cassie put her foot in his hand and he boosted her into the saddle.

"I thought we'd ride around the lake," Jake said, and they took off at a slow canter to the lake that was the centerpiece of the Castles' valley. Jake didn't say anything and Cassie missed the playful banter they usually shared.

When they reached the far side of the lake, Jake stopped Bright and pointed. Off in the distance Cassie saw a line of elk. They watched as they crossed the valley and disappeared back into the mountains. Jake continued on and Cassie followed until they came to an outcropping of large flat boulders gathered on the lakeshore. He stopped Bright and reached up to help her down.

"Let's talk," he said.

Cassie walked out onto a boulder that lay half in the water and sat down. She startled a peeper and it jumped into the water with a quick splash. A mother duck and her line of ducklings quack-quacked, and they all took off to investigate the splash. Cassie watched them with a bemused expression on her face. She was curious what Jake had to say.

The problem was, he wasn't saying anything. He was just sitting on the boulder tossing pebbles into the water, which had the mother duck swimming in circles.

"You got something on your mind, Jake? Or did you bring me out here to watch you torture that poor duck."

"I've got something on my mind," Jake confessed. "It's you."

"Me?"

"You aren't going to make this easy, are you?"

"Hey, I'm just sitting here," Cassie said. "You're the one who wanted to talk."

Jake took off his hat and ran his fingers through his hair. Then he sat his hat aside. "May I?" he asked and took her hand. His was twice the size of hers. She knew he could crush it if he wanted to, but he held it like it was one of Laurie's china teacups. "I have a confession to make," he said, and his eyes bore into hers. They were as clear a gray as she'd ever seen them, calm instead of stormy. Why did she always think about the sky when she looked at his eyes?

"I'm in love with you, Cassie Parker."

"Ah . . . oh . . ." Cassie began, but Jake put his finger to her lips.

"I don't want you to say anything today. I know you've been through a lot lately and it's not fair that I'm telling you this so soon after you lost your mother, but, dang it, Cassie, you're all I think about, since the moment I met you on the trail that night." He turned her hand over so that her palm was up and he rubbed his thumb across it as he looked at her hand.

"I know you lost your home and your family. I know you may be thinking about a fresh start someplace else," he said, and then he turned his eyes upon her once more and Cassie saw the storm gathering in them. "I just want to let you know that you will always have a home right here." He took her hand and put it over his heart. He held it there for a moment, long enough for Cassie to feel it pounding in his chest, long enough for her to see that love shining for her. For her. "Whenever you are ready for it, Cassie. I'll wait as long as it takes."

Cassie was too overwhelmed to speak. She didn't know what she had done to deserve his love. He was such a good man, a strong man, a kind man, and he loved her of all people. He deserved better. He deserved someone who was whole and not damaged like her.

As if he'd read her mind, Jake dropped her hand and grabbed her forearms. He pulled her close and she saw the storm had come full force into his eyes. "Don't you dare use what happened to you in the past as an excuse," he said. "I know you were hurt, but it is over. You need to put it behind you and live your life. Whether it is with me or someone else isn't as important as the fact that you quit letting it rule your life. You are a beautiful woman, Cassie Parker. It's time you quit hiding it and started acting like one."

Cassie opened her mouth to protest, but instead Jake kissed her. It was just like the first time he kissed her. Wild yet gentle, firm yet yielding, full of emotion. And her body responded for all she was worth, until they finally broke apart just to breath, and Jake leaned his forehead against hers.

"One more thing," he said.

For the life of her Cassie couldn't imagine what he was about to say.

"Will you be my date for the dance?"

TWENTY-SIX

A week had passed, and Cassie still didn't know what she was going to say to Jake tonight. Even though she'd agreed to go to the dance with him, she still wasn't sure how to respond to his confession of love. Every day she rode Puck around the lake in hopes of finding an answer, but she had yet to discover one. She went to visit Manuel and Rosa, and both assured her they were fine and that she needed to concentrate on herself now.

That was the problem; she'd been concentrating on nothing else for the past week. She had no excuse not to attend the dance either. If Eden could go with her crippled leg, then Cassie couldn't use the excuse of not having anything suitable to wear.

What are you so scared of? Cassie stared out the window of the Castles' parlor. The only thing she knew for certain was that she was going back to her place tomorrow. It would be cramped quarters for a while with three of them living in the bunkhouse, but they would survive it. A new house and barn weren't going to build themselves and she couldn't keep on expecting Manuel to do all the work by himself.

"Cassie?" Eden came up beside her. Cassie hadn't even realized she was in the room until she spoke. "Come with me," Eden said. "I have a surprise for you."

"A surprise?" Cassie said. "You've done enough for me."

"We can never do enough for our friends," Eden said. She took Cassie's hand and led her to her room. A blue dress lay upon her bed. "It was always my favorite," Eden explained, "which is why I kept it, even though it got too small. I've been working on it all week, for you to wear to the dance." Eden picked up the dress and handed it to Cassie. Then she turned her around so that she faced a floor-length mirror.

It was beautiful, with a rounded neck framed in a delicate row of lace and capped sleeves. The color was the same as the sky, and it made Cassie's eyes seem bluer. It was perfect.

"It's so pretty," Cassie said. "How old were you when you wore it?"

"Fourteen. I grew a couple of inches over that winter. Through here mostly." Eden blushed as she waved her hands over her breasts. "And taller too."

Eden was tall, especially when compared to Cassie, whose head just reached Eden's shoulder. To Cassie, Eden was elegant and graceful, yet Cassie recognized that she felt inadequate because of her noticeable limp. Just as she felt inadequate because of the wounds she carried on the inside. But Eden never used her limp as an excuse. She lived her life instead of hiding away or just staying in a chair. Maybe Cassie should take that as inspiration.

You are a beautiful woman, Cassie Parker. It's time you quit hiding it and started acting like one.

"Why don't you try it on?" Eden asked.

"I will," Cassie said. She gave Eden a quick hug. "Thank you so much."

"Let me know if you need any help," Eden said as she left and closed the door firmly behind her.

It had been so long since Cassie had worn a dress. Over two years, since the trial. She had nothing to wear beneath it, but she had a feeling Eden and her mother would make sure that was taken care of. She noticed a pair of blue shoes on the bed. Another remnant of Eden's childhood.

The thought of walking into the dance terrified her, but she had nothing to lose by just trying on the dress. Cassie jerked off her boots and stripped down to her camisole and knickers. They seemed ragged and dirty next to the dress, so she took them off as well. Cassie caught sight of her body in the mirror as she turned to pick up the dress.

Her skin was pale all over, except for her face and hands, which were a golden hue from the sun. She was suddenly very self-conscious of her hands, which were rough from hard work. She'd spent so much time hiding the fact that she was a woman, she'd almost stopped thinking of herself that way. Except it was hard to deny it now, when her breasts were right there in front of her. They were larger than she remembered. The last time she'd looked at them like this, they'd been covered with bruises. Now they were pale white and unblemished, with the veins showing blue beneath her skin.

She ran her hands down the flat plane of her stomach as she looked in the mirror. Her ribs were visible, not because she was starved, but because she worked hard and it showed. Her waist nipped in before flaring gently over her narrow hips. Her legs were thin, like a young girl's. Her eyes avoided the place between. The place that had been violated.

"Why did I think I could just stop being a woman?" she asked the reflection in the mirror. There was no answer, just a startled look reflected back at her. Cassie touched the chopped ends of her hair that brushed against her shoulders. Cutting it off hadn't changed anything. Just as living in a state of denial for the past two years hadn't changed anything either. There was no erasing what had happened to her. She'd been raped. Did she want to spend the rest of her life hiding because of it?

Cassie picked up the dress. It was already unbuttoned down the back. She stepped into it and pulled it up. She pushed her arms through the sleeves and settled it on her shoulders. On a fourteen-year-old girl the lace-trimmed round neckline would have been modest. On a woman full grown, even a petite one like Cassie, it showed quite a bit of cleavage. Even without buttoning it, Cassie could tell the waist was an inch or two too wide, but the length was fine once she put the shoes on, and the color was perfect.

"Cassie?" Eden knocked on the door.

"Come in," she said. "I need buttoning up."

"Oh, it's nearly perfect," Eden said. "Momma, come see."

Laurie came into the room as Eden fastened the dress up the back. "You look lovely," she said. Laurie pinched it in at the waist. "This won't take any time at all to fix." She touched Cassie's hair. "And a good washing and trimming and a few turns with the curling iron will make all the difference in the world."

Cassie grinned at her reflection in the mirror. She had a lot of time to make up for, and she didn't want to waste a minute more. "Let's get started," she said.

*   *   *

Jake couldn't recall a time in his life when he'd been more nervous. He'd laid it all on the line with Cassie last week and then told her he didn't want an answer until tonight. Dang it, he should have just thrown her on the back of Bright and taken off with her. Or maybe he should have kissed her senseless. He knew what that was like. He was downright senseless when he kissed her.

Jared and Laurie had outdone themselves with the dance, as Jake knew they would. Jared made a good living with his cattle and more so with his horse breeding. He'd even asked Jake to let Bright cover some of his mares and promised Jake the pick of the bunch in return. Jake was anxious to see what came of it when the mares finally delivered. But not as anxious as he was to see Cassie.

He'd made himself stay away all week and lost himself in his work. He caught a glimpse of her one time, on Puck, as she went to her place, and dang if he didn't waste the entire morning watching to see if she came back by, which she did. He'd been afraid she'd just take off altogether, and he'd never find her if she did.

The entrance to the Castles' ranch was lit up with candles stuck in Mason jars. The drive had jars hanging on hooks at equal distances along the way, and there were more scattered among the outbuildings and barns below the Castles' house. There were even candles floating on the lake. It was a pretty sight on the moonless night.

There were several buggies parked outside the barn, and the sound of the musicians tuning up mingled with the soft chatter of those who were gathered around the tables outside. Tables covered with food and drink. There was no mistaking the silhouettes of Leah and Cade among the guests talking and laughing.

Jake handed Bright off to one of Jared's cowboys. He looked at the barn and he looked at the house. Soft lights shone through each of the windows, and more Mason jars with candles sat along the railing of the porch.

Cassie was still at the house. He'd bet money on it.

And he would have won. Cassie was waiting on the porch when he walked up. He had to take a moment. He was so stunned by her, standing there in the candlelight, in her pretty blue dress and her hair . . . it was pinned up in the back into a riot of curls. Her eyes were as blue as the sky and there was color on her cheeks, and her lips looked downright luscious, so much so that he wanted to kiss her then and there. But he didn't. Instead, he held out his hand to her and she took it without hesitation and Jake guided her down the stairs.

"You are a beautiful woman, Cassie Parker."

"Just because you are right this one time doesn't mean I'm going to let you make a habit of it," Cassie replied tartly.

"Does that mean we have a future together?"

"I refuse to answer that question until I've seen you dance."

"Believe me, Cassie, I can dance," Jake said.

"That remains to be seen," she said.

He tucked her arm into the crook of his and they walked toward the barn. Jake glanced down at the top of her head but was suddenly distracted by what was under her chin. He'd always thought she was blessed, but now that her breasts were out there for everyone to see . . . he wasn't so sure how he felt about that. While he appreciated the view very much, he knew he didn't want anyone else gazing upon her blessings.

"What am I going to do with you, Cassie?" He sighed.

"I thought you always had a plan, Jake."

"I always think I do, until you show up and knock everything sideways."

"How about if we don't worry about it right now and just enjoy the dance?"

"That's my problem, I'm afraid everyone is going to enjoy the dance just a little too much at my expense."

"It must be a hard life you live," Cassie said with some satisfaction.

Jake tugged on one of her curls and watched in fascination as it sprung back into place. How in the heck did women do that? "It's a burden," he said with a grin.

They'd come to the barn and Jake kept a tight hold on Cassie's arm. Ward tipped his glass in a toast as they walked up and Jake grinned at him. Dang if Cassie wasn't the prettiest girl here, and there were a lot around. Everyone in the area had come, people from town, all of the outlying ranches, all the cowboys, except from Watkins's spread, and even some of the miners.

"Cassie, you look absolutely stunning," Leah said.

"Thank you." Cassie smiled. "And thank you for all of the help you gave us after the fire."

"That's what we do around here," Leah said. "We look out for each other."

"That's one of the things I like best about Angel's End," Cassie said. "The way the people look out for each other." She gazed up at Jake and his heart swelled. He was beginning to think things just might go his way.

"Oh look," Leah said. "Rosa and Manuel are here."

"They are?" Cassie turned around. Sure enough, Rosa and Manuel were walking up to the barn. "I didn't think they'd come."

"I asked them to," Jake said. "After all, they are a part of this community too."

"Did Jake tell you about the barn raising?" Cade asked.

"No," Cassie said.

"It's supposed to be a surprise." Leah poked her husband.

"Sorry," Cade said, and rubbed his arm where Leah had prodded him. "It's next Saturday at your place. We figured we'd worry about the house after that."

"We'll have everything done before the first snow," Jake said. "If it all goes according to plan."

Cassie nodded. Jake could see there were tears in her eyes, but she quickly blinked them away as Rosa and Manuel arrived.

"My Cassie," Rosa said. "You look so beautiful."

"She does, doesn't she?" Jake watched her as she talked to Rosa and Manuel. She positively glowed with happiness. It was a sight he never thought he'd see.

Jared came up. "Jake, you want to do the honors and welcome everyone to the dance?" he asked.

"It's your place, Jared. You go right ahead." Jake wasn't leaving Cassie's side for anything tonight.

Jared went to the makeshift stage, set up in the middle of the barn, and everyone filed inside. Jared welcomed everyone, and the trio of musicians, Silas on the guitar, Gus on the fiddle and one of Jared's cowboys on the bass, began to play a lively song. Couples moved onto the dance floor and soon everyone was dancing, and those that weren't were clapping and stomping along. A passel of kids, most of them the Martins', with Banks among them, looked down from the hayloft and laughed at the adults' antics.

"Would you care to dance?" Jake asked Cassie.

"I thought you'd never ask," she replied sassily.

Jake whirled her out onto the dance floor. As tiny as she was, he could have just picked her up and gone with it, but she was nimble and quick and she kept up with him. Jake had learned how to dance at the private school his mother scrimped and saved to send him to and he wasn't afraid to show it now. Soon Cassie was laughing breathlessly as they twirled around the floor, and her joy was infectious. He couldn't help but grin from ear to ear at her, and he was conscious of people nudging each other and pointing their way.

He could care less. He knew without her telling him what her answer was. He could read it on her face. She was ready to face the future.

The song ended and a waltz began. Jake put his hand on Cassie's waist and once more spun her around into the dips and glides of the waltz, and she stayed right with him.

"So," he said. "What do you think?"

"About what?" Cassie asked.

"My dancing. You said you were going to base your decision on how good of a dancer I am."

"I don't need to tell you how good you are," Cassie replied. "Or else your head would be too big for this barn."

"So I am a good dancer."

"You know you are."

"Which means . . ."

Cassie stopped suddenly, so fast that he almost stumbled—almost—and she looked up at him with a wondrous expression on her face. "I'm ready for a future with you, Jake," she said. "If you still want me."

Did he still want her? That had to be the most foolish thing he'd ever heard her say, but he didn't feel like arguing

with her at the moment. Instead, he wanted to kiss her senseless. But to his surprise, and more than likely everyone's
there, he did something he wasn't planning on at all. Jake
slipped to one knee, took Cassie's hands in his and said,
"Will you marry me?"

Cassie looked as stunned as he felt. And for one brief
second Jake realized he'd set himself up for a lot of humili-
ation. But then she smiled, and then she cried and she put
her hands on either side of his face and said, "Yes. I will
marry you."

Jake jumped to his feet and picked her up. He swung her
about and the music suddenly started up in a fast tune and
everyone was pounding on his back and offering up congratulations, while Cassie clung to his arm as though trying
not to be swept away by the tide of well wishes.

"I didn't know that was part of your plan," Ward said
when Rosa and Manuel descended on Cassie. "But it was a
good one."

"I got to confess," Jake said so only Ward could hear. "It
sort of just came to me."

"You'll never be wrong if you follow your heart, Jake,"
Ward said, and offered him his hand. "Congratulations. I
will be the best man, in case you are wondering."

"I never doubted it for a minute," Jake said.

A toast was raised to them and then they were expected
to dance, and finally they were able to escape outside. Jake
pulled Cassie around to the side of the barn for a kiss, but
she stopped him by placing her hand on his chest.

"I've decided to start living my life, Jake. It wasn't an
easy decision to make. God knows I was scared. But I'm
not scared anymore. I want to start living, and that means
now. Tonight. With you. I can't think of any reason in the
world to wait. Can you?"

Jake opened his mouth to speak, but words failed him at the moment. But it didn't matter because Cassie wasn't done. "I almost forgot the most important part," she said. "I love you."

"Are you sure Cassie?"

"I'm sure Jake. I'm ready to start living my life, and I want to start living it with you."

"Then welcome to my home," Jake said. He slid off Bright and put his hands up. Cassie put her hands on his shoulders and he lifted her from the saddle as if she weighed nothing. Cassie felt like she was floating on air. She had been, ever since the first dance.

For the first time in a long time she felt alive, and she didn't want this feeling to ever go away. Jake took her hand and they walked up the steps and across his wide front porch. He pushed opened the door and a puppy ran to them, all waggly tail and sniffing nose. Jake picked the puppy up. "This is Josie," he said.

"Pleased to meet you, Josie," Cassie said. She put her nose to Josie's and the puppy licked her face. Cassie wrinkled her nose and Jake laughed. It was such a happy sound, and his face was almost boyish. Cassie smiled wistfully at him, seeing the boy who'd had to be so serious in his youth, who'd worked so hard to make something of himself, which he had. His house was warm and comforting and solid, like Jake. It would survive whatever the world threw at it; she knew it without a doubt. Cassie held on to Josie, who wiggled contently in her arms as Jake showed her the main room of his house. There was a huge sofa on one side of the stone fireplace, and two chairs, with a table between them, on the other. Lamps hung on the wall and gave off a soft and cozy light. Jake opened a door to the left of the entrance to reveal an office. One entire wall was nothing but books.

"How wonderful," Cassie said as she peeped into the room.

"Feel free to read as much as you want," Jake said.

"Mr. Jake?" someone called from the back of the house.

"I'm here," Jake said.

"You home early." A Chinese man walked into the hallway. "With company," he said with a smile.

"Cassie, you remember Fu," Jake said.

"Pleased to see you again, Fu," Cassie said, and the man bowed at her.

"Fu, do you mind taking care of Bright for me?" Jake asked.

"I will," Fu said with a wide grin. He bowed again at Cassie and started talking in Mandarin as he went out the door.

"He's interesting," Cassie said.

"He is," Jake said. "But not as interesting as you." He touched her cheek and then picked up one of her curls and pulled it straight. He released it and it snapped back into place. "I think I could play with those all day."

"Enjoy them while you can." Cassie gave her head a shake. "They'll be gone come morning."

"Just as long as you are here come morning," Jake said. "And every morning from here on out."

"I'm not going anywhere, Jake," Cassie said. She put her palm on his chest right where his heart pounded against it, and spread it wide. "I finally found a place where I belong."

Jake bent and kissed her and she lost herself in it. Except she was no longer lost, she was found. Jake found her and brought her in from the cold and now she belonged somewhere. All these years she'd been looking for a place to belong, only to find it wasn't a place so much as who was in that place.

Josie whimpered, because she was being crushed between them. Jake put Josie on the floor and picked Cassie up, and once more she felt as if she were floating on air. He carried her through a door and by the low glow of a lamp she saw a huge bed with a high mattress. Jake sat her down on the edge of the mattress, pulled off her shoes and tossed them aside.

"There's still time to change your mind," he said.

"Why, are you having regrets?" Cassie said, because she couldn't resist teasing him. Their easy bantering one of the many reasons she fell in love with him.

"Nary a one," Jake said as he kissed her again. "Of course that could change at any time."

"Oh, it could?" Cassie said between kisses. Jake gently guided her onto her back as he leaned over her with kisses. Soon his knee was on the bed and she was prone beside him. "When did you know, Jake? When did you fall in love with me?"

He toyed with a curl. "I fell in love with you that night you ambushed me on the trail," he said. "But it took me awhile to admit it to myself." He was being honest with her, as he promised, as she wanted. "When you told me not to come around anymore, I realized I couldn't live without you. But I couldn't quite figure out what to say to convince you to see things my way."

"There wasn't anything you could say, until now," Cassie confessed. "I had to come to the realization on my own. I had to decide what I wanted my future to be like."

"Just remember, Cassie, I'll never force you to do anything you don't want to do."

"Just remember, Jake, I trust you with my life and with my heart."

"Both are the greatest gift I could ever receive," Jake said. He kissed her again and Cassie put her hands on his chest and then moved them to the buttons of his shirt. Jake gave a slight intake of breath as she slowly spread his shirt open and ran her hands over his solid chest. It was hard and unforgiving, all planes and angles, yet she knew it well as a soft place to lay her head, those many times he'd offered her comfort.

Now she wanted to give to him in a way that made her ache inside. She rose up and kissed him in the ridge at the base of his clavicle, and Jake sighed with pleasure. With that encouragement Cassie continued, slowly kissing every bit of skin she could reach.

Suddenly he pushed himself up. "No fair," he said. "I want to touch and kiss you too." A thrill shuddered through her body at the thought of Jake's lips on her body. He looked at her with a devilish grin, and Cassie sat up and presented her back to him where a row of buttons fastened her dress. "Help yourself," she said.

"I hope you don't regret saying that," Jake said as he started on the buttons.

"That's entirely up to you," Cassie replied calmly, even though calm was the last thing she felt. Luckily Jake's fingers were nimble and he soon had her dress open and falling off her shoulders. He kissed the top of her spine and moved around the back of her neck to her shoulder as he slowly eased the dress off her arms. Cassie leaned back against that very solid chest, and Jake's hands came around and cupped her breasts. His thumbs slowly moved over them and she arched into his hands.

What had she been so scared of all these years? Being with Jake was nothing like what happened to her. Paul Stacy took advantage of the fact that he was stronger than her. He abused her. That had nothing to do with this wonderful thing that was happening between her and Jake.

Somehow, without her even realizing it, the straps of her petticoat were down and Jake's hand was on her bare skin. She felt every one of the calluses on his fingers as he lightly caressed her while kissing her neck. She wrapped her arm around his neck and pulled his face to hers so she could kiss him.

Jake put a hand under her hip and moved her into his lap. Without stopping the kiss, he pulled her dress, camisole and petticoat down over her hips, leaving her in nothing but her stockings. With a lopsided grin, Jake smoothed his hand along each leg, taking the stockings with him as he went.

"You're very good at that," Cassie said. "Should I worry that you've had so much practice?"

"I just so often imagined doing it with you that it comes naturally," he said, and he laid her down on the mattress. A sudden chill chased through Cassie at the intensity of his eyes upon her. If before she'd thought his eyes stormy, then now they were possessed of a whirlwind.

"You are so beautiful," he said. It had been so long since she'd thought of herself in that way that it shocked her, but she knew by the look in his eyes, by the way he yearned for her, that he meant it, as he dipped his head and kissed her again.

"So are you," Cassie said. She tugged at the waistband of his pants. "I want to see more." Jake didn't waste any time obliging her, yet he suddenly became cautious.

"Cassie?" he said questioningly. She didn't speak; instead, she put her arm around his neck and pulled him too her.

This was strength, she realized. She, who had always been so small, had the power to make this strong man tremble with need. She felt it as he braced himself on his arms so he wouldn't crush her. She didn't want him to hold back, she wanted all of him, and her arms weren't enough to capture him, so she wrapped her legs around his hips and pulled him against her.

"Cassie." He sighed this time, and he kissed her again and again and again as his hands stroked everywhere he could reach. Everywhere he touched she burned until she was certain she would ignite into a bundle of ash and drift away on the wind. And then he was inside her and it felt so very, very right. All the empty and lonely places she carried inside of her were full, and before she spun off into the heavens, she realized that Jake was exactly where she belonged.

Jake looked down on Cassie. Dawn was just breaking through the sky and the first golden rays of the sun danced across her body. Her hair had lost all its pins during the night and he'd spent the past few minutes gathering up each one he could find and putting them on the nightstand. Now her hair sprung out every which way, flying out in all directions in wisps and curls. He loved it. He wanted to wake her just to hear what she had to say, but the sight of her so comfortable in his bed was one he wasn't ready to give up.

"Every day for the rest of your life," he said quietly and toyed with one of the curls.

Cassie slowly opened her eyes and smiled up at him.

"No regrets?" he couldn't help but ask.

"It's a little late for that, don't you think?" She sat up and kissed him, slowly, in a very tempting way. "I never want to live with regret again," she said. "It's a very lonely companion, and it does nothing to keep you warm at night."

"I promise to always keep you warm."

"I will hold you to that," Cassie said. "Especially on those long winter nights."

Jake kissed her again and was just getting down to more important things when he was interrupted by Josie whining by the bed.

"Dang it," he said. "I best let her out. She's just now getting the hang of it."

He got up, found his pants and took Josie outside. It was a beautiful morning with just a hint of a chill in the air, one that made him smile at the thought of keeping Cassie warm.

Josie finished up her business and joyfully bounded back into the house. Jake stopped by his office on the way to his room and picked up Cassie's grandfather's Bible. He heard Fu banging around in the kitchen and grinned at knowing the cook would outdo himself this morning to impress Cassie.

"Dang it!" Jake said when he walked into his bedroom.

"What's wrong?" Cassie asked. She looked very pretty lying there among the pillows.

"Josie got your shoe," he said. He picked up the mangled slipper and showed it to her.

"That could be a problem, Jake," Cassie said.

"I reckon I'll have to buy you some new ones," he said.

"I reckon you will."

Jake scooped up Josie and put her on the bed. "I didn't think about it last night, because she usually sleeps with me."

"Poor Josie," Cassie cooed at the pup. "You've been replaced." Josie wiggled up next to Cassie and gave her a quick lick on the face. "But I believe there's room for both of us, if you don't mind sharing."

"She doesn't mind at all," Jake answered for Josie. He handed Cassie the Bible. "This was your grandfather's."

Cassie took the Bible and opened it to the first few pages where all the births and deaths were written down. "I should probably add his," she said as she looked at the page.

"Just as long as it's not the final entry," Jake said. He sat down beside her and pointed to her name. "We got plenty more to add. A wedding, and I hope some births of our own, and then a long, long life, together with grandchildren eventually."

Cassie pulled him close for a kiss. "It sounds like a good plan."

A few weeks later . . .

Jake couldn't recall a finer day in Angel's End. The sun shone brightly and the breeze was enough to keep the weather comfortable. The air smelled fresh and clear and there wasn't a cloud in the sky. The church looked as if it had been scrubbed, and there was a wreath of gaily colored flowers on the door.

His buggy had been polished and washed until Dan and Randy dared anyone to find a speck of dirt on it, and Darby had flowers braided into her mane and tail, and someone had strung bunting and hung a sign on the back that said *Just Married*.

Even Lady had a bow around her neck. Ward just grinned at him as he joined him on the porch of the diner. "You ready to do this?" he asked.

Jake looked at the church where the circuit preacher and most of the population of Angel's End was waiting. Shoot, if he wanted to, he could walk across the street to Cade and Leah's house and see Cassie there, but he was kind of looking forward to watching her walk down the aisle in her pretty blue dress. He wanted to see the flowers in her flyaway hair and the look of love that now glowed in her pale eyes.

"I'm ready," Jake said.

"Laurie asked me to give you this," Ward said. He pulled a handkerchief from his pocket and unwrapped a twist of flowers. "Don't ask me to pin it on," Ward growled.

Jake laughed as he attached the flowers to his lapel and they stepped into the street.

Jake hoped Cassie was looking out the window. He hoped she was as excited as he was.

"Jake!" Jake turned to see Jared coming his way from the post office.

"I thought you were already inside," Ward said.

"The women have me running errands," Jared said. "So I hid out in the post office. I got this letter and I wanted you to have it."

"Letter?" Jake asked when Jared handed it to him.

"Remember when I said I had a friend down in Texas and I'd write to him to see if there'd been any trouble before Cassie came here? Well he wrote me back. He didn't explain anything, he just said for me to give this news to Cassie. I thought you should be the one to deliver it, since I have no idea if this was a friend of hers or not."

Jake's eyes scanned the page until a sentence jumped out at him.

Please tell Miss Parker that Paul Stacy was found dead in New Mexico. His body was staked out in the desert and it was apparent that he'd been tortured before he died. They are blaming it on the Apaches. The letter continued. *I hope Miss Parker finds the peace that she so deserves in Colorado*, and then it was signed by Jared's friend.

"Does that mean anything to you?" Jared asked.

"It does," Jake said. "But it means much more to Cassie."

"Anything we should stop the wedding for?"

"There's no dang way you're going to stop this wedding," Jake said.

"Well then, let's go." Jared smiled and they walked into the church, and Jake wondered if there was a wildflower left on a stalk around Angel's End. They should have gotten married in a meadow and saved everyone the work. He knew everyone sitting in the pews, the Martins and their six kids all shiny and clean, along with Nonnie, who smiled broadly and nodded her head when he walked by. Gus and Bettina, who was fanning her face as if she were about to boil. She wore a huge hat with a bird sitting on top of it. Then there was Margy Ashburn the schoolmarm and Zeke Preston the assayer, and the young man from the bank, who looked mournfully in Margy's direction. Dusty was there, Bob and Pris, along with Dan and Randy and the rest of his men; the only one missing was Fu, who stayed home to make sure the honeymoon suite lived up to his expectations. Fu's, not Jake's. Fu had taken an instant liking to Cassie and couldn't wait for her to officially join the household. Rosa and Manuel sat in the front row in a place of honor as Cassie's family. They were his family now too.

Cade and Jared slipped into the pews, and there were a few titters of laughter at Lady, who followed after Ward, Jake's best man.

"I hope you didn't give her the ring," Jake said to Ward.

"I did," Ward said. "It's tied in her bow."

Jake would have checked to make sure it was still there, because he was careful that way, but just then the door at the back of the church opened and the circuit preacher told everyone to stand. Little Hannah came in with a basket of flower petals and was very precise about dropping them on the floor. Then came Eden, and her beauty was breathtaking, so much so that Jake didn't even notice her limp. Easy enough because he looked past her to where Cassie stood in the doorway with Laurie on one side of her and Leah on the other.

He was right. There were flowers in her hair. And when she raised her face to look at him, a wide smile danced across her lips, and her love for him shone in her eyes.

For something he wasn't planning on, she sure did turn out to be a fine thing. A fine thing indeed.

KAKI WARNER

Heartbreak Creek

A RUNAWAY BRIDES NOVEL

From Kaki Warner comes an exciting new series about four unlikely brides who make their way west— and find love where they least expect it . . .

Edwina Ladoux hoped becoming a mail-order bride would be her way out of the war-torn South and into a better life, but as soon as she arrives in Heartbreak Creek, Colorado, and meets her hulking, taciturn groom, she realizes she's made a terrible mistake.

Declan Brodie already had one flighty wife who ran off with a gambler before being killed by Indians. He's hoping this new one will be a practical, sturdy farm woman who can help with chores and corral his four rambunctious children. Instead, he gets a skinny Southern princess who doesn't even know how to cook.

Luckily, Edwina and Declan agreed on a three-month courtship period, which should give them time to get the proxy marriage annulled. Except that as the weeks pass, thoughts of annulment turn into hopes for a real marriage—until Declan's first wife returns after being held captive for the last four years. Now an honorable man must choose between duty and desire, and a woman who's never had to fight for anything must do battle for the family she's grown to love . . .

Praise for the novels of Kaki Warner

"Emotionally compelling." —*Chicago Tribune*

"Thoroughly enjoyable." —*Night Owl Reviews* (Top Pick)

"Compelling and beautifully written."

—Debbie Macomber, *New York Times* bestselling author

FROM *NEW YORK TIMES* BESTSELLING AUTHOR

JODI THOMAS

THE COMFORTS OF HOME

A HARMONY NOVEL

Twenty-year-old Reagan Truman has found her place and family in Harmony, Texas. But with her uncle taken ill and her friend Noah lost and disheartened with his life, Reagan is afraid of ending up alone again—and she's not the only one. When a terrible storm threatens the town, the residents of Harmony are forced to think about what they truly want. Because making the connections they so desperately desire means putting their hearts at risk...

M1008T1011

LOVE
ROMANCE
NOVELS?

For news on all your favorite romance authors,
sneak peeks into the newest releases, book
giveaways, and much more—

"Like" Love Always on Facebook!
 LoveAlwaysBooks

M1063G0212

Discover Romance

berkleyjoveauthors.com

See what's coming up next from your favorite romance authors and explore all the latest Berkley, Jove, and Sensation selections.

See what's new

~

Find author appearances

~

Win fantastic prizes

~

Get reading recommendations

~

Chat with authors and other fans

~

Read interviews with authors you love

M1G0610